The Big Fang

A Harbor Humane Society Anthology

Edited by Melissa H. Blaine and Allison M. Deters

Harbor Humane Society

Contents

Foreword

Harbor Humane Society was founded in 1956 and is located in West Olive, Michigan. Harbor sees over 4,000 animals come through its doors annually. In addition to being a safe haven for every stray animal (dogs, cats, chickens, bunnies, even snakes!) in our county, we also transfer in dogs and cats from in need areas in our state and beyond. We are dedicated to strengthening the human and animal bond through a variety of community programs including an open adoption program, a robust foster network, humane education for youth, monthly vaccine clinics and pet food pantries for those in need, canine behavior classes and consultation services, and public spay and neuter services. We strive to be in the forefront of progressive sheltering in the United States. While we maintain a live release rate of over 90%, which qualifies us as "no-kill" status, we don't like to use that terminology, as it can demonize other shelters who don't meet that standard, but are doing all they can with the pet population their community is faced with. Instead, we lend a helping hand whenever we can and transfer in animals from shelters like these, in order to ease their burden.

If all this sounds like a lot of work, trust us, it is! We have a dedicated staff of 50 team members, and an annual operating budget of $1.8 million. The majority of our financial support comes from individual donors, as our county funding only provides for around 10% of our annual budget. This means every year we need to come up with new and engaging fundraisers... like this! This anthology is the brainchild of Melissa Blaine, one of our volunteer fosters. Having penned a number of short stories herself, she suggested we compile an anthology of cozy capers, each involving an animal and a "big bang" change, and sell it as a fundraiser for the shelter. And thus, The Big Fang was born! It took us nearly two years and one global pandemic, but we are so excited to present to you this unique collection of stories. Many of our authors are self-professed animal lovers and advocates and it has been an absolute pleasure putting this collection together with this talented group of writers.

For more information on Harbor Humane Society, visit our website: harborhumane.org. We can also be found posting all our real life crazy animal capers on Facebook, Instagram, and Tiktok!

Landing on His Feet

Catrine Kyster

"This is your big day! I'm so excited for you!" Jennifer scratched Peanut's chin softly, just the way he liked it. She beamed as the cat jutted out his chin in contentment. Peanut had come such a long way since he first arrived at *Cats & Cups*. The gray-and-white shorthair cat was seven years old and shy. Jennifer had been worried that it was going to be challenging to find a new home for him, but Peanut was a great example of how spending time with staff, volunteers, and customers helped socialize cats from the animal center for adoption. And today, it was finally Peanut's day to join his FURever family, as Jennifer liked to phrase it when she wrote on the café's social media pages.

Jennifer left Peanut in his favorite spot on the armrest of the oversized couch and went to the back of the café to check that everything was ready for Mrs. Parker to pick him up later: Peanut's favorite toy, food, a carrier, a vet visit voucher, and a page on how to help Peanut acclimate to his new home.

Jennifer was sure that Peanut would make a great companion for Mrs. Parker, an elderly lady who lived by herself in a rather large old house close to the small town's waterfront. Mrs. Parker had come into the café a little hesitantly. Her husband had passed away a few years earlier, and she thought a cat could maybe help her feel less alone, but she worried that she was perhaps too old to get a cat. Low-maintenance Peanut, a senior himself, had turned out to be the PURRfect match.

Just then, the doorbell rang, alerting Jennifer to the first customers of the day. She hurried into the front room to sign them in and explain how the café worked. A small fee entitled guests to an hour of petting and playing with the café's cats – there were currently ten that were all available for adoption – and a cup of coffee or tea or a soda. Many customers also bought a slice of cake or some cookies, which were made by Jennifer's sister-in-law Amy, who owned the local diner, or they purchased something from the café's selection of cat-themed mugs, books, stationery, socks, clocks, and trinkets.

As Jennifer unlocked the glass door, a police car rushed down the street with flashing lights and sirens. Jennifer furrowed her brow. The small police station was just around the corner, but she rarely saw flashing lights and sirens at 10 o'clock in the morning.

***

When the afternoon volunteer arrived at 3 PM, Jennifer doublechecked that everything was ready for Peanut's departure, as Mrs. Parker was scheduled to arrive around 3:30. But, an hour and a half later, Mrs. Parker had still not turned up. Jennifer checked her phone to see if she'd called or sent a text. Then, she dialed the number on the adoption paperwork, but instead of reaching Mrs. Parker, the phone was answered by a man. Jennifer asked to speak with Mrs. Parker. The man hesitated a moment before he answered.

"I'm afraid that's not possible right now, but may I ask who you are and why you're calling?" The voice sounded familiar, but Jennifer couldn't quite place it.

"I'm Jennifer Lee from *Cats & Cups* Cat Café on Main Street. I was expecting Mrs. Parker here today to pick up a cat for adoption."

"Oh, Jennifer. This is Doug. Sergeant Doug Turner from the police department."

Jennifer knew Doug a little bit. She sometimes picked up shifts as a waitress at Amy's diner to make ends meet, as the cat café barely broke even, and she'd often seen him there reading through files and scribbling in his notebook while eating a large blue-plate special. But what was the police doing at Mrs. Parker's house? She soon got the answer.

"I'm afraid Mrs. Parker has been murdered."

***

Jennifer had just fed the cats when Sergeant Doug Turner arrived at *Cats & Cups* the next day. Looking at the shadows under his eyes, Jennifer guessed that he'd been up all night working, trying to solve the murder of Mrs. Parker.

"Sergeant, I was so sorry to hear about Mrs. Parker. Such a tragedy. And she seemed like such a lovely lady." Jennifer gestured for Doug to sit down on the couch. To her surprise, he sat down on the side that Peanut was on and began slowly stroking the cat from his forehead to his tail. She didn't know that Doug liked cats. All she really knew about him was that he lived alone and seemed dedicated to his work. Maybe that was it. Maybe she was a suspect, and he was just trying to put her at ease? Peanut seemed to think he was genuine enough though.

"I also feel sad for Peanut here," Jennifer added. "He's old and usually somewhat shy, so he's not the easiest cat to find a new family for."

"This was the cat she was going to adopt?" Upon hearing Doug's deep voice, Peanut looked up, but he seemed happy enough to let Doug continue stroking his back. But then Doug had to stop to pull out a notebook and pen.

"I was actually hoping that I could pick your brain a bit, Jennifer. We haven't yet been able to speak with anyone who knew Mrs. Parker well, and I was wondering if she had perhaps said anything while she was here? Anything that could point to someone wanting to hurt her."

While he located the right page in his notebook, Doug gave her a quick summary of what they knew so far. Mrs. Parker's body had been discovered by her cleaning lady. The alibis of the cleaning lady, the gardener, and the handyman all checked out. It seemed that Mrs. Parker didn't see many other people. A nephew who lived a couple of hours away was named in her will, but they hadn't been able to interview him yet.

As Jennifer thought back on her conversations with Mrs. Parker, she gazed up at the wall across from them which held pictures of all the cats they'd been able to find homes for since the café opened a few years ago. People came for the cats, but Jennifer also knew that many customers enjoyed talking with her. Looking at the cats, petting them and playing with them, somehow made people feel comfortable telling her things about their lives. Perhaps they also knew her reputation for not gossiping – which could not be said for everyone in the small town.

"She really didn't talk much about herself, but yes, I also got the impression she kept herself to herself. And that she was a bit lonely too. She and her husband had had just one child, a daughter, and she passed away some years ago from cancer." Jennifer shook her head slowly. "I'm sorry that I can't help you more. She did seem like a kind person. Peanut definitely took to her."

Just then, Doug gave a happy little squeal. "He just licked my hand!"

Jennifer laughed. "He seems to be taking a liking to you too. You know, he's usually quite timid."

After giving Peanut a few more firm strokes, Doug got up. "Well, thank you anyway, Jennifer. And I'll see you over at the diner soon, I'm sure."

But just as he reached for the door handle, Jennifer remembered one thing that could be relevant. There was nobody else in the café at the moment, but she still lowered her voice. "I wouldn't normally repeat unkind things that someone said, but as this is a murder case..." Jennifer removed one of the cats from the front desk and placed it gently on the floor before she continued. "After Mrs. Parker left, Mrs. Green – you know the woman who used to work at the supermarket – said that Mrs. Parker's sister's son probably couldn't wait for the old lady to die so that he could get his hand on the property. She made it sound as if the nephew is a bit of a good-for-nothing, and I guess the house is worth a good amount of money, with the location and all. I think Mrs. Green's exact words were that the nephew 'would finally land on his feet'."

"Thank you, Jennifer." Doug nodded at her. "I'll look into it, and if you think of anything else, don't hesitate to give me a call."

After Doug left, Jennifer sat down on the couch and stroked Peanut's back. Poor Mrs. Parker. Poor Peanut.

***

The next day was busy in the cat café. Jennifer had only had time to skim the article in the newspaper about Mrs. Parker's murder, but she'd shuddered when she'd learned how Mrs. Parker had been killed. Shot at close range. Who would do something like that to an old lady?

Jennifer had just finished serving a customer a cup of coffee and a chocolate chip cookie when a very tall, hulking man burst into the café, slamming the door so hard behind him that the glass rattled. Wearing a battered camouflage cap, dirty jeans, and a worn-out shirt, his face red with anger, he didn't look like a typical customer either. Taking a quick steadying breath, Jennifer walked over to him. He raised his hand and pointed at her in response.

"Are you the lady who told the police that I can't wait for my aunt to die so I can get my dirty hands on her money?"

Jennifer shook her head, trying to look bolder than she felt. This had to be Mrs. Parker's nephew, and he was obviously very angry.

"I'd like you to know ... In fact, I'd like everyone to know." The man paused while he looked around the café to make sure that everyone was listening to him. "That I didn't kill my aunt!"

For a moment, Jennifer wondered if she should call the police before the situation got out of hand, but the hurt look in the man's eyes gave her a feeling that it wouldn't be necessary.

"Please, Mr. ... Would you like to have a seat and a soda or a cup of coffee? You must be very upset about losing your aunt."

Caught off guard, the man followed Jennifer over to a small table with two comfy chairs around it. He sat down and accepted the cold drink that Jennifer quickly fetched for him. After a minute or so of hesitation, the other guests in the café started talking among themselves again and resumed petting and playing with the cats. Several people laughed when two of the kittens chased a ball across the room.

Jennifer sat down across from Mrs. Parker's nephew. He didn't say anything for a while but just looked around and watched the cats. Then he finally looked directly at her and spoke.

"You know, it was actually me who recommended my aunt to get a cat. My girlfriend has allergies, so we don't have any ourselves, but I love cats."

Just then, one of the kittens started playing with Jennifer's shoe. She picked up the kitten and offered it to the man, who took it gently in his big hands. As he stroked the kitten tenderly, he asked her to tell him more about 'this place', and Jennifer gave him her usual two-minute presentation about the cat café. The man sat up in the chair.

"I spoke with my aunt just a few days ago, on the phone, and she was so excited to be adopting a cat. She told me that she'd already bought loads of toys and food and stuff for it. They won't let me into the house now, but once this is all settled, I'll gather up all the cat stuff and bring it by. You can make good use of it, right?"

"We sure can – thank you!" said Jennifer. "It's very kind of you to think of us."

As the man continued petting the kitten, Jennifer decided that it was safe enough to dare ask a question and try to find out more. "What are you thinking of doing with your aunt's house?"

"I'm going to sell it. My aunt told me a couple of times that there's this developer who wants to buy the property. He's offered her a lot of money – several times in fact – but she's always refused. She said to me: 'Jake, once I'm not here anymore, you can do whatever you want with this house, but as long as I'm alive, I'm going to stay in this house surrounded by the memories of my husband and daughter'."

The man petted the kitten's cheeks just behind its whiskers and smiled as the kitten purred loudly. Then his face went serious again. "The police think I killed my aunt because they know I don't have a lot of money. But I knew that money would eventually come to me. There was no rush. I may not have much, but I have enough. My girlfriend and me – we get by."

***

After Mrs. Parker's nephew left, Jennifer called Doug. Instead of talking on the phone, he offered to come by. Now, he stood in the café and looked around. "Where's Peanut?"

Jennifer pointed up to a high shelf where Peanut was snoozing in a soft basket. Although he was an older cat, he was not afraid of a bit of climbing. Doug went over and took a good long look at the sleeping cat before returning to the front desk to find out why Jennifer had called him.

"Mrs. Parker's nephew came in today. He was very upset."

Doug whistled. "We interviewed him earlier today. I hope he didn't scare you."

"No, he was fine. But he told me that there's a developer who's tried to convince his aunt to sell the property?"

Doug nodded. "Yes, he told us that too. And we've looked into it. It's that guy who built the big hotel by the harbor a few years ago. You know him, right? Tom."

Jennifer didn't count Tom among her friends, but she'd met him several times at receptions and grand openings and other community events. It wasn't that she didn't approve of newcomers to the town, but she always thought that his red sports car and tailormade suits were a bit over the top.

"He wants to turn that area with the old houses into apartment buildings. Expensive ones with water views," Doug explained. "But apparently, he can't build there until he owns Mrs. Parker's property too."

Jennifer lifted her brow. "Well, that sounds like he could have a motive, doesn't it?"

"Yes, but we've already interviewed him. He was home with his wife at the time when the murder happened. And his office is working on several other projects. It seems that the waterfront apartments aren't as important to him as Mrs. Parker's nephew seems to think."

***

Half an hour later, Jennifer said goodbye to the cats before locking up. Peanut had woken up and returned to the couch. He looked up at her as if he was wondering about something, and Jennifer had to remind herself that Peanut didn't know that he'd been about to get adopted, so he couldn't be sad about that. She knelt down and petted him. "What is it, Peanut? What's on your mind?"

Then, as she got up and went to turn out the lights, the words of a conversation that she'd overheard came to her. It was a few weeks ago. Camille, the wife of the property developer, and their little girl Penelope had visited to play with the cats. The girl had fallen in love with two of the little black kittens and had started to cry when her mom wouldn't agree to buy them. Camille had hissed to her daughter that they just couldn't afford it. In hindsight, that seemed an odd thing to say as the family were known for a more lavish lifestyle than that of most other people in their town.

Jennifer rubbed her hands together as a thought ran through her head. Could it be that Tom and Camille were more down on their luck than anyone knew? Could it be that Tom, despite what he'd told the police officers, just couldn't wait any longer for Mrs. Parker to sell her home so that he could begin building?

Jennifer looked at the large cat-clock on the wall. Doug could probably check Tom's financial records, but, right now, Doug was most likely tucking into his dinner at the diner. Well, it could wait until tomorrow – it was probably a thin idea anyway. Instead, she should try to get some steps in before heading home. The cakes in the café were often too tempting to resist, and Jennifer tried to make herself take a brisk walk at the end of each workday.

***

As Jennifer walked down Main Street, heading for the waterfront, she realized that Tom and Camille's home was not far away. Of course, she didn't expect a big sign in front of the house saying 'I did it' but it couldn't hurt to walk by the house – she still had 2,000 steps to go to reach her daily goal, and the upscale neighborhood would also make a change of scenery from her usual route.

When she was almost right in front of the property developer's large white villa, Jennifer heard a car coming up rather slowly behind her. Instinctively, she pressed herself close to the trunk of a tree on the sidewalk, out of sight from the car. The large black SUV turned into the driveway of Tom and Camille's house. Jennifer recalled Camille driving a large dark SUV, but to Jennifer's surprise, at the same time, Camille came running down the front steps of the house, stopping the car before it drove into the garage, which was slowly opening. Jennifer was expecting to see Tom's red sports car in the garage, but it looked empty, and it was Tom who stepped out of the black SUV.

Jennifer wished she could hear what the two were talking about. Judging from their body language, it didn't look like a friendly conversation. But, she could hardly sneak into the yard, could she? That would be trespassing. What if they discovered her and called the police? What if they killed her? Even if the couple were completely innocent and had never done and would never do anything nefarious, it could still end up terribly embarrassing. Word could easily get around that Jennifer was not just a cat lady but a crazy one. That could cost her the café. It could put the happy futures of the café's cats on the line.

Jennifer bit her lip. Rightly, Mrs. Parker should be home enjoying Peanut and not lying on a cold slab in the morgue. And Peanut should be in his FURever home. She remembered how the old cat had looked at her earlier that day. Didn't she owe it to them both to do everything that she possibly could to try to find out who killed Peanut's mom-to-be? Taking a deep breath, Jennifer stepped into the large front yard.

Tiptoeing carefully from one meticulously landscaped bush or tree to the next, Jennifer made her way closer to the garage as fast as she could. Even though they were arguing, Tom and Camille were trying to keep their voices down, and Jennifer had to get all the way up behind the rose bush closest to the house before she could make out what they were saying. It seemed that Tom had promised to be home earlier because Camille needed to use the car.

"If you hadn't sold your car, we wouldn't have this problem!" Camille slammed the trunk.

"Don't you go slamming doors on me," Tom shot back. "If it hadn't been for your constant vacations and new furniture and new I-don't-know-what, we'd still have enough money."

Camille stopped in her tracks and turned to stare at him. "You're just blaming me again. But I guess you didn't mind me covering for you. Well, if that money doesn't materialize as soon as you promised, maybe I'll tell the police the truth: that I have no idea where you were that evening!"

Jennifer felt blood rush to her face and her pulse beating faster. Camille had just put her husband in the frame for Mrs. Parker's murder. Now all Jennifer had to do was get away safely and call Doug.

Jennifer tried to be as quiet as a cat as she began walking backwards from the rose bush. But the ground was dryer than she thought and as she stepped on a twig it made a distinct cracking sound.

"Who's there?" Tom yelled and began walking in the direction of the sound. Jennifer tried to think fast. She couldn't hide, and she was unlikely to be able to outrun them. Perhaps they even had a gun. There was just one thing she could do. She stepped right out in front of Tom.

"Oh, I'm so sorry. I didn't realize than anyone was here – I thought I saw Coco. The cat."

"What are you talking about?" Tom narrowed his eyes as he seemed to be trying to figure out what to do.

"Coco was adopted a few weeks ago by a family who lives just a few streets away from here, but she ran out the door today and hasn't come home. The family called me to come and help look for her. Coco may remember me from the cat café and trust me, you see."

Camille had caught up with them now.

"Tom, I've seen this lady before. ... I think she's actually telling the truth. Penelope plays with the daughter of the family who just got Coco – that's how she got the idea that we should go to the cat café. This lady owns that place."

Tom cleared his throat. "Well, whoever you are, you shouldn't be on someone else's property. Now, get out of here before I call the police!"

Don't worry, I'll call them myself, Jennifer thought as she smiled apologetically and left the garden as fast as she could without seeming suspicious. She walked down the street calling for Coco, until she was well out of sight of Tom and Camille. With a deep sigh of relief, she reached into her purse for her phone and called Doug.

***

A few days later, Doug came into *Cats & Cups*, beaming. He followed Jennifer into the office, away from the customers. "Well, I thought you'd like to know that we found the gun that killed Mrs. Parker when we searched Tom and Camille's house. Apparently, he'd not gotten around to getting rid of it yet although that was his plan – and when we confronted them with the ballistic results, Camille recanted her alibi, and then Tom confessed."

Jennifer sank down in her office chair, relieved. "I'm so thankful that he didn't get away with it. He did Mrs. Parker and her family a great wrong. And Peanut too."

"Yep. Now there's just one loose end."

Jennifer looked at him puzzled. It seemed to her that the whole case was pretty tight and tidy. They had the murder weapon, a motive, and a confession.

Doug cleared his throat. "I've been thinking about what's going to happen to Peanut... I was, in fact, wondering if you think he might make a good pet for a busy police officer?"

Jennifer's mouth dropped. "You want to adopt Peanut?"

"Yes, sometimes the house just feels a bit empty, you know." Doug's face had turned slightly red.

Jennifer reached over and got out a copy of the adoption application from the animal center. With a smile, she put it in front of Doug. "You know, I think Peanut has just landed on his feet one more time!"

Born and raised in Denmark, Catrine Kyster now lives in South Carolina. She and her daughter love to visit the local cat café which provided the inspiration for the fictional cat café featured in her short story in this anthology. In 2018, Catrine won the Danish Kær-Lit Award, and her short stories and non-fiction articles have been published in both Denmark and the United States. Catrine is currently working on her first romantic historical mystery novel. You can follow her on Instagram @catkyster and at catrinekyster.com.

The Parrot from Primrose Lane

Shari Held

"Help! Help! He's gonna kill me!"

Casey Kelly dropped her bag of groceries to the ground and sprinted down the alley in the direction of the cry for help. She stopped when she spotted a parrot with a sunshine yellow head and brilliant turquoise body perched on a wooden fence. A barking dog, the alleged "killer," was on the other side of the fence.

"Help! Help! He's gonna kill me!" the parrot repeated, bobbing its head back and forth between Casey and the dog.

Casey had grown up with her father's parrot and was familiar with the drill. While talking softly to the frenzied bird, she slowly extended her arm. As the bird stepped onto her hand, she grasped the second and third digits on its foot and carefully moved it toward her chest and began walking toward her car. When she reached her VW Beetle, she gently set the bird on the passenger seat.

"I hope you're used to riding in a car. Now, stay here while I get my groceries. Then we'll go home and figure out what to do with you."

The parrot screeched in response but didn't try to escape.

Once Casey arrived at her Broad Ripple duplex, she deposited the parrot in her screened-in porch where it perched on top of a floor lamp.

"You're certainly a beauty. But your timing isn't very good. It's Friday evening. The vet's closed. And Barry should be arriving for our date any minute now."

"Pretty lady! Gimme kiss!" the parrot said.

Just then, the doorbell rang and Barry let himself in, bottle of wine in hand.

Casey greeted him, grabbed his hand, and led him to the screened-in porch. "Look what I found." The bird immediately squawked and started flapping its wings.

"What the heck is that?" Barry asked. He couldn't have looked more disgusted if the bird had pooped on his Gucci loafers — while he was wearing them.

"An Amazonian parrot, I believe. I rescued it in the alley behind the grocery store. Poor baby. He must be terrified. I'll take him to the vet's tomorrow morning to see if we can find the owner."

"Loser! Loser!" the parrot said.

Barry's lip curled. He took a step back and put his hands in his pockets. "It's not going to spend the night here, is it? You know birds give me the heebie jeebies. Don't you have a cage you can put that thing in?"

"I don't usually keep a spare cage lying around in case a parrot in need happens to appear. I'll call Woods and see if he has any suggestions."

A few minutes later, Woods, Casey's landlord, who lived in the other side of the duplex, appeared.

"I've got a large dog crate that should work short-term," Woods said. "I'll bring it over."

"Why don't you take the parrot?" Barry said to Woods. "That seems more logical to me."

Casey bit her lip. And more convenient for you. "Would you mind, Woods? I've got some grapes and bananas for him. And I'll take him off your hands first thing tomorrow morning."

"No problem. Bring it on over, then." As he left, Woods barely nodded toward Barry.

Casey coaxed the parrot onto her arm and cradled it against her as she followed Woods next door.

"I hope you don't mind. Barry and I are getting ready to leave for Shakespeare in the Park, so —"

"You don't have to keep making excuses for that schmuck," Woods said. "If I were you, I'd keep the bird and get rid of the jerk."

***

"Romeo and Juliet, not one of his better plays — and certainly not executed brilliantly," Barry said as he guided Casey toward his BMW. "What a waste of time."

Leave it to Barry to pull her out of the moment. "I thought it was sweet," Casey said. "Such a tragic ending. It always gets to me."

"You're letting sentimentality obscure your better judgment. You should be more discriminating."

They entered Casey's duplex and she turned on the lights. The hair on the back of her neck rose to attention. She did a quick assessment, noting a few subtle changes. The sliding door to the screened-in porch was open, and the neat stack of bills on her desk was now askew.

"I think someone's been here."

"Probably Woods needed something." Barry sat on the couch and stretched his long legs in front of him.

"No, he wouldn't do that without leaving a note. Someone's been in here snooping around." She went to the front door. "See?" she said, pointing to the scratches on the lock. "I think the lock's been picked."

"Great! I guess that means you'll be calling the police and they'll keep me up all night. You know I have an important presentation to prepare for." He glared at her.

Casey was tired and not in a space to cater to Barry's mood. She glared right back. "There doesn't appear to be anything missing, so I'm not going to report it. And, for your information, it's not like I planned this."

"You don't have to. Wherever you go, trouble's one step behind or one step in front of you." He threw up his hands and stood up. "Your life's just too complicated. That whole parrot thing's the last straw. I know you. If no one claims it, you'll keep it, no matter how I feel."

Casey opened her mouth to object. Then stopped. She couldn't deny it.

"I think it would be best if we stopped seeing each other," Barry shouted over his shoulder as he walked out the door.

That was sudden. Although not unexpected. Barry had just been going through the motions for weeks. Casey sat down and conducted an internal assessment of her feelings. Devastated? Nope. Sad? A little. Happy? Maybe a little. Ah, that elusive feeling she was trying to pin down — relief! ▯▯▯▯

***

Bright and early the next morning, Casey showed up at Harley's Pet Wellness, a Salted Caramel Mocha from Starbucks in one hand, the parrot in the other.

"Hey, Harley," she said, handing him his favorite Starbucks concoction. Harley and she were in the same graduating class at Broad Ripple High School.

"What have we here?" he said, eyeing the parrot.

"What's up?" the parrot said.

"I rescued this little guy behind the grocery store on Primrose Lane yesterday. Not an area where someone would be likely to own an exotic bird. Can you check if he's microchipped?"

"Sure thing. Put him on the counter."

Harley grabbed his scanner and slowly approached the parrot, crooning softly.

"Call a lawyer! Call a lawyer!" the parrot said.

"He has an unusual vocabulary. At least he's not calling you a loser. Has anyone reported a missing parrot?"

"Not to me." Harley examined the band on the parrot's right leg. "It's a male according to the sexing band. Hmm, that's odd." He aimed the scanner at the bird's chest. "Here we go. I've got the code. I'll call this in and have an answer for you Monday."

"How often are parrots united with their owners?"

"It's not a sure thing, even with microchipping. But it's much better than it used to be. We'll see."

"So, I should leave him here until then?"

"Could you possibly keep him until Monday? There won't be anyone here to care for him. I'm catching a plane as soon as I see my last patient, and my assistant has already headed out of town for the weekend."

Casey didn't respond immediately.

"I can give you a loaner cage and some treats," he added as an incentive.

Casey nodded, then turned toward the bird. "I bet you're more fun than Barry, anyway."

"Pretty lady! Gimme kiss!"

When Casey got home, she thought how worried and frantic the owner must be to find the parrot. She decided to put up a few flyers around the Village. Just as a backup to the microchipping.

***

"Hungry! Gimme apple?"

"Good morning, to you, too," Casey said. "Let's clean your cage." She tore a sheet from the Sunday paper and started to put it in the cage, when a headline, "Homicide in the Village," caught her eye. According to the paper, a man named Palmer Scudder was found dead near Primrose Lane, soon after Casey had rescued the parrot.

Casey put the paper down. Poor man. Broad Ripple was not the quiet little village it once was. The crime rate was rising. Maybe she should have reported her suspected break-in. Nah. At this point she wasn't even sure her duplex had been broken into. Maybe she'd brushed up against the stack of bills and moved them. It's possible she'd left the door to the porch open. She'd certainly been on edge that night. And the scratches on the lock could have been there for weeks, even months. She'd just continue to do what she'd done before, place a chair under the doorknob.

She jumped when her doorbell rang. She went to the window and peeked out. A tall, lanky guy stood there, his back turned to her. It looked like Barry. She opened the door. It wasn't.

The man held a flyer in one hand. "I'm Gerel Gibbs," he said, extending his other hand. "You have my bird, I believe."

The parrot started shrieking, "Help! Help! He's gonna kill me!"

The man smiled. "That's Salty, all right," the man said. "He learned that line from his previous owner. Of course, I'll give you a reward for caring for him." He pulled a thick wad of bills from his jacket pocket and offered it to her.

"Actually, I can't release the parrot. I'm just keeping him until the vet gets the microchip results back on Monday. Do you have a card so we can contact you?"

The man handed her his card and walked off without so much as a goodbye to her or "Salty."

That's weird. On impulse, Casey grabbed her iPhone and snapped a picture of him and his car, being sure to get the plates.

Soon after, her doorbell rang again. This time it was a couple standing on her porch, flyer in hand.

"Hello, ma'am, we're the Faggs. We've come for our parrot," the man said.

"Here, Cheese-It!" the woman called, as they entered Casey's duplex.

"Cheese-It" squawked and called out, "Cops are coming! Hide the loot!"

Casey told the Faggs the same thing she'd told Gibbs. When she asked for their information, they balked and inched out of her front room backwards. Casey snapped a photo of them and their car anyway.

She went through several alleged "owners" inquiring about the parrot. Again, she followed the same routine, taking photos of them and their vehicles.

***

Monday morning Casey showed up at Harley's with "Salty," aka "Cheese-It," "Baldy," "Littlefinger," "Fido," and "Myrtle."

"We've got a name for the parrot's owner," Harley said.

"Make my day!" the parrot said.

"And I've got a bunch of alleged owners who've claimed him," Casey said. "What?"

Casey told Harley how she'd put up flyers.

"I'm not surprised you had takers. I should have warned you not to advertise. Parrots are a hot commodity. Well, with any luck, we'll get this little guy back to Palmer Scudder soon."

"Did you say Palmer Scudder?" Casey sat down hard on the chair.

"Yes. You know him?"

"No. I read about him in Sunday's paper. He was murdered on Primrose near where I rescued the parrot. The same day."

It was unnaturally quiet in Harley's office for a few seconds, like a tribute to the dead. Even the parrot was silent for once.

"That so?" Harley finally said. "Looks like you'll be keeping him for a while — unless you want me to keep him. I can, now."

"No, that's okay. He can stay with me until we locate the owner's next-of-kin. That should show up in the obituary. Meanwhile, if anyone else shows up I'll let them know we found the owner."

When Casey arrived home, she put the teakettle on for a cup of ginger tea. It was known for increasing cognitive function, and she'd need all her "little grey cells" if she was going to fit the pieces of the mystery together.

She'd rescued the parrot on Primrose Lane soon after his owner, Palmer Scudder, had been found murdered. What if the parrot had been repeating what his owner had said right before he died? Could that mean the killer was still there when she rescued the parrot? She shivered.

If the killer saw her, he might have tracked her back home. Maybe he had broken into her duplex looking for . . . for what? The parrot? No, that didn't make sense. Her? What if the killer thought she'd seen him and was tying up loose ends? She didn't even want to go there. Besides, that was a long shot, and there hadn't been any further attempts to break in.

What if one of the people posing as the parrot's owner was the killer? Maybe he wanted to gauge her reaction — see if she recognized him. At the very least, all of them were would-be thieves. Casey decided to check out the contact information each of the "owners" had given her. Not surprisingly, the phone numbers were disconnected or belonged to someone else.

"Well, now, what are we going to do?" she asked the parrot. "Make yourself useful. Who did it?"

"Wasn't me!" the parrot replied. "I was framed!"

Casey mulled over her questions. One minute nothing held together, the next, every solution she'd thought of made perfect sense. She couldn't winnow down the list.

"I'm going to need help," Casey finally said. She hightailed it over to Woods' half of the duplex. As an ex-Marine who kept in contact with a network of veterans, he knew people with many useful skills.

"Woods, you know anyone who could track down a few license plates for me?"

"You meddling again? Remember what happened last time."

Casey had a knack for stumbling upon and getting involved with crimes. And a track record with the police to prove it. Especially with Jack Morgan, a drop-dead gorgeous detective she always seemed to butt heads with.

No, she wasn't a big fan of the police. They never seemed to take her seriously. Neither was Woods. She'd never asked him why. Better not to know.

"Keep bringing that up and your new nickname is 'Barry.'"

Woods fake-shuddered. "Give them to me. I'll see what I can do. You going to fill me in, or what?"

"These people all showed up claiming the parrot."

"And you just happened to be practicing your camera skills as each one left?"

"Let me catch you up on what's been happening. First of all, Barry's no longer in the picture."

Woods slapped his knee and beamed. "Well now, that's the best news I've heard in a long time. How you doing?"

"Fine. With this mystery surrounding the parrot, I haven't had much time or inkling to wallow in misery."

"The mystery? Oh, trying to find the owner?"

"Not exactly. Harley tracked down the owner. Turned out to be some guy who was killed on Primrose Lane. I'm going to try to locate his next-of-kin. Until then, I'm keeping him."

"Here we go again," Woods murmured, not quite under his breath.

"I'm going to see if my friend Jane can get me some info about the owner, Palmer Scudder. She has access to all kinds of databases at the paper. If anyone can find his next-of-kin, she can. You haven't heard of him, have you?"

"Palmer Scudder? Hmm. Don't think so. I'll get on the license plates ASAP. I'm almost afraid to ask, but anything else going on with you?"

Casey hesitated. "Well, I'm not sure, but I think my front door lock may have been tampered with. Could you check on it and see what you think? A few things looked out of place Friday night when Barry and I got home. That was such a weird day — I found the parrot, Barry and I broke up. I could have been mistaken."

"You should have told me sooner. Of course, I'll check it out."

"Good. I'm going to drop by the paper and see Jane. See you later!"

"While you're gone, I'll keep an eye on the duplex," Woods said. "How 'bout if I sit on your front porch?"

Casey felt her shoulders relax a little. She hadn't realized how tense she was. It was so nice to have someone she could count on. Woods was more than a landlord. He was a confidant and a father-figure, albeit a non-traditional one. "Would you? I'd appreciate it."

"No problem. Just protecting my property."

***

"I can't believe you're asking me to find a gangster's next-of-kin," Jane said. "What the heck have you gotten into now?"

"A gangster?" This situation was going from bad to worse. "What kind of gangstering did he do?"

"He didn't kill anyone, if that's what you're worried about. At least, it's not on his record. He was a climber. He moved up the food chain by getting the goods on members in competing gangs and then blackmailing them. He must have blackmailed the wrong person this time."

"I see."

"You still want me to track down his next-of-kin? Have you considered how dangerous it could be for you to contact them? What do you need them for, anyway?"

"Well, maybe not a next-of-kin. But someone in his family. Someone local, preferably. I rescued his pet parrot. Now I need to get him to his new owner."

"Wow." Jane pursed her lips and drummed her fingers on her desk. "Why don't you just keep it? Or sell it? They're worth a lot of money, aren't they?"

"I couldn't sell him. It wouldn't be right. I love all animals, but I think I'm more of a cat person at heart than a bird person." Casey shrugged her shoulders. "See what you can find out. Last resort, Harley can return the little guy to the breeder."

***

As soon as Casey and Woods walked in, the parrot called to her.

"Pretty lady! Gimme kiss!"

Casey laughed. Maybe she should reconsider keeping the parrot.

"Hey," she said. "I'm going to put the teakettle on. You want a cup of chamomile tea?"

"I'll pass. But thanks for asking. Two things. I looked at the lock. It's scratched, but that doesn't mean it was picked. You say nothing was taken?"

"No, nothing. And the place wasn't tossed, just a few things were misplaced. What could they have wanted?"

"It happened Friday night, right? Assuming someone did break in, maybe they were after the parrot. They could have seen you take it. They wouldn't have known that I kept it for you Friday night. It's possible. Anyway, Mack found one person of interest in the plates you gave me. The car Gibbs was driving was reported stolen a few days ago."

That didn't sound good. Casey switched to ginger tea, extra strong, and sat down at the kitchen table.

"Casey, what haven't you told me?"

"Palmer Scudder was a local gangster who had a penchant for blackmailing other gangsters. His parrot is now my roommate."

Just then the parrot came to life and started squawking. "Cops are coming! Hide the loot!"

"Let's say Gibbs was looking for the parrot," Casey said. "When he didn't find him, he came back with a flyer and tried to claim the little guy."

"But why would he want it?"

"Good question." The afternoon sun glinted off the parrot's band. Casey remembered what Harley had said when he was examining the parrot.

"I've got a hunch." Casey picked up her purse and the bird cage. "Want to come with me to Harley's?"

"I'm in, as long as you can drop me off at the yoga studio on the way back," Woods said.

Thankfully Harley was available when they arrived. "Any luck finding Scudder's next-of-kin?" Harley asked.

"Not yet," Casey said. "Hey, when you examined the little guy the other day, what was it you thought odd about his band?"

"Put him on the counter and I'll show you."

"Make my day!" the parrot said.

Once the parrot was ready to be examined, Harley explained. "Bands bear a code designating the issuing organization. I would have expected the code to begin with SPBE for the Society of Parrot Breeders and Exhibitors. But this code doesn't match anything I've ever seen."

"What exactly is the code? Casey asked."

"It's a bunch of numbers and letters — 53R23L55R7L26R8L."

Casey wrote it down. "Thanks, Harley."

"Sure, anytime."

On the way to the yoga studio, Casey kept running the numbers through her head.

"Got it!" she said. "I'll bet it's a safe combination. The parrot has the combination to Scudder's safe!"

"I hate to say this, but I think it's time to call in the cops," Woods said.

"Yeah, I think you're right."

After Casey dropped off Woods, she called Detective Jack Morgan. She'd had his number on speed-dial ever since she'd helped solve a prior case for the Indianapolis Metropolitan Police Department. After she explained the situation, he promised he and his partner, Gordie, would meet her at her duplex within a few minutes.

***

Casey opened her door and maneuvered the birdcage inside, setting it on the kitchen counter.

"There you go, pretty boy. Whew, I need to change your papers again. Let's just put you and your cage in the bathtub for now." She carried the cage through the hall and deposited it in the bathtub. Then she checked out her hair in the bathroom mirror and started to apply her favorite lip gloss.

"Help! He's gonna kill me!" the parrot started shrieking and flapping its wings.

Out of the corner of her eye, Casey glimpsed movement in the hall. She slammed the door. Locked it. Then she pushed open the small bathroom window, saying a silent 'thank you' that it had no screen. If she could flag down Jack before the guy broke through, she'd be okay. If not . . . she didn't want to go there.

"Look, lady," said a man's voice from the other side of the door. "All I want is the bird. Put the cage outside the door and I won't bother you."

"Help! Help! He's gonna kill me!"

"Very funny, bird," the intruder said. "I'm gonna wring your neck if you don't shut up."

Casey saw Jack's car pull up. She tossed out a roll of toilet tissue, which unfurled leaving a trail of white behind it, and waved her arm out the window to get his attention.

"Help! Help! He's gonna kill me!"

Casey joined in the chorus, her and the parrot crying for help in perfect harmony.

"Casey? Is someone in your house?" Jack asked from the other side of the window.

Casey nodded, never so glad to see the police.

"Help! Help!" the parrot said.

"Shut up, both of you," the guy behind the door shouted, pounding on the door. "If I have to come in there and take that darn bird forcefully, I'm not gonna be happy."

Jack motioned for Casey to respond while he and Gordie circled around to enter through the front door.

"Sorry. You're scaring him. I'm trying to calm him down. Give me a minute."

"Get a move on," the guy said. "I don't have all day."

Casey heard shouts and thuds, groans and crashes. No gunshots, thankfully. What seemed like an eternity later, Jack knocked on the door and told her it was safe to come out.

Just as she suspected, it was Gibbs who was handcuffed in her hallway. Gordie was reading him his rights.

"You okay?" Jack asked.

"Sure," Casey said, hoping he wouldn't notice her wobbly legs. "Thank you for getting here so soon."

"Thanks for the tip. We'll get out of your hair now." He turned to follow Gordie and Gibbs.

'Wait, I've got something else for you." Casey grabbed a piece of paper from her purse and handed it to him. "This should be the combination to Scudder's safe. I bet you find something interesting there."

***

The following evening Detective Jack Morgan showed up at her door.

"I take it you are off duty?"

"Umm, yes. I was in the neighborhood and thought I'd stop by and give you an update."

She poured a glass of wine and handed it to him, motioning him to sit on the couch. "So, what did you find out?"

"We got Gibbs for Scudder's murder. Gibbs works for a competing gang. We uncovered Scudder's safe and found enough dirt to put away members of both gangs for a long time." He smiled. "And to think, their downfall was all due to a chatty parrot."

As if on cue, the parrot chimed in. "Wasn't me! I was framed!!"

"You still have that bird?" Jack asked.

"He's only going to be here momentarily. I was able to locate Scudder's niece who was delighted to get, brace yourself, 'Capone.' She should be here soon to pick him up."

Just then, a young woman came to the door. Casey opened it before she had time to ring the doorbell.

"Hi, I'm Zelda. I'm here to pick up my uncle's parrot," she said when she came inside. "Is that Capone?"

"That's him," Casey said.

"Great! Oh, and thanks for letting me keep the cage until I get the one from Uncle Palmer's place." Zelda leaned down toward the parrot. "You're such a pretty boy, aren't you? We're going to get along just fine, aren't we?"

"Pretty lady! Gimme kiss!"

"Let me get the door for you," Casey said, stepping out on the porch so she could open the door wide. She practically bumped into someone standing out of sight on her porch.

"Barry?" Casey asked.

He had the grace to blush.

"Oh, Barry, sweetie!" Zelda said. "Meet Capone. He's so cute! And he talks, too! Aren't you just going to love having him around? Here, take his cage, please."

"What?" Barry stammered, backing away. "No, no, you keep it. I'll just go get the car door open for you." Without giving her a chance to reply, he hightailed it to his BMW.

"Loser! Loser!" the parrot said.

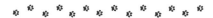

Shari Held is an Indianapolis-based freelance journalist, editor, and author. Her short stories have been published in numerous anthologies, including: "Pride and Patience" in The Fine Art of Murder (2016), "Murder Most Merry" in Homicide for the Holidays (2018), "Lost and Found" in Circle City Crime (2019) and "Deception at the Double D Convention" in Murder 20/20 (2020), for which she also served as co-editor. When not writing, she cares for feral cats and other wildlife, knits, and thinks up imaginative ways for her characters to get into all manner of trouble!

Catastrophic Crime

Steve Shrott

I was the one who discovered the body, despite the fact that others want to take the credit. Slime balls!

The name's, Roxy. I'm a tabby cat. I have black stripes, swirls, and spots. Some of the other felines have said I'm a hottie. And I did not pay them any mice to say that.

The dead body was human, by the way. I found it behind the Townsend library we have here in Hilltop County. That's my usual hangout. It's odd since I've never been much of a reader.

All the kids who go to the library try to pet me, but I'm usually able to scootch away before they get their sticky fingers all over my velvety-soft fur. I don't like kids. Too needy, too grabby, too loud. And no, I'm not an old grouch. I'm only four.

As I headed toward The Hungry Pig, one of our county's fantabulous restaurants, I could smell the delicious aromas emanating from the trash cans outside. That's when I heard a gunshot and I...uh ...uh...sorry, lately my memory hasn't been working so well. I'm also getting tired much easier. I don't know what's up with that.

I do remember living with this old lady. She used to say that I was a rescue or maybe it was that I rescued her. Yeah, that sounds like something I would do. You know, like pulling her from a burning building, diving in the ocean to save her from drowning, pushing her out of the way of a speeding car. The only problem with any of that is I'm afraid of fire, water, and cars as well as pulling, diving, or pushing anything.

She fed me, told me stories. Got me this red collar with rhinestones that I wear around my neck. Some of the cats on the street got their noses out of joint about it, saying, "Roxy thinks she's something special now that she's sporting jewelry."

Hey, you can only be who you are. I'm actually quite humble. Although when I pass a mirror, I have to say I do look fine.

Now, I remember, I was talking about the dead body, right?

So when I heard the gunshot, I jumped into one of the garbage cans. I figured the bullet was meant for me. Hey, I did some rough stuff back in the day, and thought my nemesis, Fluffy might still have a vendetta against me. She's a tough cookie. You make one tiny meow when she's having a siesta, she'll come at you hard.

I quickly climbed out of the trash to see what was happening. Then I saw a flash of blue as someone raced away. On the ground was a human, not breathing. Blood all over him. It was grisly. Forgive me, but it looked like something the dog dragged in.

I had come there just to search the garbage and get some takeout, but after what I saw, I had no appetite.

Of course, that never stopped me before, and I dived back into the garbage can and helped myself to some spuds with bite marks and a few morsels of sautéed vegetables. It was great cause I'm vegan. Well, part-time. Otherwise, I'm a steak-a-holic. After all the munchies, I was completely stuffed, which meant I would be hungry again in five point two milliseconds. But right now, I knew I had to get justice for the dead guy. I'm very socially conscious that way. After all, he was probably some cat's pet.

So I started investigating the area. You know, I think I could have been a great detective except for the fact that I'm not so keen on blood, guns, crooks, or investigating.

I meowed as loudly as I could, hoping that it would bring attention to the body.

A few moments later, people started showing up, and after a while, there were several policemen. A handsome cop began talking to a plump bald man.

"How did you discover the body, sir?"

"I just came out of the restaurant and there it was."

I shook my head at the man. Really, that's how it happened? I didn't do anything? I don't remember you straining your esophageal sphincter meowing like a crazy person.

I meowed again just to make my point. Handsome Cop heard it, then noticed me on the ground. "Hey kitty...how are you?"

Now, I have to tell you that being called, 'kitty' is one of my pet peeves. It's just so demeaning. For some reason, we don't get respected like dogs even though they drink out of the toilet then pee like a fire hose wherever they darn well please. Go figure.

Handsome Cop examined my collar. "You must belong to someone."

Then he picked me up. Geez, would this horror never end? My other pet peeve is being picked up by strangers.

But actually, this was kinda nice. It was warm and he did have soft, strong hands. Ah, what the hell. Being cuddled by an attractive man was number two on my bucket list. Number one was hiring Lady Gaga's esthetician so I wouldn't have to groom myself and get freaking fur all over my tongue.

He took me to his home. Quite nicely decorated, I must say. I was put off a little by the photo of him and this little girl hugging an enormous mouse at a place called Disney something or other. What the hell are they feeding that thing? I knew I was gonna have nightmares about that monster. Handsome Cop said, "Tomorrow we'll try and find your owner."

I doubted my owner would even remember me. I had been travelling on the dark, dissolute streets for uh...I didn't really remember but it seemed like years.

Besides, I'd already kinda gotten used to the cop's luxurious pad and didn't want to leave. But the next morning he took me down to the police station.

I heard the cops working on the murder. I really didn't think they'd ever figure it out. I mean cops are smart, but we have a bit more upstairs, if you know what I mean. You think those mice we bring you as gifts just fall from the sky? There's planning, navigating, mathematical calculations, and a lot of fancy footwork. Oddly enough, even with that, I'm not a great dancer—four left feet. Ha Ha Ha. That's my favorite joke. Hey, I'm here all week, folks!

After a while, I got bored being in the office with nothing much happening. So when the door opened, I slipped out of the police station and went back to the Hungry Pig. I wanted to see if I could dig up evidence. Okay, I also wanted to see if I could dig up some half-eaten pork chops in the garbage.

A few moments later, I saw a tall man heading toward me. I was sure he was the perpetrator. He was wearing blue like the guy who had run away from the body. What other clues did I need? I chomped down hard on his leg. He screamed like he was having quintuplets without anesthetic.

I thought, now I've got him. But when I looked up, I saw that the man I had bitten was... the Mayor of Hilltop.

What had I done? I dashed away behind the garbage can, hoping he hadn't seen me. If this got in the papers my reputation would be ruined—especially with any eligible bachelors. No one likes a tainted lady.

Maybe it was the stress of biting the mayor that did it, but I started playing with this small round thing on the ground beside the garbage can. I liked rolling it around. It had been a long time since I had toys. I felt my eyes moisten. I missed toys... and the old lady who I took care of.

I couldn't think about that now. I had work to do. I left the toy behind the garbage, then searched again to see if there were any other people wearing blue. I didn't find anyone and was about to give up my investigating when two men entered the area. One was a thin guy and the other, burly. Burly Man was wearing a blue jacket.

Could this be the murderer?

He surveyed the ground for a few moments, then started looking in the garbage as Thin Guy watched. Their dialogue sounded like this, although probably not exactly. Hey, I'm a cat with limited linguistic abilities.

Thin Guy said, "Did you have to kill him?"

Burly Man replied, "He saw us rob the bank. He would have told the cops and we'd be in jail for a long time. You want that?"

"No, but what are we doing here? The cops already have the body.; They ain't coming back."

Burly Man pulled numerous items out of the garbage can and threw them onto the ground. "Who knows, they might. And if they find it, we're in trouble."

I checked the objects on the ground for hard evidence and to see if they had any bacon grease on them. Me loves the bacon grease.

I didn't know what they were looking for, but a light went off in my head. It was Burly Man. Doesn't the killer always return to the scene of the crime? I snarled at the men like I was hopped up on catnip. (That stuff is delicious, but diabolical.) Burly Man screamed, "Get away cat." Then he kicked me. I was about to bite him, but then I realized that I didn't want to end up like dead guy. I was in my prime and still had a lot of napping to do.

Burly Man picked me up. Geez, twice in one day. I did not like the feel of his hands and they smelled like a Doberman Pincher who hadn't seen a bar of soap in months.

Thin Guy shook his head. "What are you doing with him?"

Burly Man replied, "He saw us looking for the evidence. He's a witness."

"He's a cat. He can't tell anyone about us."

"You never know."

Thin Guy rolled his eyes.

I tried to get out of Burly Man's arms, but he held me tight as they jumped into some old car. Immediately, he threw me into the back seat and Thin Guy started driving.

I wasn't going to take this lying down. I jumped onto Thin Guy's head and grabbed a strand of greasy hair in my teeth. Then I slid down and swung in front of his eyes like I was one of the Flying Walendas.

He shook his head from side to side, trying to shake me off. But I held tight like his hair was a mouse dipped in fish pate.

The next moment, the car swerved out of control, and we crashed into a stop sign.

I was dazed, and the two men looked unconscious, but I saw they were still breathing. I looked at Burly Man's blue jacket, and suddenly I knew what to do. I scampered out the now shattered windshield and onto the mean streets of Hilltop.

I needed to go to the police station. But first I had to make a quick stop at that garbage can, and not just to look for another rib-eye. Although while I was there, what would be the harm?

***

I jumped onto the hands of Handsome Cop as he sat at his desk in police headquarters. They were still warm and strong. I could get used to this.

"You're back. Guess you missed us." He said, a smile on his face. Then he started stroking me.

So good.

"What's that you've got?"

I opened my mouth and dropped my toy onto his desk.

At that moment another officer entered the room. He was wiry with a tiny moustache. "Is that a button?"

"Yeah, it's from the cat."

"They pick up the stupidest things."

I stared at Moustache Dude. I just solved the case, buster. How's that for stupid? This button was what the two guys responsible for the dead body were looking for at the scene of the crime. Got it? It matches the blue buttons on Burly Man's jacket.

Moustache Dude said, "You know what? That button has what looks like blood on it."

Handsome Cop nodded. "It does. And the cat was near the body the other night."

This was taking them way too long to figure out.

Finally, Moustache Dude said, "That button must be from the killer's jacket."

About time, Einstein.

At that moment the phone rang and Handsome Cop picked it up.

"Uh huh. Two men at a stop sign...and a cat?"

Handsome Cop looked over at me.

"Let me ask you a question...," he said to the guy on the phone. "Is one of the men missing a button from his coat?... Thanks." A moment later, he hung up, a stunned look on his face.

"Was he missing a button?"

Handsome cop slowly nodded. "Not only that, he said that witnesses told him a cat jumped out of the car when these two guys crashed into a stop sign. They said the cat had a rhinestone collar." Handsome Cop spread his hands. "This cat stopped the crooks, found evidence, and solved the murder."

They both looked at me as if a cat could never do all that. I just shook my head in pity.

A moment later, Handsome Cop patted me. "Good work, kitty."

I still hated the name, but at least I got some credit for all the detective work I did. I hoped this would encourage them to get more cats to join the force. They could pay us in bacon grease.

***

The two men were arrested and went to jail. A week later, the officers found the gray-haired old lady who I took care of. Her name was Lilly and she had a big smile on her face. She picked me up and hugged me tighter than a wrestler who's trying to stop his opponent from breathing. She said her place is going to be my forever home after I'm fixed. I really didn't understand that as nothing is broken. I'm not sure they can make me better than I am now, but, hey, if they can, I'm sure it will be a delightful experience.

But it was sure nice to have a forever home.

She told the cops that I'd only been gone a few days, not the eternity I had thought. I guess that was my memory playing tricks on me. She said she had looked everywhere, worried sick because I was...pregnant.

Pregnant? Me? No way. Kids? Not on your life. Still, that would explain all my issues with not remembering and being so tired. I heard being a mom really affects your mind.

A week later, I gave birth to six kittens. They're so needy, grabby, and loud. But between you and me, I love them.

I'm hoping I can help the cops in future cases. After all, I now have a team of deputies-to-be.

Steve Shrott's short stories have appeared in numerous publications including Sherlock Holmes Mystery Magazine, Mystery Weekly, and Black Cat Mystery Magazine. In Flame Tree Press's Mystery and Crime anthology, Steve's story, The House, appears alongside tales by Author Conan Doyle and Charles Dickens, His comedy material has been used by well-known performers of stage and screen. As well, he has written a book on how to create humor (Steve Shrott's Comedy Course.) Two of his humorous mystery novels have been published (Audition for Death and Dead Men Don't Get Married,) and some of his jokes are in the Smithsonian Institution.

Where All the Bodies Are Buried

Gabriel Valjan

P eople expect to find death in a cemetery, not a murder.

Paul Specter and his dog discovered the body inside the grave dug for Olive Goodrich on Sunday morning. Paul was the town's gravedigger and groundskeeper. Cerberus was an adult wolfdog, orphaned after someone had shot his mother dead. The late Mrs. Goodrich was Prospect Bay's first centenarian. In the space for her final destination, the earth received, instead, the town's mailman and journalist, Harold Munster.

Paul was out that morning to put flowers on his wife's grave and say a few words. Her death and her absence hurt man and dog alike. She'd died at home, and not in some godawful hospital room at County Hospital twenty-five miles away. When he was done, Paul reached into his pocket for his cell and called Police Chief Shelby.

"We've got a problem," he told the lawman and long-time friend.

"Let me guess. Vandalism, or some kids rode through the mud on their mountain bikes?"

True, it had rained overnight but there was more to it than that. Planted upright in the mound in front of Paul, like a scarecrow, was his spade. He could've sworn he had returned the tool to his shed.

"No kids, but there's plenty of mud."

"What then?"

"Murder."

Paul heard the chair creak. Murder seldom visited Prospect Bay. The town saw its share of mischief, from pranks to barfights throughout the year, but not homicide.

"How do you know it's murder, Paul?"

"Someone's in Olive Goodrich's grave, and it isn't her."

"Who then?"

"Harry."

"Munster? How can you be so sure?"

"Aside from his head bashed in, Harry was defiant to the end."

"Come again?"

"Face down and his can is in the air. I'll wait here with Cerberus."

Paul ended the conversation and pocketed his cell phone. He knew the chief had to call the County Medical Examiner, the funeral home, and the Goodrich family. There was a good chance that he might rein in Doc Perkins, the town's veterinarian. Doc might find clues before County arrived and poached their case.

Cerberus stayed with Paul until Doc Perkins arrived. Paul and Ellen had never had children, due to her health. Cerberus was the closest thing to a child they'd had. Ellen had doted on the pup, and the dog matured into a majestic beast, a creature that was protective of his humans. With his massive head, thick body and enormous paws, the wolfdog possessed expressive blue eyes and an acute sense of smell. He would trail Ellen everywhere. After she died, he followed Paul everywhere.

***

Cerberus stood guard at the gate to the cemetery, while Chief Shelby photographed the perimeter of the grave with his iPhone. Budd Perkins asked to borrow the phone, saying he wanted to record his observations of the crime scene, after they gloved up.

"Victim is Harold Munster. Caucasian male, age fifty-two and found knee-to-chest in a recent grave. Excavated depth is," and the doctor looked to Paul, who said, "Nine feet. A family plot."

"Nine feet. Heavy rain has rendered the site muddy, possibly impossible to scale once the victim fell inside." Perkins looked. "What?"

"Possibly impossible?" Chief Shelby asked. "Is that even English?"

Perkins paused the recording. "Did you understand what I said when I said it?" Shelby nodded. "Then it's proper English. Shall I continue?"

"Chief Shelby has photographed the victim and a shovel. What is it now, Paul?"

"It's a spade."

"Correction. Gravedigger Paul Specter has identified the instrument at the scene as a spade. Pending forensics, the spade is assumed to be the murder weapon. The decedent's head has sustained blunt-force trauma, consistent with a spade. Caretaker Specter stated that he returned the spade to his toolshed after digging the hole for the imminent interment of Olive Goodrich." The doctor returned the phone to the lawman.

"Imminent interment...isn't that alliteration?" Shelby asked.

"Shut up Shelby, how's that for alliteration?"

"You know what?" the police chief said. "The heck with waiting for County. Paul, get us a ladder."

Whoever killed Harold had hit him on top of the head the way a strongman used a mallet to ring the bell at the top of the High-Striker amusement at the annual carnival. Paul looked down at the body. "Harold could've drowned. Let's say he was brained, fell into the hole unconscious, and then tried to get up but couldn't."

"Would explain his butt up in the air," Shelby said.

The doctor considered the theory. "The ME will check his lungs for water. Either way, your spade killed him."

"You don't think I..."

"You have means." Chief Shelby pointed to Paul's house, next to the cemetery.

"And half of this town has motive," Paul said.

Cerberus lifted his head and howled an ancient song he'd inherited from his canine ancestors. The county sheriff and medical team had arrived.

***

Paul Specter was correct, in that the other half of the town disliked the victim. Harold Munster was Prospect Bay's monster in-residence. 'Handsome Harry' was his byline at Prospect Bay Today. The mailman was a self-taught journalist, an autodidact, who claimed Ben Franklin and Jay Gatsby as his inspirations. With time, everyone in Prospect Bay either wanted to see Handsome Harry struck by lightning like Franklin or floating in the pool for the big swim like Gatsby.

He played the town's Agony Uncle, offering advice to the beleaguered and besotted. Advice soon degenerated into observation, and observations deteriorated into malignant gossip. Handsome Harry's had reached the peak of infamy when he became the town's self-appointed critic and reduced the masthead of PBT to a joke, as in Painful Butt Today.

***

They watched the body and gurney disappear into the black car. County Sheriff Cox walked over. Shelby said nothing. The two men had been rivals since high school, captains of their respective teams on the gridiron, on the basketball court, and the baseball diamond. Cox may have won the election to become sheriff but he lost his girl to Police Chief Shelby.

"Your ME give an approximate time of death?"

Cox answered. "Maggie says the liver temp places Harry's death somewhere between eight and eleven, about the time the rain started and stopped." Cox started to walk away and turned to have the last word. "My guys dusted the inside of the toolshed, which I bet will match Paul's prints, once he gives us a set. Total wash, no pun intended, on the spade, though. Good luck with what's left of your investigation, Chief Shelby."

Cox did the proverbial tip of the hat and walked away. The County ME still had an autopsy to perform. Paul provided a set of prints to the tech. Budd Perkins excused himself, saying he had to tend to his bovine patients.

Cerberus returned to the graveside. He pawed the ground and pried something loose and sniffed at the mud. Paul asked, "What've you got, boy?"

The stone was uncommon to the area, and pink. Shelby approached, Evidence bag ready. Paul used the spent gloves in his pocket to grasp the rock and slid it into the paper bag. Shelby looked. Paul answered, "Quartz."

"A geologist, in your spare time?"

"I'm a groundskeeper, remember?"

"Groundskeeper where all the bodies are buried. Come with me, and bring the dog."

***

Handsome Harry had made enemies the way a bee gathered pollen, but he'd never aimed any malice at the Specters, because they'd adopted Cerberus. The man had cared more about animals than he did about people.

Cerberus' mother Mabel was a local fixture. Wolfdogs are social creatures, and Mabel would wander into town to socialize with the other dogs. Once, while she was sauntering down Main Street, Harry had leashed her and took her to Dr. Perkins for a full checkup. That was when the town learned that Mabel was pregnant. When Mabel died, her killer a mystery, Harry unloaded both lobes of his infuriated brain, outraged that someone would murder a mother and orphan her child.

***

Their first stop was to see Harry's widow. Paul entered the room after Shelby had delivered the awful news. The officer was skilled enough to offer his condolences and question her as a potential suspect without offending her.

"We'd like to establish a timeline, his whereabouts on Saturday."

"I saw him last in the afternoon, around five or so."

"You didn't have dinner together then?"

"No. I had to attend a parent-teacher conference. We came home together after the conference."

"We, as in you and Penny?" Shelby asked.

"Yes, I picked her up at her girlfriend Nancy's house."

"About what time was that?"

"Let's see," Elizabeth Munster said. "The conference ended 8:30ish, and I talked to the Wilsons and the Flanagans. It'd started to rain, and I thought I could wait it out. Unfortunately, the rain worsened. I'd say I left the school ten to nine, picked up Penny at the Bowers around nine o'clock, and came home."

"And Harry?"

"Out, reviewing something or finding his next story, I suppose."

"Any emails, texts or phone messages?" She shook her head. "Was Harry upset recently, preoccupied?"

"Peeved was Harold's natural state of existence, so no."

"You said finding his next story. Was he working on anything in particular?"

"Follow me," she said and led the way into Harry's study. She unhinged the man's laptop and unlocked it with a password. Neither Paul nor Shelby said a word about the fact that she knew the password. She clicked on the icon for Word and moved the cursor to the menu and selected File and then Open Recent.

And they read. They read about who may have helped Harry into the hereafter.

Suspect one. The minister Wakefield was having an affair. Harry provided the names of B&Bs and hotels outside of Prospect Bay. He listed the dates for the encounters between the town's Dimmesdale and his Hester Prynne.

Suspect two. The mayor was embezzling from the city's coffers. Harry offered little proof, only innuendo. His article called for an investigation. Chief Shelby closed the cover and said, "Let's visit the minister and mayor."

The chief asked Elizabeth if she would print the two files for him and told her that if anyone asked, the laptop was with him. They thanked her and left.

Cerberus slobbered, happy to be a part of Clue Crew.

***

The reverend was somewhat new to Prospect Bay. His predecessor had died of natural causes. The town advertised for a new shepherd. Interviewed by the parish's board, Reverend Wakefield was hired. He was paid a modest salary, and the town provided him with a house. He met and married local girl Dorothy Windstrop, and they had a child, Daniel, who was now five years old, a spoiled brat, and the closest thing to a howler monkey in human form. Common sense said Dorothy's salary carried the family.

Reverend Wakefield received them in his kitchen. He said his wife was out with their son. Police Chief Shelby and Paul Specter marveled at the décor. Dorothy Wakefield demonstrated an aptitude for home design.

"I assume you've heard the news," Shelby said.

"That Harry is dead? Yes, I have. I plan to visit Elizabeth after Dorothy returns."

Shelby reached into his pocket, chose the right piece of paper, and handed it to the reverend. "You should read this."

Wakefield's eyes moved left to right, like a typewriter. There was no bell with the carriage return, no appearance of alarm in his expression.

"Is it true?" Paul asked.

"Harry certainly knew how to sell copy."

"True, but you know what they say about stuff once it's online. Content lives forever. Is it true or not?"

"Gossip or not, an affair is grounds for motive," Paul said.

"You think I killed Harry?"

"Funny," Shelby said. "I never said how Harry died."

"The man was found headfirst in a fresh grave, in the cemetery. Not what I'd call natural causes."

"You seem cavalier about life and death. A man is dead."

"Look, Chief Shelby. Harry had enemies. Wave a salacious piece of gossip in anybody's face, and you won't find much sympathy."

Paul stepped forward. "A salacious piece of gossip you didn't deny."

"I won't dignify idle talk with a response. Now that you've made the purpose of your visit known, I'd suggest you get to your point."

"Fair enough," Shelby said. "Account for your whereabouts last night."

"An alibi, is that it? I was with Daphne Strickland, five to eleven."

"Doing what?"

"Does someone need to spell it out for you and include a stick drawing?"

"Humor Chief Shelby, and answer the question," Paul said.

"Counting raindrops. Satisfied?"

"And your wife?" Shelby asked. "Public humiliation is—"

"Now she's a suspect? Is that how you pivot when I've just given you an alibi? If you must know, she's been with her mother since Friday night. She would like our son to have a relationship with his grandmother."

"I see," Paul said. "The fox visited the henhouse while the wife was away."

"Judgmental much?"

They heard a door open and close, a child crying. Dorothy walked in with Daniel in her arms, said hello to them and excused herself. She said something nasty about the large dog in the backseat of the police cruiser frightening her son but disappeared too quickly for them to hear her exact words. The reverend escorted them to the door, saying he wanted to spend time with his wife and child. Shelby and Paul walked back to the vehicle.

Cerberus, head hanging out the car window, howled. He may have preferred Hester Prynne to Dot Windstrop.

***

Mayor Huntley lived on Prospect Hill, the affluent section of Prospect Bay. As the cruiser drifted down the driveway, crushed stones bristled against the underbelly of the car. When they exited the vehicle, Cerberus nosed the ground and picked up one of the many rocks in the driveway and brought it to Paul. He held up the stone for Shelby to see it. The sheriff shook his head while Paul pocketed the stone.

The butler inside informed the mayor that the police chief, the gravedigger, and a large dog were there to see him. The three of them heard the oft-quoted line from the movies, "This way, please."

In a hallway fit for a Caesar, they passed rare paintings and commissioned portraits of the mayor and his wife, Arianna, and of their children. Politics paid well.

The butler closed the door. Shelby and Paul each turned his head when they'd heard it click behind them. Cerberus snapped and snarled at the rifle on the wall. The wall displayed trophies. Elk. Moose. A mountain lion. A wolf.

The mayor approached for the handshake. His hand was soft as the seasoned leather of a baseball glove. Cerberus found himself a sunspot on the area rug and lay down.

"Harry Munster is dead," Chief Shelby said.

"I heard," Huntley said. He turned and pointed to the phone behind him. "Dale called me, about an hour ago, and Maggie is doing the autopsy as we speak."

"I wasn't aware you were on a first-name basis with the County Sheriff and Medical Examiner," Paul said.

"All in the spirit of cooperation. Now, how can I help you?"

Shelby reached into his jacket. He pulled out a piece of paper and handed it to Huntley. The mayor asked, "What's this...a subpoena?"

"No, but it might lead to an arrest warrant. It's from Harry's computer."

Huntley unfolded the paper and scanned the page. "Harry always exercised a flair for the dramatic."

"So, you're not interested in running for the Senate?" Paul asked.

"Of course I am, but my campaign funding is aboveboard."

"Then open up your books and prove Harry wrong," Shelby said.

"It doesn't work that way, gentlemen."

"How does it work then?" the chief asked.

"First of all, donors are entitled to privacy until I declare my candidacy. Second, political funding is a matter for auditors. If you want access to my campaign financials, you'll need the proper legal papers. Need I remind you that I'm acquainted with all the judges."

"Convenient." Police Chief Shelby reached into his coat pocket and pulled out the Evidence bag. He shook it as if it were a bag of peanuts. The mayor squinted at first and then sighed, "Is that supposed to mean something?"

Paul reached into his jacket. "Cerberus found this in your driveway. It's the same kind of rock that's inside the chief's bag. I bet they both can be traced to the same quarry. Pink quartz."

"What are you two, the rock police?" Huntley said. "I'm confident that the same quartz and quarry can be found in several driveways throughout the state. Anything else?"

"Where were you last night, between eight and eleven?" Shelby asked.

"Here probably. I'm sure my wife or Horace can confirm it. Satisfied?"

Chief Shelby smiled. "Your wife can't testify against you. Horace is the butler, right? The man probably signed a nondisclosure agreement to never discuss whatever happens in this house."

"I'm done being amused," the mayor said. "Unless you have a subpoena or a warrant—"

"I'll get both. Oh, that's right: you know all the judges."

"And don't forget that a police chief serves at the mayor's pleasure. Now, if there's nothing else, I suggest you leave."

"Actually, there is one more thing," Paul said. "Chief Shelby has Harry's laptop under lock and key at his office. First thing Monday morning, a bunch of computer geeks will be scouring that laptop's hard drive. All it takes is one little speck, one little spark, and your house burns down to the ground. You may end up wishing you had jumped in and joined Harry. The plot accommodates three."

Before they left, Paul whispered into Cerberus's ear. The wolfdog took a big whiff of the mayor before leading the way out the door.

***

In the car ride to the station, Paul explained his plan to Shelby, but the chief wasn't sold on the strategy. "What if he thinks we're bluffing about Harry's laptop?"

"He'll do nothing then." Paul looked over his shoulder at Cerberus. "You in or not, buddy?"

The dog blinked his big blue eyes and continued panting. Paul asked that they make a stop at the local Piggly-Wiggly for provisions and Milk-Bones for Cerberus. They spent the next few hours in the parking lot, killing time, and reminiscing about their wives.

When the time had come, they parked the car behind the police station and entered the building from the rear door. The layout was as simple as applesauce. There was a wooden desk from the last century, a phone, a computer monitor, and a printer. The place could've passed as the set for The Andy Griffith Show, except for the contemporary technology, from a high-speed internet connection to the digital camera for the rare mugshot. The bathroom down the hallway was unisex and clean. The one item in the whole joint that did seem as if it'd leapt out of a western was the jail cell, which consisted of a bunk bed, two thin mattresses and two lumpy pillows. There was a small sink, a toilet, and the cheapest and most abrasive roll of toilet paper, courtesy of the taxpayer. The door to the jail cell and the window, high above the street, were thick with iron bars.

Paul set his laptop on the desk and cracked the blinds wide enough for a view to the sidewalk. They'd wait in the dark, sitting on the floor with Cerberus in the corner. As it grew darker and their snacks dwindled, they tossed treats at Cerberus to keep him entertained. They would continue this stakeout and see whether the mayor had bought the lie that Harry's laptop was here.

Cerberus rested his head on his paws.

Traffic on Main Street died down around ten. There was a false alarm at eleven when some kids passed the station, dribbling a basketball and talking smack with each other. At midnight, the laptop reflected a bluish glow from the streetlamps. All of Prospect Bay seemed asleep.

Then they heard it.

The doorknob rattled. Paul leaned over for a look and Shelby peered around a corner. Paul threw another Milk-Bone to confirm that Cerberus was awake. The dog's ears twitched at the sound of another noise, a subtle crack, and the sound of glass splintering. Someone had broken the windowpane above the doorknob.

The chief watched a gloved hand dip inside and then the crook of an elbow angle downward for the knob. Shards of glass glittered on the floor. The dog's blue eyes looked up. His hindquarters shuffled from side to side in preparation for the pounce. His nostrils flared as if he recognized a scent.

The silhouette walked cat-like to the desk; glass crunched underfoot. When the gloved hand touched the laptop, Cerberus sprang and arced through the air. The burglar crashed with a loud scream. The chief threw the light.

Mayor Huntley.

***

The mayor talked for the better part of an hour. His wife was old money and he needed new money. There wasn't a senator who wasn't a millionaire, and it took serious cash to fund a war chest. Huntley explained that he had 'borrowed' from the city coffers and swore that he'd be able to replace it when he was elected by bringing big money to small Prospect Bay.

Harry had caught on to his scheme. They'd agreed to meet. The mayor was certain that Harry would be open to a sum and that the matter would be settled. Handsome Harry refused, the mayor said.

He claimed Harry accused him of killing Mabel with the rifle on his wall. The mayor said he tried to reason with Harry, but Harry wouldn't listen.

They argued. It rained. The mayor shoved Harry. Harry fell into the grave. The mayor said he looked around for something to help Harry out of the hole. He saw the toolshed. He ran over to it, found it unlocked, and opened the door. He saw the ladder.

He chose the spade.

Gabriel Valjan lives in Boston's South End. He is the author of the Roma Series and The Company Files (Winter Goose Publishing) and the Shane Cleary Series (Level Best Books). His second Company File novel, The Naming Game, was a finalist for the Agatha Award for Best Historical Mystery and the Anthony Award for Best Paperback Original in 2020. Gabriel is a member of the Historical Novel Society, International Thriller Writers (ITW), and Sisters in Crime.

Five-O

Tracy Falenwolfe

Robert "The Hammer" Shelhammer knew the trio on his front porch were cops, but he called out anyway. "Who is it?"

"Uh oh. It's the cops! Five-O. Five-O. Squawk. It's the cops."

"Chuck!" Hammer warned. "That's enough."

The African Grey parrot ignored him, shuffling from side to side on his perch. "Uh oh. Squawk."

"We're coming in, Sarge." Hammer's squad trooped into the kitchen uninvited. Working in Vice, they didn't look much like cops, but they were all seasoned pros.

"Here." Jackie Barber handed Hammer a cup of coffee from the food truck outside the station. Her badge hung from a chain around her neck.

Chuck bounced up and down when he saw it. "It's the cops! Squawk!"

Chris Hanson and Phil Donnelly hid smiles behind their coffee cups.

"How are you, Chuck?" Jackie said to the bird.

He gave a wolf whistle. "She'll like it too." Then a sexy purr.

"Enough," Hammer said. "Behave yourself, or you're out of here," he said to the bird.

Hanson and Donnelly snickered.

"What?" Hammer drank some of his coffee, his mood still foul two weeks after he'd been sidelined by a bungled drug bust, leaked body cam footage, and Chuck—the bird who never stopped talking. "What are you two giggling about?"

Chuck shuffled from side to side and cocked his head toward Donnelly. "Be the envy of other men. Squawk!"

"You know it," Donnelly said to the bird. Donnelly wore his long, gray hair in a ponytail and dressed like a biker.

Hammer shook his head.

Hanson, the youngest of the squad, always dressed in flannel and sported a man bun. He bent his head and peered into Chuck's cage. "He looks a little better. How does Lena say he's doing?"

Chuck gave another wolf whistle. Then a racy growl.

Donnelly and Hanson laughed. "He sure has your number," Donnelly said. "Even the bird can see you're into Lena."

"Get out of my house," Hammer shot back.

"Sorry, Sarge. We'll be serious." Donnelly put the cap back on his coffee cup. "Tell us, how is he doing?"

Hammer leaned back against the counter and folded his arms across his chest. "Lena says he's still traumatized. But he's stopped pulling out his own feathers, so that's good."

Lena Jimenez was the animal control officer for the county. She'd been called to remove Chuck from the drug dealer's house after the bust gone wrong. When she told Hammer they would have a difficult time placing the bird, but that she'd be willing to work with whoever fostered him, Hammer had volunteered for the job.

Jackie finished her coffee and tossed the empty cup in Hammer's trash. "So when are you coming back to work?"

The question gave him hives. Two weeks ago, he and the team had set out to bust a ring of drug counterfeiters. Warrant in hand, they'd arrived at the home the ring had been operating from. Before they even knocked, Chuck, the parrot, outed them. "Uh oh. It's the cops! Five-O. Five-O. Squawk! It's the cops."

The counterfeiters attempted to run out the back door. Hammer plowed through the front and yelled, "Hands in the air! Don't move a muscle, sucker."

One of the counterfeiters escaped. The other was caught, but only because he stopped to laugh at Hammer. It was embarrassing. He couldn't say why he'd blurted out such a cheesy line. Adrenaline, maybe. Or maybe the bird threw him off his game. Twenty years on the job and he'd never felt this humiliated.

The ring of drug counterfeiters turned out to be two brothers slapping male enhancement pill labels on bottles of off brand ibuprofen. Then, as if he hadn't taken enough guff from the guys at the station, Hammer's body cam footage was leaked online and he became an overnight internet sensation. He couldn't even grocery shop without someone pointing at him. "Hands in the air! Don't move a muscle, sucker." Everyone said it now.

"I'm thinking about hanging it up," Hammer told Jackie.

"You're not serious." Donnelly's leather vest squeaked against the back of the chair when he leaned forward. "Come on, Sarge. It'll pass. People will forget about it."

"Not cops. Cops never forget."

"Uh oh. It's the cops! Five-O. Five-O. Squawk. It's the cops."

Hammer sighed, and shook his head at Chuck.

"Look," Jackie said. "It wasn't for nothing. The one we have in custody is singing like a—" she stopped and looked over at Chuck. "Well...you know. They were selling party drugs, too. Real ones. It was a big stash. They'll both do time."

"The burn out you collared thinks he's getting off the hook." Hanson mopped up a drop of spilled coffee with the tail of his flannel shirt. "But his deal is only good if we pick up his brother as a result, and so far he's in the wind."

Hammer nodded. Righteous bust or not, he was still feeling disgraced. "Shouldn't you guys be getting back?"

Jackie looked defeated. "Why don't you come with us?"

"Not now," Hammer said.□

Donnelly and Hanson rose from the table. They each clapped Hammer on the back as they filed out. "Take it easy, Sarge," Donnelly said. "We'll be back tomorrow."

Jackie stopped at the door and turned back. Her badge caught the sunlight. "The squad isn't the same without you."

Chuck gave another wolf whistle. "Squawk! You can go all night!"

Hammer closed his eyes and sighed. "I'll see you later."

***

When Lena came over that night to check on Chuck, Hammer admitted what he couldn't say to his squad. "I don't think he likes me."

"He likes you just fine." Lena tore open the packet of arugula she'd brought. "African Greys are not cuddly birds. They tend to bond with one person, and this one may have been bonded with one of the drug dealers. Give him some time." She placed some of the arugula in the bowl on the kitchen table. "And give him this with his pellets. He'll like it."

Lena had the kindest eyes Hammer had ever seen. They were big and brown and soulful, with long lashes that didn't need mascara. Animals loved her, and so did everyone else. Hammer had been planning to ask her out, but that was before his body cam footage had gone viral.

"Has he been out of his cage today?"

"Yes," Hammer said. "For a couple of hours."

"What did he do?"

"He flew around the bird room. He climbed on the ladder. He beat his wings." The bird room was Hammer's spare bedroom, which Lena had helped him make safe for Chuck to spend time in out of his cage.

"Those are all good things. Why do you think he doesn't like you?"

Hammer shrugged. "I don't think he likes cops." Plus, he shied away when Hammer put his arm out. Chuck wouldn't sit on his finger or on his shoulder, and he wouldn't let Hammer get very close to him.

Lena put the arugula in Chuck's cage. "You like Hammer, don't you, Chuck?"

"Uh oh. It's the cops! Five-O. Five-O. Squawk. It's the cops."

Lena laughed. "You're naughty."

Chuck did his sexy purr. "Light her fire."

Hammer felt his face turn red.

Lena laughed. "His former owners must have discussed what to print on their labels in front of Chuck."

"He should come with an adult content warning."

"It would be hard for him to unlearn words and phrases he already knows, but you could teach him new ones. He's a very smart bird."

Hammer watched Chuck eat his arugula.

"He's hungry," Lena said.

"He only eats when you're here."

Lena smiled at him. "Then maybe I should come around more often."

Hammer liked the sound of that. "Maybe you should."

Chuck gave a wolf whistle. The bird could really read the room.

Lena laughed. "You're a character, aren't you, Chuck?"

Hammer ran a hand across the back of his neck. For a bird, Chuck wasn't much of a wingman. He kind of stole the show.

***

It was one o'clock in the morning when something woke Hammer. He'd fallen asleep on the sofa in front of the television, but now he was on high alert. All of his senses pinged, as if he were in the middle of an operation. Then he saw why—his body cam footage was playing on a late night talk show. He'd awoken just in time to hear his now infamous line. "Hands in the air! Don't move a muscle, sucker." The audience roared with laughter. The late night host cracked a joke.

"Uh oh. Squawk. Uh oh." Chuck sounded tired, but didn't miss an opportunity to offer his two cents from his cage in the kitchen.

Hammer was reaching for the remote when the body cam footage was replaced by a still shot of him with a bag of groceries in front of his house. Then one of him in his fatigues from when he was in the corp. He sank back into the sofa. "Cripes," he said to the television. "You forgot to show my colonoscopy." He turned off the television, and pinched the bridge of his nose, where the tension was building. His ringtone broke the silence.

"Yeah?"

It was Donnelly. "Sarge, we got a problem."

"I saw it."

"Saw what?"

Word of Hammer's appearance on late night television would get around in a hurry, but if Donnelly hadn't seen it yet, Hammer wasn't going to bring it to his attention. "What are you talking about?"

"Leo Simpson. The kid from the bust."

"What about him?"

"He made bail."

"We figured he would."

Donnelly hesitated. "He freaked out about his bird."

"His bird's okay."

"Yeah, except it's not his bird anymore. Lena cited him for neglect."

Hammer glanced over at Chuck. "So what's the problem?"

"He called the station and said he and his brother were going to kill Lena for taking his bird and you for busting him. Thinks it's your fault about the bird. Vowed to get him back."

"So pick him back up and charge him with making criminal threats."

"We tried to."

The back of Hammer's neck started itching. "What do you mean tried to?"

"We went by his house and he wasn't there. It was cleaned out. We think he skipped."

Hammer muttered a curse as he paced to his window.

"That's what I said," Donnelly told him. "We have a car on your house."

Hammer pulled his curtain aside and spotted the unmarked sedan across the street. "Forget about me. What about Lena?"

"We have one there too."

He let the curtain fall back into place. "Keep me in the loop."

"Will do, Sarge. Watch your back."

Hammer got himself a glass of water and stood next to Chuck's cage.

"Uh oh. Squawk. Uh oh."

"Yeah, I hear you." Hammer drank his water. "Lena went out on a limb for you. I hope it doesn't cost her."

"Squawk." Chuck moved from side to side. He did his racy growl.

"Yeah, her," Hammer said. He opened Chuck's cage and stuck his finger inside. Chuck hustled to the far side of his perch, as far away from Hammer as he could get.

Hammer closed the cage. "I'm trying, buddy. I'm trying."

Chuck bobbed from one foot to the other. "Uh oh. Squawk. Uh oh."

***

The next morning, Hanson, Donnelly and Jackie Barber sat around Hammer's kitchen table. "So far, we've had no luck finding either one of them." Jackie sipped her coffee and stifled a yawn. "We were out all night."

Donnelly emptied his cup and leaned back in his chair. He was in his leathers today. Ride or Die was stitched across the back of his jacket. "If the Simpsons really intend to get the bird back, somebody must be putting them up locally."

Hammer leaned back against the sink. "Have you checked in with the known associates?"

"No dice," Hanson said. He wore forest green flannel today. "Maybe it was all talk and they're halfway to Mexico by now."

Hammer looked at Chuck. Chuck chattered and paced.

"Or maybe they think we're stupid." Jackie turned her phone so the others could see her screen. A neon green flyer advertised a rave, with party favors compliments of the Simpson brothers. "We just got this on the tipline."

Hammer dumped the rest of his coffee in the sink. "When is it?"

Jackie looked at her phone. "Tonight."

"Uh oh," Chuck said.

***

Hammer's squad was not an undercover unit, but they could blend in when they had to. After Hammer's fifteen minutes of fame, he'd never blend again. That's why he would be sitting home while his squad sat in a van around the corner from the rave, waiting for a signal from the undercover team inside.

It bothered Hammer not being a part of the action, but he was making the most of it. He'd invited Lena over for dinner. She showed up with a pizza and a bottle of wine, and a mango. "I brought you a treat," she said to Chuck, holding up the mango.

Chuck gave his sexy purr.

"Behave yourself," Hammer said.

Lena peeled off her animal control windbreaker and hung it on the back of a chair. "How has he been today?"

"About the same." Hammer dealt out paper plates.

Lena smiled as she opened the pizza box. "It takes time to get to know each other, same as it does with people." She laid a slice of pizza on each of the plates.

Chuck gave a wolf whistle, then immediately launched into his racy growl. "You can go all night."

Hammer's face felt as red as Chuck's tail feathers. Lena looked amused. "Any word from your squad?"

"Not yet." Hammer looked at the time on his phone. "The rave doesn't start until late."

"So we have some time to kill?"

Hammer didn't want to assume anything. He opened his mouth and closed it again.

"Be the envy of other men. Squawk."

"That's why you invited me, right?" Lena had worn her hair down tonight. Waves of it spilled over her shoulders.

Hammer glanced at Chuck before meeting Lena's eyes. "Excuse me?"

"Because your team is all at the rave. You had no one to watch my house, so you're keeping an eye on me yourself."

"Well..." Hammer was momentarily speechless. "That wasn't the only reason."

Chuck let out a long descending whistle and finished with a garbled noise that sounded like radio static. Parrot-speak for crash and burn.

Lena laughed.

Hammer was mortified. "That's a new one."

"He must be feeling more comfortable," Lena said.

"Listen," Hammer said. "I didn't invite you just because of the threat."

"That's good, because you know I can take care of myself."

Chuck started his crash and burn sound effect again, but Hammer shushed him mid-whistle this time. "I've been meaning to invite you since the day I met you."

Chuck gave a wolf whistle.

Lena drank her wine. "Good."

Hammer breathed a sigh of relief.

"You know," Lena said. "I've been threatened before. It's part of the job. People feel strongly about their animals."

They finished the pizza and opened a second bottle of wine while they talked. Hours passed like minutes. Chuck made snoring noises. Hammer turned to look at him. "Are we keeping you up?"

Chuck snored some more.

"He's right," Lena said. "I can hardly keep my eyes open."

Hammer looked at his watch. It was 3am. "Take my bed," he said.

Chuck gave his racy growl.

Hammer waved him off. "I'll stay down here on the sofa. Neither one of us should be driving."

"You're probably right," Lena said.

"The rave should be pretty hot right now. Hopefully we'll pick up the Simpson brothers soon."

"Good."

Hammer showed Lena upstairs and then returned to the living room and made sure the doors were locked. He checked his phone, but there was no word from his squad. He texted Jackie. Anything?

She texted back. Zip.

He stretched out on the sofa to wait. He dosed off, but came awake an hour later when he heard Chuck chattering. It sounded like he was talking in his sleep. Hammer sat up and rubbed his eyes. He schlepped out to the kitchen. Chuck paced back and forth on his perch, but he wasn't talking. Hammer opened the door to the cage. "Chuck?"

Chuck cowered at the far end of his perch. He plucked out one of his own feathers. According to Lena, Chuck had been plucking his own feathers for some time. She attributed it to either boredom due to neglect or emotional trauma caused by his former owner's lifestyle. Either scenario made Simpson unfit to keep the exotic bird.

"Don't do that to yourself," Hammer said.

Chuck squawked. It was out of the ordinary for him to be so shrill and so loud. He bounced up and down on his perch. Hammer heard his phone vibrate on the coffee table. Then he heard a footstep on his front porch. He shushed Chuck just in time to hear a board creak on his back porch. He was unlocking the kitchen drawer where he kept his gun when he heard the snick of the lock on his front door. "It's okay," he whispered to Chuck.

But he had a problem now. Two intruders—he'd bet they were the Simpson brothers—but only one of him. He hoped the text his phone had received was from his squad saying they were outside, but he couldn't be sure of that.

He watched a slim hand reach in and jimmy the chain on his kitchen door. He let whichever Simpson it was step inside before he cocked his gun. "Get down on the floor."

The intruder let out a defeated sigh, then dropped to his knees.

Hammer heard a noise behind him as he was cuffing the elder Simpson to the refrigerator.

He spun, but Leo Simpson was too close.

"Hands in the air! Squawk! Don't move a muscle, sucker."

Leo Simpson took his eyes off Hammer for a second to look at Chuck, and then let out an oomph, before he fell to the ground.

Lena stood where he'd just been with an empty wine bottle in her hand.

Chuck gave a wolf whistle, then flew out of his cage and landed on Hammer's shoulder.

Lena smiled. "You two make a good team."

"I need to call this in," Hammer said.

"I already did." Lena flipped the empty wine bottle into the air and caught it on the way back down. "Right before I saved your tail feather." She smiled.

"Then I guess we three make a good team."

Sirens whined in the distance.

Chuck rubbed his head against Hammer's cheek and made kissy noises.

Lena winked. "Told you he was a smart bird."

Tracy Falenwolfe's stories have appeared in Black Cat Mystery Magazine, Flash Bang Mysteries, Crimson Streets, Spinetingler Magazine, and more. She lives in Pennsylvania's Lehigh Valley with her husband and sons. She is a member of Sisters in Crime, Mystery Writers of America, and The Short Mystery Fiction Society. Find her at www.tracyfalenwolfe.com

Sweet Revenge

Michele Bazan Reed

The sparrows were chirping, and the late-April breeze brought the scent of bluebells, as I settled in with the *Burlington Free Press* and a steaming mug of Earthback coffee. I was savoring the moment, when my morning's peace was shattered – literally – by the sound of breaking glass mere inches from my Adirondack chair.

I lowered my newspaper just in time to see Kara Sampson roaring away in her red pickup, shaking her fist out the driver's side window. "I'm done with you, Jake," she shouted. "You can't pawn that swill off on me. You're gonna ruin my reputation!" The truck vanished in a haze of dust as she gunned the engine and headed out toward Route 7.

I looked down and saw a bottle of Jake's Reserve, my finest, lying near a pile of window-glass shards glinting in the late morning sun. The top had come off in the impact and a pool of amber-colored liquid was forming on the plank floor.

With a sigh I swigged down the last of my coffee and scooped up the bottle of precious liquid. With maple syrup going for more per barrel than crude oil, I figured I could salvage what was left of this bottle to use in my own coffee. I flashed back to hours in the sugar house tending the kettle, stung by Kara's comment about "swill."

After cleaning up the sticky pool so it wouldn't draw ants and flies – or worse yet that pesky raccoon that was hanging around making Sacha crazy – I swept up the broken glass. My rescue Plott Hound was on high alert inside the house, leaping up toward the window and barking for all she was worth.

"It's all right, girl. Go back to sleep." If there's one thing Sacha hates more than that raccoon, it's anything that disturbs her slumber. And Kara's well-aimed missile had certainly done that.

I squeezed through the screen door without letting Sacha out, scratched between her ears, and set the bottle on the kitchen counter. Time to go find out what Kara was upset about, I guess. I pulled on a clean T-shirt, the one with a cow appliqued in flannel. Since Kara had sold it to me when I first came to town,

I thought it might mollify her. Checking in the doorway mirror to be sure I was presentable, I ran my fingers through my spiky sandy-colored hair and assessed my trim figure in profile. Dark bags under my eyes attested to long nights in the sugar house, but now that the season was over, I might just get a little rest.

Sacha had seen me grab the car keys and was already at my side, glancing from the door to my face and back again, calling shotgun with silent eye commands.

Settling into the driver's seat, I glanced over at my copilot. Sacha already had her head out the window, barking for all she was worth. That's my girl! The family from the ritzy suburb who left her at the shelter said it was because she barked too much. So did the other two families who adopted and returned her. When I got her, she'd been at the shelter for six months and had a bit of an attitude. But I didn't care. With her sleek black fur and huge dark eyes, I thought she was the most beautiful girl at Helping Hounds. And now, out here in the Vermont woods, she could bark to her heart's content, with no one but me and that dang raccoon to hear her. I loved her "singing" voice and, frankly, I didn't care what the raccoon thought.

On the short drive to Kara's, I thought about her comment on the bottle of syrup, and what this might mean for my business, but most of all, for our friendship. Not that there was anything much there yet. But a guy can hope. Kara's Kitchen was why I settled here. Little more than a pitstop for tourists heading south from the ferry crossing over Lake Champlain, Kara's served up a helping of Vermont hospitality with every slice of apple pie, chunk of cheddar or stack of maple-drenched pancakes. It was a dog-friendly place, too, with an outside tap, water bowls, and tables where guests could enjoy the company of their furry friends with their own meals.

I had stopped on my way up Route 7 from the bridge at Crown Point, having left New York behind with only my clothes, my laptop, and my canine best friend, after my girlfriend Amy's constant jealous fits had gotten too much to bear. I hadn't known where I was headed when I stopped for a break at Kara's. A cup of Earthback and a piece of apple pie, along with the warm welcome she gave Sacha, and I knew I had found my own little slice of heaven.

It was on Kara's bulletin board that I'd seen the sugarbush for sale. I knew nothing about maple syrup, but how hard could it be? And I figured the secluded setting and once-a-year production schedule would give me plenty of peace and quiet to write that mystery novel that had been percolating in my brain on the long drive north.

Once Jake's Maple Heaven was up and running, Kara offered to serve my syrup with her pancakes and sell it in her gift shop alongside the marble cheese boards, pottery mugs, aged cheddars, and maple wood trivets. It was a great budding partnership, and I hoped it might blossom into a partnership of a different kind. Now, something had happened to put it all in jeopardy.

I arrived between the breakfast and lunch rushes, although out here that word took on a whole new meaning. I could see Kara through the pass-through from the kitchen, prepping veg for lunch. Even with her wavy auburn hair pulled back in a sloppy ponytail and a big green apron over her T-shirt and shorts, she looked beautiful as she concentrated on dicing carrots and onions for the soup du jour.

She glanced up as the bell on the door rang, then looked back down quickly. "Go away, Jake. I have nothing to say to you. That was a dirty trick and I expected better from you."

My head reeling, I plunked myself down at the nearest table. "Kara, please. Can we talk about this?" I must have sounded a little desperate, because she looked up then. Seeing my face and slumped shoulders, and Sacha whimpering as she stared up at me, Kara relented. Wiping her hands on a dishtowel, she grabbed two mugs, filled them with coffee and came over to my table.

"You have a lot of nerve showing up here." Her lips barely moved; her teeth clenched tightly. If the mug hadn't been good Bennington Pottery, she probably would have snapped off the handle with her grip.

"Kara, trust me, I have no idea what you mean."

"I'll just bet. Pawning off colored sugar water as pure maple syrup, and your best grade at that! That's just big-city sleazy."

That stung. I'd struggled to be accepted here where the locals had a healthy distrust of strangers. I'd made some inroads. But I'd always thought I was safe with Kara.

"Sugar water? What are you talking about? And you've had my syrup here for months, enjoyed it yourself, you said. Why now?"

"You couldn't even face me with it, could you? Dropping it off at my kitchen door before opening last Thursday? I should've been suspicious, but no. I never suspected your switcheroo until a local returned a stack of pancakes as inedible." She drummed her fingers on the tabletop. "You know some people around here even carry their own jugs of syrup to restaurants. Not in my establishment. They've come to trust me. But if word of this gets around . . ." She twisted strands of her ponytail between her fingers as she stared off over my shoulder, avoiding my eyes.

"Kara, you know me. I'd never just leave a case of syrup at your door without delivering it to you in person. For one thing, it's too valuable to just leave out where someone could steal it." For another, I silently admitted to myself, I'd miss a chance at seeing Kara. □

She stared down at the grounds in the bottom of her cup. "I guess that's true. But then, why does it have your label on it? And why does it taste like that garbage they sell in the supermarket, the one they have to label 'pancake syrup' because it doesn't have any maple at all?"

I knew the kind of junk she was talking about, created from high fructose corn syrup and artificial flavors and colors. The shelves at big chains were lined with it. People snapped it up because a quart could be had for $3 or less, while pure Vermont maple syrup went for $15 a pint. Worth every penny, but that wasn't the point right now. Or maybe it was.

"If word of this gets around, people will stop eating here. And they won't buy the stuff I sell in my shop. If the syrup is fake, they'll believe I import the cutting boards from China or repackage grocery store cheese as real aged cheddar." Her fist was starting to clench again, and I could see she was biting back tears. "I'll be out of business in no time. And you will, too."

"Say, do you have any of the new batch around? Could I see it? Taste it?"

"You're lucky. It's in the garbage bin, but hasn't been collected yet." This time she managed to meet my eyes. Maybe she was starting to believe me.

Kara brought over a familiar maple leaf-shaped bottle with two shot glasses. The label read "Jake's Reserve" in 20-point Bookman Bold over a picture of Sacha's smiling face. I'd spent days working on that label. If anyone could resist the sweet lure of Vermont maple syrup, they'd be hard-pressed to turn away from my pup's gorgeous mug.

As Kara poured a little in each glass, I could see at once it wasn't Jake's Reserve. My prize syrup had a rich, amber color that marked the syrup from a late-season tapping, when it becomes darker and tastes more caramelized. I put many a sleepless night into stirring that batch, hiring a couple of trusted neighbors to take turns with me so we could all get some shut-eye. The kettles couldn't be left untended for any length of time or the syrup would burn to the bottom of the vessel, and the batch would be ruined.

See. That was Number 1 of the five S's needed for syrup judging, followed by swirl, smell, sip, and savor.

I swirled to release the bouquet, like a fine wine, and sniffed it. Again, it lacked the depth of aroma that signaled a really good batch of syrup. I sipped and instead of savor, my fifth "S" step was spit.

"Ugh! You're right! That is swill." Now I was the one with clenched fists. "And it's not mine."

Kara had stopped at swirl. Looking down at the table, she dragged her fingers through the rings left by our coffee cups.

I thought of that smashed bottle on my porch, something niggling at the back of my mind. "Can you bring me an unopened bottle? I want to check the cap." I used a distinctive gold-colored screw top on my bottles. It cost a bit extra but made my product stand out on store shelves as a little more luxe.

"You can have the whole darn case back for all I care." In a minute she was back and slammed the box down, causing my mug to rock slightly on the wobbly table. Sure enough, the caps were all standard-issue black ones.

"Bingo!" My shout made the dozing Sacha jump and bang her noggin on the bottom of the pine tabletop. "That's not my cap. Check the old stock in your shop – you'll see I use gold tops."

Her eyes lit up. "You're right, Jake! But why would somebody do this? Why fake a bottle of maple syrup?"

I was studying the box. It was from a delivery of lettuce to a local grocery store. No clue there. Whoever did this had obviously grabbed it out of a dumpster behind the store. There was no handwriting sample anywhere on the box, and Kara had already told me it was just dropped off, with no bill or note.

"I don't know why, but more importantly, who? Who would want to hurt my reputation, and yours? We've got to get to the bottom of this."

"Knock yourself out. I've gotta go finish prepping for lunch." I looked over the box of faux syrup. Despite her brusque words, Kara was grinning at me and gave a conspiratorial wink.

Who, indeed? I wracked my brain but could think of no one who would have it out for me. Sure, some locals were a bit stand-offish, but I expected that, as a newcomer in a tight-knit New England community. Yankees weren't all friendly on the outside, but once they got to know you and trust you, you could count on them till the end. I knew it would take time to earn that.

As I walked out through Kara's gift shop, I glanced at the shelves. Sure enough there was my Jake's Reserve with the familiar gold cap in a place of prominence. There were also a couple of bottles of Peterson's, relegated to a lower shelf. Walter "Pete" Peterson was my biggest rival. He'd practically cornered the maple syrup market in our little part of the world before I came along. His syrup was in similar leaf-shaped bottles and topped with a black cap. I'd be suspicious, but I knew there were only so many suppliers and a lot of us favored the glass bottles that showed off the color of our syrup, even though the popular plastic jugs weighed less and kept the syrup from light, enhancing its longevity .

"Hey, Kara! What's up with Pete's syrup? Didn't he have any for you this season?" I had to shout to be heard over the whirr of her immersion blender pureeing the soup.

"Yeah, funny thing. When folks got a taste of Jake's Maple Heaven, sales of Pete's fell off, and I mean dramatically." She switched off the blender, so she didn't have to shout. "When I reordered for this year, I cut his numbers way down. I felt like I had to stock some, of course, with him being local and all. I can tell you, he was not happy about it. Said he'd get you for this, or words to that effect."

I took the offending bottles out to the car and headed for Triple C's, the local printer. Brothers Chris and Craig Carpenter printed all the flyers around town, wedding invitations, even the local weekly newspaper. It's the only game in town, and where I'd always had my labels made, along with my advertising flyers.

Craig looked up as I entered, his smile turning to a puzzled look as I slammed the bottle down on his desk. "I take it by your frown and the forceful way you placed that bottle on my desk, that's no free sample as thanks for a job well done?"

"What can you tell me about that label, Craig? Where did it come from?"

His brow furrowed and he looked at me like I was speaking Martian. "Came from the order you placed last week." He picked up the bottle and squinted at it, studying the label. "You stuck a note on my door before opening, said you needed 100 more labels in a hurry, but you were too busy with sugaring to come and get them, so to just put them in your mailbox and send you the bill later. Figured you were anticipating a higher than usual level of production."

Must be the prankster had been watching my mailbox and pulled out the labels before I checked my mail. I did a little quick math. One hundred labels meant whoever did this could make 8 cases of 12 with a few labels left over for error. I did a quick run through of my local clients.

I explained to Craig what had happened. "So, this isn't genuine Jake's Reserve, but I'll bring a bottle of the real stuff when I come in to pay the bill. I've got to run and see if I can find out who did this before he dumps them on any more of my clients."

In the parking lot, I nearly bumped into Pete Peterson, exiting his black SUV, parked nearby.

"Morning, Pete," I said. Hoping he'd stop and chat, I angled myself to get a look in the back of his SUV. I could see two boxes crammed with glass bottles topped with black caps, but I couldn't make out if the labels on the bottles were his or mine.

"You've got your nerve, New York, being all friendly." Pete seemed more interested in his shoelaces than my face. When he looked up, the glint in his eye told me all I needed to know. "Kara cut my order and so did June. I don't like rookies coming in and taking away my business."

Sacha moved protectively between me and Pete, growling ever so softly. I knew that growl. Pete didn't want to know what came next, if he were to threaten me physically.

I knew it wasn't wise to antagonize him, but I couldn't help myself. "Well, Pete, when people taste a superior product, they just naturally want it. What can I say? I expect as word gets around, my syrup will get even more fans."

His laugh was more of a bark. "We'll see, Jake. We'll just see about that." Pete turned on his heel and headed for the main business district.

Making the rounds of my customers, I called on Grandma June's Gift Shop, Maple Artisans Gallery, Tom's Ice Creamery, and two local hotels which stocked Maple Heaven products for sale to guests. All had suspicious deliveries, and all were glad to get rid of the offending bottles. I promised fresh stock of the newest vintage in the next few days and finished making my rounds.

All but two of my regulars had been scammed. Beckett's B&B and Aunt Rita's Bake Shop were probably due to get their deliveries tonight or tomorrow. Rita thought I may be right with suspecting Pete. Based on the pattern of deliveries, we both figured her shop was next on his list. The baker dusted flour off her hands onto her apron and took me around back to show me a good spot to hide behind her freestanding brick oven, with a clear line of sight to the back porch.

"With his MO, I suspect the perp will leave the counterfeits by the back door." Rita loved her mystery books and obviously relished doing a little sleuthing of her own. "He'll be lured in by the fact that it's dark back here, but the motion-detecting lights will come on as soon as he gets to the top step and you'll have a clear view of the bad guy's face."

"Sacha and I will be out there shortly after sunset and stake the place out," I promised, as she handed me a paper bag of apple-maple muffins and homemade cheddar dog biscuits to sustain us in our vigil.

***

The night wore on, and even a thermal mug of coffee wasn't enough to keep me awake. Crouched down with my big dog for warmth, I dozed. I don't how long I'd been asleep when a soft growl from Sacha woke me up. Her superior hearing and sharp hound nose had alerted her to the intruder. "Hush, girl," I whispered and peeked around the curve of the brick oven. A dark SUV, with a silhouette like Pete's, had coasted to a stop in the alley leading to the back of the bakery, its lights switched off. Must be he didn't want to alert anyone who could identify him.

Sacha had great eyes, having been bred for night hunting, and she saw something that had her riled up. She was straining to get at the intruder, despite my tight grip on her collar.

I heard the clang of thick glass bottles banging against each other as the driver crept up the uneven cobblestone path, punctuated with a whispered "Oof!" as he stubbed his toe and nearly lost his grip on the carton. With the box safely delivered, he turned and as the security lights came on, I had a clear view of a face that made me suck in my breath.

I had to put my hand on Sacha's neck to calm her from barking, and bite back an expletive of my own. Despite the baggy overalls and ball cap pulled low, I recognized that driver. It was none other than my ex, Amy.

***

The next morning, at a table at Kara's Kitchen, I laid out my findings. Kara, June, Rita, Leslie and Craig were gathered around with mugs of their own and some of Rita's best maple-walnut cookies. Sacha chomped another of Rita's biscuits with a bowl of fresh water.

"I don't get it. Why is she doing this?" Kara shook her head, her lips set in a grim line.

"It's hard to explain about Amy, but she's into revenge. It's why I had to leave." I told them about her volatile temper and her penchant for getting even – sometimes when she only imagined an offense.

"I was a reporter in New York, so my cell was filled with strange phone numbers – my confidential sources. One day, Amy called one and a woman answered. I had to do a lot of work to get that city council member to even talk to me again. Amy plotted revenge, and poured a 2-liter of Mountain Dew into my gas tank." Heads nodded around the table. "Joke was on her, though. Mike down at the dealership told me I was lucky. I'd filled up the car the day before. If it had been near empty, that little trick would've ruined my engine."

I paused for a big gulp of coffee. "Then there was the time she threw all my clothes out in the rain and mud, because she found a receipt for lunch for two at a fancy Manhattan restaurant in my pocket. I'd been meeting a source for a secret exposé of some industrial espionage. Amy wasn't buying my explanation." I shook my head at the memory of my stained shirts and ties.

"But this is the worst she's ever attempted. I'm convinced she's out to destroy my new life here, in retribution for leaving her. If I don't stop her now ..." My voice trailed off leaving their imaginations to fill in the blanks.

My new friends agreed that Amy had crossed the line and were eager to help me teach her a lesson.

"I've got to stake out the B&B tonight. It's my last chance to catch her sticky-fingered, as it were."

"We'll help. What do you need?" Good old Rita, always ready in a pinch.

Leslie, the owner of Beckett's, was as mad as I was. A retired teacher, she was used to taking charge. "If anyone knows how to deal with a bully, it's a teacher. Leave it to me. I've got a plan." If I were Amy, I wouldn't like the look of that grin Leslie flashed just then.

The B&B was in an 18th-Century inn converted for the tourist trade and a popular stop on the Vermont ghost tour. It was reputed to be haunted by the wife of a Captain Otis, a Revolutionary War soldier who came home and found her, clad in a nightgown, in the arms of another man. She protested that the man was just comforting her as she grieved what she thought was a report of her husband's death in battle. Unconvinced, the enraged soldier strangled her then and there. To this day, it is said, the wronged wife walked the grounds of the inn in her nightgown, weeping.

Although some guests reported strange noises in the night and objects moved from their usual spot, Leslie swore she'd never seen the ghost. But that didn't stop the tourists from flocking there in the hopes of being the first to catch a glimpse of the spirit.

"You, know," Leslie said. "Legend has it that Mrs. Otis had a beautiful hound dog, much like our Sacha here. When she was killed, her loyal hound howled his grief to the heavens. It is said that he lived out his days curled up on his mistress's grave." She stooped to scratch Sacha between the ears as we all digested the tale of the wronged wife.

Ever the teacher, Leslie passed out assignments for each of us. We clinked our mugs, broke the huddle, and agreed to meet in Beckett's kitchen at sunset.

***

At 8:30 that evening, the mood in the kitchen was giddy. June cut tags off one of her special "Colonial Lady" nightgowns, a flowing white gauzy number with a matching robe that she promised would flutter nicely in the evening breeze. She fussed about as Kara slipped the gown over her shorts and a white T and helped the younger woman let her hair out of its ponytail, tousling her locks to enhance the wild look.

Rita chuckled as she sprinkled flour over Kara's hair, face and hands. "You look like a credible specter," she told her as they all surveyed the results in the mirror hung by the back door.

On her cell phone, Leslie keyed up the app that she'd found to play horror movie noises. "Listen to this one!" She broke into a guffaw as the sound of wind and moaning filled the kitchen.

"That's perfect! I can't wait to see her face." Rita snapped the top back on her flour canister.

Leaving Kara in the kitchen near the back door with a quick "Break a leg!" the three women headed to the living room to find a good place to hide with a clear view out the window to the front porch.

I crouched down behind the stone wall Leslie had built with good Vermont slate, Sacha on a tight leash at my side, to wait for our mark.

Once it got good and dark, I heard the now-familiar sound of Amy's rented SUV, followed by the clinking of bottles. She grunted as she hoisted the box of syrup and headed up the slate pathway. Soon, she was right in front of the porch steps.

I started to worry. Where was Kara? Our plan depended on perfectly orchestrated timing. At this rate, Amy would be gone and we'd miss our only chance. Why was Kara dawdling?

Suddenly the air seemed chillier than it had before, and I wished I'd brought a fleece. The forecast on my phone said it would be a low of 50 degrees, but this seemed like early winter weather. A breeze picked up, and I could hear the sound of wind in dry branches followed by a low moaning. Well, at least Leslie was doing her job.

Sacha set up a howl fit to raise the dead. The hair on my arms stood on end. Amy stopped in her tracks, her head twisting from side to side, obviously shaken.

Suddenly a figure appeared around the corner, white nightgown flying out behind her in the breeze. Her sleeves fluttered, and her hair streamed out behind her. Her mouth open in a silent scream, she pointed directly at Amy with a shaking finger, her arm at full extension.

Oh, man! Kara was playing it to the hilt!

Amy gasped, a sharp intake of breath. "Stop! G-g-go away!" Her voice shook as she started backing away from the "ghost" advancing on her. This was getting to be fun!

Soon, Amy was in full panic mode. She shrieked and threw her arms up in the air, bottles flying out of the cardboard box and shattering on the slate pathway. My ex was drenched in faux-maple syrup, and she was scrambling on the slippery paving stones, going down on one knee, then recovering her footing as she ran for the vehicle. I could hear her swearing as the engine misfired, but she finally got it going and peeled out of there, laying rubber and causing lights to come on in houses across the street. I figured that was the last I'd see of my ex.

Rita, Leslie, and June ran down the front steps, laughing uproariously. We were all high-fiving and patting each other on the back. Sacha was jumping up on everyone, tail wagging and tongue hanging out in glee.

"Weird, my phone's battery died right as I went to press 'Play' on the sound effects." Leslie looked sheepish. "But I guess we didn't need them after all."

"Not with Kara's awesome acting job!" Rita sounded full of admiration.

"Great job, Kara," I said, turning to where I'd last seen her, to give her a hug. But my arms encircled empty air. She wasn't there.

"Hey guys, sorry! I heard that vehicle backfiring. Was it Amy?" Kara was just coming around the corner of the house.

"I hope I didn't ruin everything, but I couldn't get the back door open. It stuck, almost like it was locked, and for a few minutes I couldn't budge it for love or money. Almost crashed to the ground when it did give way a few seconds ago." She looked down at her white gown, the hem now trailing in sticky syrup. "Why is it so cold out here? And where did this syrup come from?"

She searched our faces, one by one.

"I guess Miss Sacha really does have a voice that could raise the dead," said Leslie. "And that earns her a pancake. C'mon in, everyone, I'm cooking breakfast – with genuine Jake's Reserve."

Michele Bazan Reed's stories have appeared in *Woman's World* magazine and several anthologies, most recently *Malice Domestic 15: Mystery Most Theatrical*, *Masthead: Best New England Mysteries 2020*, *The Eyes Have It* and *Crazy Christmas Capers* in the Holiday Hijinks collection. Her story, "The Hot Dog Thief," featuring her son's late rescue hound, Jerome, was published in *Chicken Soup for the Soul: Life Lessons from the Dog*. A member of Sisters in Crime and the Private Eye Writers of America, Michele dotes on her once-feral cat, Charlie, and her three rescue "granddogs": Brit, Max and Sacha.

The Midnight Crier

Kate Fellowes

When I first went to look at the four-family apartment building for sale on Hollander Drive, I took along a list of questions copied from a library book. Is the basement damp? How old is the furnace? Vinyl or aluminum siding? I clutched the list nervously as I climbed from my car, still not 100% sure about the idea of becoming a landlord. I only knew the old family home was too big for just me and it was time to make a change. I wished again my daughter, Jaynie, could be with me. But she had to work, so I was on my own.

On my own. It was a phrase I'd thought more and more recently, every time I realized how true it was. At sixty-two, I was more than old enough to be on my own, but it was still a new mantle I wore like an itchy wool scarf—one I wished I could just shrug off.

The building was lovely. Red brick, it had evergreens in the front yard and maples along the road. It sat between two other red brick multi-families that made them look like a family of their own. Hollander Drive was a quiet street, close to the city park and far from the business district. Tidy, safe and, according to the real estate advertisement, "highly desirable", it seemed welcoming enough in the weak spring sunshine.

The man who answered the door of the manager's apartment was tall and thin and nearly bald. He looked about eighty and when he greeted me, there was a hint of whistle from his teeth.

"Mrs. Newsome? I'm Jack Modowski. Glad to meet you. Please, c'mon in." He held the door wide and I stepped inside.

For the next hour, he told me about the building, the neighborhood, and the garbage pick-up. He gave me a very grand tour that left me gasping at the end of it, when I had already made up my mind.

My checklist was covered now with scrawled notes, nearly every question with an answer written beside it. I glanced down, reading, and asked, "Do any of the tenants have pets?"

Now, I don't know why I even bothered to ask that, except to get his insight as a landlord. I don't have any pets. Never had, except as a child. I like animals, of course, and send money every year to the local humane society. I just never had any of my own.

"Cats only," Jack Modowski stated. "Nice and quiet. No barking and no messes in the yard. Do you have a kitty?"

Head bent, I was writing on my checklist. "Um, no, I don't." I looked up. "My husband is—" I paused, corrected myself, "was—allergic."

Mr. Modowski misinterpreted my hesitation. "Well, I'm sorry for your loss, Mrs. Newsome. Is it recent?"

I blinked. Then, with a smile, I told him, "Oh, I didn't lose my husband. I know right where he is. In those new condominiums on Plano." If there was a hint of bitterness in my voice, well, I hoped I'd be forgiven.

Straightening up, Mr. Modowski ran a hand through what was left of his hair. "A divorcee, hmm?" The way he said the word made it sound scandalous and sexy. He'd have twirled his mustache if he had one, I'm sure.

"That's right," I said flatly, becoming businesslike once more. "May I let you know about the property tomorrow?"

"Oh, sure." He waved a hand in dismissal. "I promise not to show it to anyone else until I've heard from you."

As he led me to the door, he pointed at the identical building just to the north and said, "You know, I own that building, too. Can't keep up the maintenance on both of 'em anymore, so I'm selling this one. But I'm right next door there, if you need me. I'm in the lower left." He jogged my elbow. "We could be neighbors."

Even as I smiled, I mentally jotted that down on my checklist, with an exclamation point behind it. He stood at the curb, waving and watching me drive off and I wondered what life would be like on Hollander Drive.

***

Inside of a month, I'd purchased the apartment building, sold the home I'd come to as a young bride and moved a greatly reduced amount of belongings into Mr. Modowski's former building. Now, if anyone knocked on the door labeled "Manager", I was the one who opened it.

My daughter laughed over that. "I hope you can manage being manager, Mom," Jaynie said.

"Well," I shot back with a grin, "I've managed to get this far!"

On the first warm weekend in May, when the sun was high and bright, I set out to work in my new backyard. Gardening is hard work, as any gardener will be happy to tell you, but it does wonders for one's spirit. I had a dozen red geraniums to plant and a flat of cheery little marigolds, too,

I was on my hands and knees, on a squishy green cushion, when a movement several yards off caught my eye. At first, I couldn't see what it had been. The area under the big clump birch was still covered with tulips in primary colors, their leaves fading and blossoms spread wide. Had that been all I'd seen—a falling petal or two? But, as I squinted and looked closer, I noticed a secondary color. Orange. Like orange marmalade. The flick of motion came again and, all at once, like one of those optical illusions, I could see a tabby cat sitting there among my tulips.

"Oh!' I said, startled. "Hello, there. Who are you?"

The cat regarded me through golden eyes for a long moment, then blinked quite slowly. The sun, warm on that lovely orange fur, was making him sleepy, I guessed. I was also guessing that the cat was a male. He looked too big to be female. His paws, tipped in white, seemed sturdy rather than dainty and the plume of his tail looked about a foot long.

I sat back on my cushion. "Where did you come from, Mister? Are you wearing a collar?" Craning my neck, I tried to see if any silver tag hung from his neck, listing an owner's name and number. But, no.

"Hmm." I set down the little trowel I'd been using and peeled off my garden gloves. Mr. Modowski, if he had looked out his window just then, would have seen me advancing slowly, an inch at a time, toward the pretty tabby under the tree.

I was on my knees, one hand extended palm up for the little cat to smell, when a voice spoke, practically in my ear.

"Mrs. Newsome? Mrs. Newsome?"

I recognized that voice. I looked up into the quizzical face of Mr. Modowski.

"Hello." I tried not to show any irritation, but he had interrupted a delicate mission.

"What are you doing?" he asked, as well he might.

"I was trying to make friends with this kitty." Turning, I gestured to a bare spot among the flowers. The cat had gone.

Mr. Modowski pointed, and I could see the thick evergreens about twenty feet away moving very slightly, as if a sleek orange body had recently passed there. A keen sense of disappointment filled me.

Rats! I thought. Instead, I said, "What can I do for you?"

"Just thought you'd like to know there've been several break-ins this week. On our block," he added.

"What?" I knew that simple question would lead to twenty minutes of conversation, but this was important news. "You're kidding."

Shaking his head forlornly, Mr. Modowski told me, "Wish I were. But, I just heard it down at the coffee shop. You know the one, next to the park."

I nodded. The one and only, it made a natural gathering point for the retired set.

"Bob heard it from Officer Willis—he was in there earlier. Cops are calling the burglar 'The Moonlight Marauder', but I don't think it's anything to make jokes about," he went on, indignant. "Two garages in the last week. Took all the tools and a lawn mower."

It was difficult to envision stealthy burglars trundling away a bulky lawn mower. Tools would be easy to swipe, though.

"How terrible! Any suspects?"

"Nope. But I just thought I'd warn you. Make sure you lock up the garage good and tight."

I pressed my lips together, thinking. Replacing the flimsy lock on the garage's side door was on my list of things to do. I'd have to move it up to top priority.

"Thanks, I will. I'll call the locksmith as soon as I go inside."

He nodded his approval. "Good enough." Looking down at my scattered gardening supplies, he said, "I'll let you get back to work. Hope your kitty comes back."

"Oh, he isn't my kitty," I told him. "All of a sudden, he was just—" I shrugged, "there."

Mr. Modowski wore a knowing look. His smile was gentle. "We'll see," he said. "We'll see."

***

Later, after I'd called the locksmith and been told he could come out in three days, I made a trip to the grocery. Quite deliberately, I turned down the pet food aisle and bought several tiny cans. There was no sign of the cat as I placed a plastic bowl of the smelly stuff there among the tulips, but I hoped he'd show up and have a little snack. What can I say? I'm a mother, so my first instinct is to offer food.

The next morning, the bowl was empty, licked clean. My eyes swept the yard, looking for the little fellow without success. Carrying the bowl with me, I went out to the garage to check for signs of a burglary, but everything looked fine.

When I turned around to head back to the house, there on the path just a few feet away sat the cat, his tail curled around his paws in classic fashion.

I can't describe how pleased I was to see him. He looked so peaceful there in the morning sun, and I felt as if he were saying, "Thanks for dinner."

"Good morning," I greeted him.

He opened a surprisingly tiny pink mouth and emitted a high-pitched squeak. Not a meow, it sounded more like one note of bird song.

"Did you like that tuna?" I asked, nodding my head.

Again, he gave that squeak. I took a step closer and bent over, extending my hand toward him. Cooing softly, I tried to get him to come to me. But, I soon learned, he had a stubborn streak and held his ground. Then, I took one step too close and he bolted, back to the evergreens, tail waving behind him like a flag.

"Rats!" I said aloud.

All that day, I made sure to sneak peeks out the window, but the orange tabby cat was as elusive as Bigfoot. Eventually, I gave up the hunt, but I made sure to refill the plastic food bowl and place it back among the yellowing leaves of the tulips.

Later that night, before I headed off to bed, I looked again, out the window over the kitchen sink. The yard lay bathed in moonlight, silent and still.

Not feeling the least bit silly, I whispered, "Goodnight, kitty," and turned out the light.

***

Hours later, I came awake with a start. I'd been dreaming, and in my dream, a baby was crying. Now, lying in bed with my eyes wide open, I could still hear the baby, wailing at top volume.

"What the—" I tossed back the covers and scurried as quickly as I could into my slippers and robe. I was still putting my arms into the sleeves when I got to the kitchen, that was how fast I went down the hall.

The crying continued, rhythmic and unabated, and I wondered what sort of mother would be outside with a squalling infant at—what time was it? I glanced at the clock. 2 a.m.

Twitching aside the curtain over the sink, I looked out into the yard, where the noise seemed to be originating. In the alley, maybe? It was too dark to see, really, with the moon hidden behind some clouds, but when I squinted, I thought I detected motion near the garage. As I watched, with one second passing into the next, a bit of moonbeam squeezed through a break in the cloudbank and I saw a figure separate itself from the shadows. The figure turned, glancing toward the house, and I could see it held not a baby, but my weed whacker!

The garage thief!

Grabbing the phone, I punched in 9-1-1.

"The garage thief is here!" I whispered, as if the person in the alley could hear me. "And there's a crying baby, too!"

The dispatcher, who had obviously heard odder messages than mine, assured me the police were on their way. I was to wait for their arrival.

She never told me where I should wait, and there isn't a mother on the planet who could stay inside when there might be a baby in trouble outside. What if the thief had stolen the baby, too? That little one needed me—now.

Very, very quietly, I eased open the lock of my apartment door and moved down the tiny stretch of hall to the back door. This, too, I carefully unlocked, all the while listening for the trill of approaching sirens.

The night air was cool and I wrapped the folds of my robe more tightly around me.

From just at my feet, splitting the darkness, came that shrill baby's cry and my heart leapt into my throat. I glanced down, fully expecting to see an abandoned newborn.

Instead, I saw the orange tabby cat. Sitting on the edge of the stoop not two feet away, he was still in the process of closing his mouth after emitting the cry.

In a blink, I understood. There was no crying baby. There never had been. It was he who had awakened me, he who had sounded the alarm, alerting me to the burglars in the garage.

"Ssh!" I hushed him now, stooping down.

He took a step closer, then another. Then, he rubbed up against my ankles and twined between my feet.

"Who's my good boy?" I whispered, stretching out a hand and stroking that brilliant orange fur for the very first time.

As if I'd been doing it all my life, I bent and lifted him into my arms. We stood there together on the darkened porch, watching in fascination as flashing lights appeared in the alley.

The heavy body in my arms rumbled, gently at first, then building to louder more thunderous sounds. I squeezed the cat tight, listening to his purrs of pleasure and feeling like purring myself.

In the yard next door, the porch light came on, and it was no surprise at all to see Mr. Modowski appear in flannel robe and bare feet. He looked my way, raised an arm in greeting, then sprinted across the lawn toward me.

His first words were not, "What's going on?", as I expected. Instead, his face gentled as he looked at the contented tabby cat.

"Well, well," he said, reaching out to pet the cat's broad forehead with the back of one finger. "Didn't I say you had a kitty? Wasn't I right?"

The cat extended his neck, eyes squinted shut, reveling in the affectionate attention.

"You were right," I agreed, looking down at my new friend. "I have a kitty."

Kate Fellowes is the author of six mysteries, most recently *A Menacing Brew-*. Her short stories and essays have appeared in several anthologies, as well as Victoria, Woman's World, Brides, Romantic Homes and other periodicals. In 2020, she won the San Diego Public Library's Matchbook Short Story contest. A founding member of the Wisconsin Chapter of Sisters in Crime, her working life has revolved around words—editor of the student newspaper, reporter for the local press, cataloger in her hometown library. She blogs about work and life at http://katefellowes.wordpress.com and shares her home with a variety of companion animals.

Follow Your Nose

Cathy Wiley

"Help me, Tracy Warner, you're my only hope."

"Wait, I'm Obi-Wan?" Tracy said. "I'd rather be Princess Leia. Better hair."

"Good point." I had fun picturing Tracy, a 50-something DEA agent with short, gray hair, with Princess Leia's signature hairstyle. While that wouldn't work, I bet she could rock the gold bikini, considering how fit she was. "But you really are my only hope." I looked down at the bundle of energy vibrating beside me. "I've tried everything with Tigger. We've gone jogging, running, hiking, everything. I'm exhausted, but he's still ready to play."

Tracy followed my gaze and contemplated my beautiful Copper Husky. When he noticed her looking, he tugged at the leash, trying to jump on her. "I promise you, Lauren, after just one session of nose work, he'll be exhausted. He'll probably fall asleep in the car."

"Really?" That sounded amazing. After doing research, I had decided I wanted a husky, since I always thought they were beautiful, smart dogs. I knew they had tons of energy, but I figured twice daily walks, longer hikes on weekends, and a large fenced-in yard would be sufficient. Even when the Husky Rescue agent had warned me that this four-month-old Copper Husky had been turned in by his previous owners because he was "too energetic," I thought I could handle it. As an active twenty-seven-year-old, I figured I'd be able to wear him out with regular walks. I was wrong. Not a problem, I had meant to start exercising more. But even running five miles every morning didn't wear him out. I'd come home from work to either a destroyed house or a dug-up backyard and an escapee dog. And a dog that wouldn't stop jumping on me. Obedience training lessened the jumping, but not enough. "Tigger has enough energy for three toddlers, even at almost a year. A tired dog sounds wonderful."

"It is. Chester also has tons of energy, although he's chilled now that he's older." She pointed toward her German Shepherd, who was calmly lying in a crate at the edge of the parking lot. "But any day we do nose work, he's as tired as, well, a dog.

Dogs love using their noses. It's what they're built for. And the brain stimulation tires them out better than physical exercise."

"That's what I read." My increasingly desperate Internet searches had pulled up nose work as the solution to my dog's energy crisis. I had tried some of the training at home and booked a session with Tracy and Chester, a former drug-sniffing dog and trainer. Make that a former trainer and drug-sniffing dog. "I haven't noticed too much of an effect yet, with the exercise you gave us, but I'm hoping that—"

"Mother, how long is this going to take?" I glanced over at the interruption, a pre-teen or teenage girl with long hair, long legs, and a long-suffering look of boredom on her pretty face.

Tracy sighed. "Sorry, I had to bring my daughter with me. It's my weekend to have her." She turned to her daughter. "Brianna, it's not polite to interrupt. And I told you it would take about two hours. Lauren, this is my daughter, Brianna. Brianna, this is my client, Lauren Chase, and her dog Tigger."

I might be slightly biased, but Tigger is a gorgeous animal. Copper-colored hair, bright blue eyes, and a happy personality. Most people had to stop and tell me what a gorgeous dog I had. But could his handsomeness counteract teenage ennui?

Brianna's glance barely passed over me: probably rated me old and boring, which hurt considering that I generally considered myself young and stylish. I suppose the fanny pack was ridiculous, but I needed a place to store the treats I was supposed to give Tigger. Still, my designer jeans, cute boots, and purple highlights in my dark hair didn't sway her. But Tigger? He noticed her, so he gave her his best puppy look, tongue dangling out on one side, and I saw the recognition of adorable, the melting of the cold teen heart to show the child inside. Then she rolled her eyes. "Is there anything I can do? I don't get a good signal here."

About twenty miles outside Washington DC, the Pebble Stream Nature Preserve was a perfect location on that breezy April morning, with the trees just starting to bloom. There were dozens of wooded trails, multiple parking lots and playgrounds, a scenic waterfall, and a miniature farm. Unfortunately, it did not have Wi-Fi.

"You could help here, Brianna. You used to enjoy helping me. Why don't you get the cotton swab ready?"

"Oh joy. I'm so luck—" A sharp glance from her mother stopped her. She shoved a food packet into her pocket. "Fine. What scent are you using?"

"It's Tigger's first time with a scent, so let's go with birch."

From my reading, I knew that Brianna was about to dip a cotton swab in essential oil. While dogs could do nose work with almost any odor, usually trainers would work with birch, anise, or clove. There were even weekend trials where dogs competed to find the scents the fastest and most accurately. My competitive soul was very intrigued with that possibility.

While Brianna opened up the plastic kit, Tracy showed me the set-up. She had laid out six square white boxes, like the ones the post office uses to ship things in, in the parking lot where we were meeting. The cotton swab would be hidden in one of those boxes. I had seen videos online of dogs sniffing out the correct box. It was impressive, especially when they would stare up at their owners — wait, the correct term was handlers — alerting them to the correct box. It looked like fun.

"You've been doing this with treats already, right?" Tracy asked.

"Yes, and he was happy to get his bacon treats. He's always happy to get his bacon—"

"Oh no!" At Brianna's loud exclamation, Tracy and I ran back over. I stopped when I saw the broken glass, not wanting Tigger's tender toes to be cut.

Tracy stopped short as well. "You dropped the bottle? Are you okay?"

"I'm fine. But I got the stupid oil all over my new shoes." Brianna stomped one of said shoes. "Daddy just bought these."

Tracy glanced around, obviously assessing the situation. "Well, we can't do training here, that's for certain. Odor is all over the place. Lauren, why don't you grab the boxes — they're cold, sorry, I mean they have no odor yet — and head over to the opposite side of the parking lot?" She lifted Chester and his crate into the back of her SUV, seemingly effortlessly. Leaning into her vehicle, she came out with some paper napkins. Stretching, she passed them over to Brianna. "Carefully pick up the glass and take that over to the dumpster over there. I don't know what we're going to do with your shoes. You might have to trash them before you get in the car. If not, it will totally overwhelm Chester."

"You care more for that dumb dog than me," Brianna complained. She crouched down, picked up the glass, and clomped over to the dumpster and back.

"That's not true," Tracy said as she picked up the kit. "I'm sorry that it ruined your shoes. We'll replace them on the way home if you'd like."

Brianna yanked a bag out of her pocket, threw more food in her mouth, and chewed noisily. She rolled her eyes again; she was obviously a champion eye roller in the Teenage Olympics.

Tigger strained towards Brianna, but reluctantly followed me when I pulled him toward the boxes. I gathered them up, and we trotted over to the opposite side of the parking lot where I spread out the boxes in the same configuration Tracy had done, three rows and two columns of boxes. Tracy followed in her SUV. After parking, she pulled out Chester, then the kit, gloved up, and dipped a cotton swab into a vial. "Sorry about that. Luckily, I have more than one vial of birch."

She placed the cotton swab in the top middle box, took off her gloves, and gestured at the boxes. "Do you want to see Chester demonstrate, or do you and Tigger just want to try it?"

"What am I supposed to do?" Brianna called from across the parking lot. She shoved more of the snack into her mouth.

"Why don't you go see the animals on the farm?" Tracy suggested. "They have goats."

"Great, goats. I'm so excited." Brianna trudged away.

"Be back in an hour, young lady." Tracy said, checking her watch.

"Fine." I was impressed with how many syllables she got out of that word. She dropped her voice to a mutter. "I wish I were with Dad. He takes me to exciting things."

Tracy snorted out a disgusted breath. "That's because he's trying to buy your love. And hurt me." Her voice wasn't loud enough for Brianna to hear, fortunately, but I wasn't certain what I should say. "Sorry," Tracy said with a sigh. "Didn't mean to drag you into that. Let's start training."

Without Brianna, the lesson progressed smoothly. Tigger performed admirably, quickly figuring out that picking the right box equaled bacony goodness.

"Dogs usually are motivated by one of three things," Tracy said while we took a break. "Attention, toys, or food."

I laughed. "Tigger is definitely motivated by food. His food, your food, my food, any food he can get his paws on. Especially if it's bacon."

"Do you feed him people food?" Tracy asked with a frown.

"Not often, but I do give him bacon. Or sometimes he just takes it. He's quite the thief." I gave him a quick scratch behind the ears to let him know I still loved him, bacon thief or not. "He also gets ice cream. We both love our ice cream."

Tracy checked her watch. After staring off into the distance, she pulled her phone out of her back pocket and frowned. "I wonder what is keeping that girl." She tapped at her phone. "I'll text her and remind her to come back. So, let me bring out a few more boxes, and I'll add odor to a second box."

This delighted Tigger, since now he got twice as many treats each time.

"You're both doing well, but you, as the handler, know where the odor is. Let's try it with you not seeing which are the hot boxes."

I turned, glancing around as I did to check for Brianna. I didn't see any signs of her. "Do you want to check on her? She was supposed to see the goats, right? I don't mind if we take a break and look for her." I could tell Tracy was anxious.

"You don't?" She smiled in appreciation. "Tigger is fine with other dogs, right?"

I nodded. "Loves them."

"Well, let me grab Chester and some poop bags and we can take the dogs for a walk. A potty break is a good idea anyway. We haven't discussed this yet, but if you decide to try competitive nose work — and I think you should since Tigger has taken to it quickly — you need to worry about potty breaks." She leaned down to open the cage.

"Oh? Tigger's always been good at that, even when he was younger."

She attached a leash to Chester's harness. "Yes, but if a dog eliminates in a search area, it's an automatic disqualification." The dogs did an obligatory butt sniffing, and once that was out of the way, happily trotted next to each other as we headed toward the farm.

"Number one or two?" I asked.

"Both. You'll get good at recognizing the signs. Then you quickly call finish and rush the dog outside of the search area."

"I've already figured out some of his signals."

"You'll really start to figure his expressions the more you do nose work. It's a really good way to bond with your dog. When you start trusting him and his nose, he trusts you more. And the more you work together, the better you both get at communicating." She sighed. "Now if I could only communicate with Brianna as well as I do with Chester, I'd be much better off. I know she's upset about the divorce, especially since, due to his problems with alcohol and probably drugs, the judge ordered that his visits must be supervised visits. And it doesn't help that he's constantly badmouthing me to her and—I'm unloading on you again. I'm sorry."

"I don't mind. I'm a Human Resources Director, I'm used to being a sounding board." I didn't bother mentioning that my mother and sister constantly complained to me as well. "And I know divorce is hard on everyone involved. Hopefully, she'll adjust soon enough."

"I hope so." She slowed down as we approached the barns.

I could see, hear, and sadly, smell, the signs of goats and chickens and other farm animals. But there was no sign of Brianna.

"She's not here." Tracy pulled out her phone again, frowned, and typed. "She'd better answer my texts. I know we don't get the best signal here, but I've got two bars." She stared down at Chester, who was sniffing at the ground. "Actually, I know just how to find her." She switched Chester's leash from the top of his harness to the back. "That leash adjustment puts him into working mode. Chester, seek!"

I could see the change in Chester's demeanor. He immediately perked up his ears and started sniffing in earnest. He must have scented the birch immediately, since he looked back up at Tracy. "Good dog," she said, giving him a treat. "Now seek the source." She followed him as he picked up his pace. "If we tried this with Tigger, he'd probably expect a treat every step that Brianna took. However, since Chester has also done rescue searching, he knows how to follow a scent, without expecting a reward each time."

As if hearing her, Tigger lifted his head from where he'd also been sniffing and stared at me until I praised him and gave him a treat. He went a few feet, sniffed again, and looked up expectantly. I gave into him one more time, okay, two more times, then tugged on his leash to get him to stop sniffing every step of the path.

Chester quickly led us away from the farm and toward a hiking trail that led to the west side of the park. I'd been hiking here before with Tigger, in my futile attempts to wear him out. We followed Chester and Tracy into the woods. The farm noises were quickly replaced by the sounds of birds and small creatures scrabbling in the forest.

After a few minutes, we came to a fork in the road, with a sign stating that the right led to the lake, the left led to another parking lot. Chester didn't hesitate, he headed toward the right fork. I started to follow, but had my arm jerked back as Tigger tried to go to the left. "Come on, Tigger," I said as I tugged him to follow me. A few yanks finally convinced him to heel, although he let out a quiet howl of protest. "Hush, Tigger. We need to find Brianna."

Chester seemed confident of the right path, so we broke into a trot as we searched for the missing girl. As we turned around a bend, I heard Tracy curse loudly and come to a standstill. Tigger and I angled around her, and I quickly saw what had made Tracy so upset. To the right side of the path, lying in the tall grass and weeds, was, not Brianna, but her shoes. Chester placed his nose almost on the shoes, then sat down and looked at Tracy. Even though she was obviously distracted, she praised him and gave him a treat.

"She must've taken them off," Tracy said. "Still, there'd be traces on her socks, so Chester should still be able to find her. Seek, Chester!" The dog immediately obeyed, completing a large loop around the shoes, sniffing as he went back and forth. But after a few minutes, he trotted back to Tracy and looked at her with, what I interpreted, was a confused expression. Maybe I was getting better at this dog expression thing.

"She couldn't have just disappeared," I said, wanting to be helpful but feeling helpless.

"No." Tracy sat down on a nearby bench, placed her head in her hands. When she raised up her head again, I could see anger in her eyes. "It has to be Erik!"

"I haven't heard Erik's name before, but I'm going to make a wild guess that that's your husband."

"Ex-husband," she said, standing up. "He's the only one who she'd go with and would know that having birch-covered shoes would help me find her. Especially since he hates the smell of it. And he'd know that he'd need to carry her so that Chester can't follow her." She pulled out her cell phone and tapped three numbers. "Hello, I'd like to report a missing girl. I suspect my ex-husband has taken her. He's threatened to do so in the past."

While I was concerned that Tracy might be jumping to conclusions, I was worried about Brianna. "Maybe we should head back, see if she returned to the parking lot."

Tracy stayed on the phone with 911 as we trotted down the path. When we got to the fork, I tried to head to the left, toward the farm. My arm was almost yanked off as Tigger violently jerked me toward the right, toward the other parking lot. "Tigger, what is so fascinating about this direction?" I asked, tugging on the leash.

Whining, he bent low, nose working overtime. After dragging me a few feet, he placed his mouth on the ground. And came up crunching. "What?" I said.

Tracy had already passed me heading down the left path, still on the phone. I called out, waved at her with one hand, while my other arm was currently being stretched to its limits.

Tigger pulled me another five feet and yet again, found something to munch on. "What are you eating?" I leaned down, tried to take it from him. He was reluctant, but I got a few crumbs. I smelled it. "Bacon?"

By this time, Tracy had made it to me. "What's the hold-up? The police are going to meet us at our vehicles. We need to go."

I stared down at my dog, who continued to pull away from me. I curled my fist around the bacon bits. "What snack was Brianna eating?"

"What? Um, oh, it was some jerky. Bacon jerky, I think. Let's go!"

I unfurled my hand, showed her the crumbs. Her eyes met mine, and she and Chester bolted ahead of me. Tigger was having none of that, and raced ahead, determined to get to the bacon first.

It took another minute before he discovered more of his favorite snack. Tracy had informed the emergency operator to redirect the police to the other parking lot. Hopefully, they'd be there in time and Erik hadn't left yet.

The forest was thinning, and I could see cars in the distance. Just as we stepped out of the woods, a scream pierced the air.

"I don't want to go to Mexico. Stop it!"

"Brianna!" Tracy yelled, then charged forward.

With the dogs in the lead, we both ran toward the parking lot. Halfway up an aisle, I saw Brianna, struggling with a tall, bearded man who was trying to shove her into a black pick-up truck.

"Erik, put her down!" Tracy demanded. She used Chester to make her point, as the formidable German Shepherd yanked at the leash, just inches away from the man.

"Easy, Chester." Erik set Brianna down on her sock-clad feet next to the open passenger door. "What's the big deal? I was just going to take her out for some ice cream. You know, since you were too busy with your class."

"That's not true," Brianna said, wiping away tears. "I mean, that's what you said at first, saying we'd just play a joke on her and get her worried."

This time, Tracy growled.

Erik put an arm around Brianna. "Yeah. It was just a little prank. No harm."

Brianna shook off her father's arm, walked over to Tracy and turned around. "But then as you carried me to the parking lot, you said we could get me new shoes when we got there. When I asked what you meant, asked since when do ice cream shops carry shoes, you said once we crossed the border, you'd get me new shoes."

It would be a while to get to Mexico, I realized, but I suspected Erik wasn't the sharpest tool in the shed.

"I was just kidding," he protested.

"You were not!" Brianna yelled. "You said that you were going to take me to Mexico, and that Mom would never see me again."

The arrival of the police probably saved Erik's life, based on Tracy's balled-up fists and lunge toward her ex-husband. I pulled her back, tugging on Tigger's leash as well.

"Excuse me, Mrs. Warner?" The police officer said as she walked up. "What is going on here?"

Three voices broke out at once, words tumbling over each other. I decided to stay out of it, trying to back away from the fray. Tigger, however, kept yanking toward the truck.

"So, you, Mr. Warner, are claiming you were just going to take your daughter to get ice cream, even though it is not your visitation weekend?"

Erik nodded as he stepped forward, away from the truck. "Yes. I understand that was not appropriate, nor was it right for me to deliberately worry Brianna's mother by doing the trick with the shoes. But when I met Bri at the farm, after she texted me that she was bored, I figured what the hell, I should worry her some since she was ignoring our daughter."

"I wasn't ignoring her, you idiot, I was trying to make some money since you—" She dropped her voice down to a more reasonable volume. "Since you just can't seem to afford child support. Although you can buy yourself a new truck."

She gestured at said truck. I turned toward the vehicle, which Tigger took as permission to explore. He placed his front legs on the truck's running board, stuck his snout on the passenger side floor, and came back with a plastic bag nipped between his teeth.

"Tigger!" I grabbed the bag from him. Glancing inside, I saw why he was interested. Inside, along with a number of candy bars and chips, were four or five bags of the bacon jerky that Brianna—and Tigger—loved. "Huh. That's certainly a lot of food for a quick drive to the ice cream shop."

"See!" Brianna exclaimed.

Looking inside the truck, I raised my eyebrows. "Don't normally need suitcases for that trip either."

The officer pulled out her handcuffs. "Erik Warner, you are under arrest for suspected kidnapping."

It took a while for everything to settle down, but I stayed with Tracy and Brianna, who had wrapped their arms around each other, as the police took Erik away.

"I'm so sorry, Mom," Brianna said in a whisper. "I had texted him that I was bored, and then he said he'd come and we'd have ice cream. I went along with him about the shoes when he said it was just going to be a joke on you, but then he got so serious, and mad, and I realized it wasn't a joke."

"It's okay, love." Tracy smoothed Brianna's hair down. "I'm sorry too, for how hard this is on you."

She turned to me. "And I'm so sorry that this has been such an unusual training session. Allow me to assure you that you have earned free nose work lessons for life. And as for you, Tigger..."

Tigger perked up at the sound of his name. And his tail started wagging as Tracy snagged the bacon jerky bag from Brianna's pocket. "All the bacon for you!"

Cathy Wiley is a member of Sisters in Crime, Mystery Writers of America, and the Short Mystery Fiction Society. She's written two mystery novels and several short stories included in anthologies, one of which was a 2015 finalist for a Derringer Award. She lives near Baltimore, Maryland, with one spoiled cat and an equally spoiled husband. Hopefully, the cat will forgive her for writing about doggies. Visit www.cathywiley.com for more.

Mullet and the Nope Rope

Melissa H. Blaine

It all started with a snake. Well, two snakes if you count both the human kind and the reptile variety.

Mullet (and yes, I know the name should have tipped me off right away but sometimes you're three margaritas in and lonely and the next thing you know, it's six months later and you're sharing kitchen space with your drunken mistake) plopped down a canvas bag on the floor of the living room and went to change out of his mud-spattered hiking clothes.

Hitting the pause button on the latest true-crime drama I'd been watching, I threw a foam ball across the room for the kitten I'd adopted the week before. Mullet had been a hard sell on the kitten, but a few tears and lots of begging had finally won him over. Reggie, a fluffy ball of orange hair with subtle stripes on his back, pounced on the ball before batting it away. It rolled toward the bag Mullet had dropped. Reggie careened after, his little legs struggling to get a grip on the slippery wood floor, making him look a little like a cartoon-version of a giraffe on roller skates.

He'd almost reached the ball and bag when he skidded to a stop, the hair on his back standing up straight as his back arched.

It probably says something that my first reaction was to yell down the hall, "Mullet, what's in the bag?" I really wanted it to be some Halloween prank for the trick-or-treaters the next night.

Silence.

The kitten swiped at the bag and jumped back, hissing. The bag returned a hiss, the bottom of the bag undulating.

I screamed, grabbed Reggie by the back legs, and curled him into my arms as I climbed on top of the end table.

Mullet ran into the room, his hands gripping a baseball bat in the swing position. He slid to a stop when he saw me standing on the sofa.

"I thought someone was breaking in, Em." Mullet lowered the bat and propped it in the corner.

I pointed to the bag. "It's moving!"

"Well, yeah. It's a snake. I thought Reggie might want a playmate." Mullet undid the string holding the bag closed. A small heart-shaped head slithered out.

"A kitten, Mullet! A playmate for Reggie is a kitten, not a snake." I wanted to look away from the gray nope rope with brown patches as it inched its way out of the bag, but if I lost sight of it, I was burning Mullet's whole house to the ground before I slept another night in it. "It cannot stay in the house. Take it outside." I'm not ashamed to say that my voice was squeaky.

"It's a baby. It's not going to hurt anything."

The nope rope was almost all the way out of the bag. It wasn't long, maybe a foot and a half, so maybe Mullet was right that it was young. But a little snake turned into a bigger snake.

That's when the rattling started.

"Mullet, that's a rattlesnake." I hugged Reggie a little tighter in my arms.

He looked at me like I was daft. "There aren't any rattlesnakes in Michigan, Em. It's just a baby hognose." He turned to look at the danger noodle. "Aren't you, you sweet thing? We can set up a tank for him in the dining room and I'll take care of him."

"I don't care. It can't stay in here. I'm not living with a snake in the house."

The snake, whatever it was, choose that moment to launch an attack on one of Reggie's stuffed mice. I screamed like a four year old, leapt from the sofa with enough height that I'm surprised I didn't give myself a concussion, and grabbed a change of clothes and Reggie's carrier before vacating the premises for my best friend Liz's house.

Mullet left about twenty voicemail messages, ranging from how he was worried that the python wouldn't survive the winter in the barn (and would get lonely) to blaming me for not getting to know Norman, as he'd named the snake, to yelling that he'd been sleeping with his ex, Tina, anyway so I could just stay gone.

This would have all been a good story to laugh about twenty years from now if it wasn't for the lottery ticket. Sure enough, twelve hours after I vacated Mullet's house, my lucky numbers came up on the BiGMONEYDRAWING. I could almost feel the $10,000 burning a hole in my pocket... except that I'd stuck the ticket in Mullet's kitchen cupboard for safe keeping earlier that week. I had been so focused on getting away from Norman and his forked tongue that I completely forgot about the ticket... well, that and the fact that I'd never won anything before so it wasn't like I ever expected that ticket to come to anything.

I needed that ticket back. It was enough for first and last month's rent. With Mullet and me done like dinner, I needed a new place to live. I might even have enough left over to buy a shelf-worth of soap to wash the Norman cooties off me.

Problem was, Mullet knew about the ticket too and about an hour after the drawing, I got a text from him with a picture of the ticket and the words "haha."

My first order of business the next morning was to sneak back into Mullet's house. It wasn't like Mullet was the sharpest tool in the box so I figured that he probably hadn't hid the ticket very well, if he'd even thought to do that.

I waited behind the barn until I saw him leave. Then, I peeked through a few windows until I saw that Mullet had set Norman up in a glass terrarium in the living room. With the coast clear, I let myself in, (thankfully he hadn't thought to change the locks yet), and turned the place over, coming up blank. I even went so far as to peer into Norman's tank. Eek! Still nothing. My hopes of finding the ticket were fading faster than my willpower with a plate of cookies. For all I knew, Mullet had taken it with him, hot-footing it over to turn the ticket in and claim the money already.

On a whim, I decided to take more more peek in the kitchen cupboards, thinking that maybe Mullet had stashed the ticket behind some of the plastic beer glasses he hoarded. I was halfway through the second cupboard when the phone rang. I froze, feeling like I'd been caught even though I knew logically that whoever was on the other end of the phone couldn't see me.

"Mullet, you there?" The voice was raspy with a little wheeze after the question. "I hid that envelope like you asked. Not sure why you dropped it off here, but I took care of it. You just get over here soon to pick it up. I'm not your personal secretary, boy."

Great-Uncle Bert. The man with hands like tentacles and a mindset stuck in the 1950s.

I'd only been to his condo once or twice with Mullet, but I knew it was located in a little retirement village on the northside. Mullet must have left the ticket there for safekeeping until he had time to cash it in himself.

I needed a new plan. One that would get me in Great-Uncle Bert's house and give me time to find wherever the heck he might have hidden the ticket. He was marginally smarter than Mullet and meaner than a hornet so I knew he wasn't just going to give me the ticket back without Mullet. Thankfully, for me, his memory was a little fuzzy most days, more from his consumption of alcohol than the ravages of time, so there was a good chance that he wouldn't recognize me. I'd have to find a way to bluff my way in.

***

Later that afternoon, after a quick trip to the pop-up costume store on Butternut, I parked my car in front of Uncle Bert's condo, a little cream-colored end unit with red shutters and an apple tree growing in the front yard.

I tugged down the white skirt of the nurse's uniform I'd rented and shut the car door behind me with a thud.

You can do this, Em. Just go up, knock on the door, give him some story to get in, and then figure it out.

My fingers found the bottle of anti-histamines like it was a life preserver. I wouldn't use them unless I had to and I'd just give him enough to make him nap. Heck, he was old; he'd probably fall asleep mid-sentence anyway.

After giving the heavy wood door a rap with my hand, I rang the doorbell and stepped back. I heard a cough and the shuffle of feet through the door before it swung open. Great-Uncle Bert looked like a man who needed not to be living alone. He also smelled like it. His undershirt was speckled with dirt and his pants probably stood by themselves when he took them off. A half-drank bottle of beer hung loosely from one hand while the other gripped a shiny black cane with a rubber bottom. Under a thread-bare beanie, thin gray hair stuck out to the side and mixed with the collarbone length beard.

"Who are you?" His eyes ran from my head to my toes before they settled on a spot that was not my eyes.

"Hi, I'm Emily. I'm from Dr. Pettingan's office to do a wellness check. You should have gotten a call last week about it?" I not only was a pretty good bluffer, but I had a poker face that champions wished for.

His eyes narrowed. "Didn't get no call. What's this all about?"

"It's just a wellness check to see how you're doing. I'll take your blood pressure and pulse rate, things like that. I'm sorry you didn't get a call." I leaned in closer. "I'd just really appreciate it if you could let me take your vitals. I don't get paid for the visit unless I come back with them and my sister's been really sick and well, you'd be helping me out."

Uncle Bert took a long sip from the bottle and squinted his eyes. "You look familiar."

I could almost feel the wheels turning in his brain. I tried to keep my breath calm. Even if he remembered who I was, Mullet might not have spilled the beans about us breaking up.

The wheels ground to a halt. He shook his head a little and opened the door wider. "Just make it snappy. My nephew's coming in an hour for dinner."

My heart sped up. This had to work and it had to work now. I wasn't going to get any second chances on this.

"Of course, Sir. I'll be as brief as possible and get out of your hair." Where would the old coot put an envelope that he had to give back to Mullet soon? "Would you like to sit in the kitchen?"

"Nah, we'll be more comfortable in the sun room, sugar." He winked.

Kill me now. "Sure, that sounds just perfect. Do you mind if I take a quick detour to get a drink of water before we get started?" I knew from the last time I was here that if I could get him into the sun room, I could look around the kitchen, bedrooms, and bathroom without him seeing.

"Grab a beer and let's make it a party!"

I laughed one of those high pitched, girlie giggles and gave his arm a squeeze. I was going to need all $10,000 of that lottery ticket to restore my dignity. First, I had to find it though.

After Uncle Bert settled in a recliner that leaned precariously to the right, I told him I'd grab another drink for him on the way back. I glanced around the kitchen, feeling like this was a wild goose chase. I was never going to find the envelope and ticket. Even if I could get Bert to sleep, Mullet was going to be here in less than an hour. I wouldn't have enough time to do much searching.

"How you doing in there? You need some help?" Uncle Bert called from the recliner. I held back a gag and walked around the kitchen, my heels clicking on the linoleum floor.

"Just fine." I opened up the first cabinet. "I'll just pour us a little drink, eh? What's your preference?"

Uncle Bert mumbled something from the family room that might have been bourbon. I was reaching into the liquor cabinet when the front door crashed open. Crap, if Mullet was early he was going to catch me and my shot at that lottery ticket was totally gone.

"Don't move, Bert. Just tell us where the drugs are and nobody has to get hurt." The voice sounded like my mom when she was scolding one of her school kids.

"Ladies, there's no need for the guns. Can't we just sit down and talk about this?" Uncle Bert sounded a little shaky under the slurring.

Ok, not Mullet, but this didn't sound like something I wanted to be in the middle of either. Guns? Count me out. But, if I left, no $10,000. And speaking of leaving, was there even a way I could get out of here? Ladies with guns at the front door and Bert in the sun room by the sliding glass door. Could I get through one of the bedroom windows if I popped out the screens? Was I a bad person for not even stopping to think about poor Uncle Bert? I didn't think so. Maybe if he'd kept his eyes above my neck. Sometimes a woman's got to save herself. If I could out, I'd call the cops on my cell and they could deal with whatever this situation was.

I chalked up another strike against Uncle Bert when I looked up to see a pistol-toting, five foot, walker-pushing woman standing in the kitchen entry. If I hadn't stop to think about him, I could have been halfway out a window instead of being face-to-face with an evil version of Sophia from The Golden Girls straight down to the mask she wore over her face.

"Rose, we got an extra guest here." The Sophia-lookalike motioned me toward the family room. Another women, also holding a gun, stood just inside the front door. She was sporting a Betty White mask. A giggle escaped my lips as the thought that I had somehow landed in the middle of *The Golden Girls* meets *Breaking Bad* reality show.

Rose eyed me, "You're not a nurse so what're you doing here?"

"What're you talking about? She's from some doctor's office to give a wellness exam." Bert scratched a hand across his chest.

"No nurse dresses like that. Pick it up from a costume shop?" The Sophia character waved her gun toward a kitchen chair. "What're you really doing here?"

I plopped down in the chair with a huff, visions of my winning lottery ticket going up in smoke. "My ex is Bert's nephew. I left a winning lottery ticket in his house and I think he brought it here to keep me from getting it back. Bert's a leech so I figured he'd let me in if I was dressed like this and then I could poke around and find the ticket."

Sophia asked, "Mullet?"

"Yeah. Not my best idea."

Sophia looked over the top of her glasses, "You think? That boy is a donkey's butt. But, you got spunk, and Rose and I need to search this place too so let's tear this place apart together."

"What? You can't do that!" Uncle Bert sputtered.

"I don't think you have a say in this, old man. Rose is going to have a little chat with you about taking what's not yours and you're going to tell us where you put the pills that you stole from us. If the girl and I find the pills and lottery ticket before you tell Rose where they are, well, she doesn't like people who waste her time."

A wave of relief washed over me. I didn't know why these two retirees were after drugs at Uncle Bert's and I didn't care. If we could find the lottery ticket before Mullet...

"He's coming here. Mullet." I sputtered. "When I got here, Bert said he'd be here in an hour." The relief was short-lived. We weren't going to have enough time. Sophia looked spry for her age, despite the walker, but this was impossible.

"Buck up, girl. No sense giving up until we have to." After motioning for me to get up, Sophia followed me into the kitchen, where she started opening cupboard doors and rifling through the contents. I followed her lead.

"Bert stole pills from you?" I asked, checking behind some cans of green beans.

"Yeah, the girls and I run over into Canada a few times a month and buy meds for people who can't afford to get them in the US or need stuff that you can't get here. Bert must have heard us talking about it, because he showed up earlier this week and the next thing we know, the pills are gone. Knowing him, he's planning on selling them or having that nephew of his do it. We would have been over earlier, but I'm the only one who owns a gun so we had to round up another one.'

I shook my head, "Bert's a sleeze."

We finished the kitchen, no drugs or lottery ticket to be found. Bert's bedroom was first down the hallway. Other than a discarded towel in the corner of the room and a bed that didn't look like it had been made in the last decade, there wasn't an obvious envelope and short of rifling through his underwear drawer, which I did not need the money bad enough for, there wasn't anything to be found. The bathroom was also decidedly gross and empty of hidden lotto tickets or drugs. I was batting 0-2.

Sophia pushed her walker down the hallway toward the second bedroom. She turned the doorknob and went in as I poked through a linen closet outside the bathroom.

"Found 'em," Sophia said. "The meds are here and I think your envelope might be under this plastic tub thingie."

I got into the room too late to help. As Sophia tugged on the envelope, the rack of plastic tubs that the envelope was stuck in swayed. She gave one last tug, as I grabbed her arm and the walker, pulling her out of the way of the teetering rack. For a minute, it looked like it might right itself. But the tubs on it had shifted just enough that the rack began to fall, pulling the next rack and then the next toward the floor like a line of dominoes.

From the middle of the pile of racks and tubs, a heart-shaped head appeared beneath a dislodged tub cover.

"Out. Out. Out." I pulled Sophia out of the room and slammed the door shut behind me. I was not sticking around to find out how many of Norman's cousins were living in those tubs. Bert could clean up the mess later, long after I'd left with the envelope that Sophia had dropped into the walker basket next to the bags of pill containers.

We hightailed it back through the kitchen to the sun room, where Rose was lecturing Bert. They turned toward us just a second before Rose's eyes got big.

Before I could even react, she pointed the gun toward Sophia and me. We froze mid-step.

"It's coming for me. Don't let it get me." Rose fired the gun, the sound ricocheting around the room.

Then all hades broke loose.

The recoil from the gun knocked Rose off balance and she tumbled into the chair with Bert. Sophia and I looked behind us to see a swarm of wiggling danger noodles coming from under the bedroom door. Rose's shot had missed the front runner... well, slitherer.

I grabbed Rose's hand, hauling her out of Bert's lap, and between she and I, we maneuvered Sophia and her walker out the front door. Across the drive, a few early trick-or-treaters huddled on a condo's front porch, the adults holding phones to their ears. The sound of police sirens in the distance indicated that Rose's shot hadn't gone unheard.

Sophia smuggled the bag of medications to Rose, who walked over to a neighbor's shrub and dropped the bag into it, pretending that she was on the verge of vomiting. I looked toward the front door, wondering if Bert was coming out. I felt a little guilty that we had left him in there with the snakes.

"Do you think we should go back for him?" I looked down at Sophia as she tucked the envelope that had started all the trouble into my hand.

"Not a chance. There had to be a hundred snakes in there." She shuddered.

Mullet pulled into Bert's drive just before the police, who ended up blocking him in. So much for any getaway he might have tried. Uncle Bert stumbled out the front door, hollering about Armageddon. He climbed right inside one of the cruisers without even putting up a fight. Thankfully, all of the danger noodles stayed inside.

The police took one look inside the condo and called in animal control and DNR officers.

As we watched them remove snake after snake after snake, I turned to Rose. "Will you get in any trouble about the gun?"

"Nah, I got old lady charm. Besides, I got a concealed permit a couple of years ago. The cop I talked to said he'd of done the same thing with that many snakes coming at him."

***

Norman's reptile cousins turned out to be eastern massasaugas, a threatened species of rattlesnake native to Michigan. The DNR officer, Kate, who I met at Mullet's house to turn over Norman, told me that it was illegal to collect the species because of its conservation status. Both Mullet and Bert were looking at some wildlife trafficking charges as well. Not only had they been collecting and selling the massasaugas, but they'd also been trading in other illegal species. Kate assured me that the snakes would all be examined and those that could be released back into the wild would be.

I could live with that. I just hoped I never had to encounter another of those danger noodles again.

Sophia and Rose, who were really Mable and Joyce, met me for coffee the next week. We celebrated the fact that they'd been able to keep the medications hidden from the cops and get them to the people who needed them. They planned to continue their trips into Canada, particularly since it seemed Bert hadn't ratted them out.

I also had some celebrating to do. The lottery ticket that Sophia had retrieved for me turned out to be a $100,000 winner and not the $10,000 that I thought. I'd already found an apartment for me and my kitten, Reggie.

And I was going to get a playmate for Reggie... but no nope ropes allowed.

Melissa H. Blaine (aka Melissa Haveman) thinks massasauga snakes are interesting, but she hopes to never see one. A West Michigan native, her mystery/crime short stories have appeared in various anthologies and her nonfiction writing has appeared in everything from textbooks to business books, including several upcoming releases on doubt and creativity . She's also a certified executive and leadership coach for creative professionals and teams. She loves fostering kittens for Harbor and has only foster failed once (with a cranky adult cat who now rules the house, including the dog). The kitten in her story was inspired by a foster kitten that both she and her niece fell in love with while she fostered him and her snakiest friend, Kate, graciously agreed to play the role of danger noodle rescuer. Melissa can be found at www.creativelycentered.com

The Fetch Connection

Tammy Euliano

"R eady to go to the lake?"

I think the dogs understand those words. My husband, Neil, thinks it's all in the delivery. We agree to disagree. The dogs leap into the back seat, Kody, the sixty pound black fur ball of a rescue dog, on the passenger side, and Pep, the golden retriever, behind me.

The forty-five minute drive from the "big city" of Gainesville to our lake house in the country town of Earleton is a trip back in time—from Publix supermarkets and Shell stations to Williamson's family grocery and Joe's Gas and Go.

Our long dirt driveway ends with a view of beautiful Lake Santa Fe, sparkling blue on this fine June morning. Before I let the dogs free, I check next door. We learned last weekend that the current renter is not a dog person. Having a rental next door has been a bigger problem than expected. Nearly every weekend is the same—new neighbors for the dogs to introduce themselves to. No fence separates our yards. It's surprising how many people are fearful of large barking dogs racing toward them at break-neck speed, but always with tails wagging. They never actually collide with anyone, more like a furry game of chicken. Most of the renters are happy to meet them, unless they've just come from a swim (the dogs, not the people), some are less eager, but Pep and Kody win them all over in the end. Or at least they did, until last weekend. He may be a dog-hater, but at least he opted for a long-term rental. He'll be here the whole month. Hopefully the dogs will get used to him...or he'll get used to them.

Dog-hater is nowhere in sight, and there are no cars in the rental's driveway, so I release my dog-shaped torpedoes to explore all the new smells in the yard. I set up my laptop on the patio and start my Friday ritual of writing, interrupted every few minutes by Pep whining that the tennis ball she placed ten yards away is stationary. *The ball's not going to throw itself, Mom.*

I don't really have time today, with a deadline looming for my response to an article on the opioid epidemic. As an anesthesiologist, I hope to explain why we can't eliminate all opioids. But I also can't say no to my annoying, wonderful dogs.

So I bang the Chuck-it, the greatest dog toy ever invented, on the tile and Kody, the older brother by several years physically, and decades in brain power, moves the ball within reach. I toss the ball for him to catch—he prefers catch to fetch—then "chuck" the ball again, into the neighbor's yard, for Pep. This routine gives me several minutes to write before the scene replays. And I wonder why I'm so far behind. Every few throws, the dogs run into the lake to cool off, often returning with a different ball. Pep must have them stored all over the neighborhood.

She begins barking, joined immediately by Kody. "Pep, Kody, come," I say sternly, as if that ever works. They've already begun their mad dash toward another new face. I move to intercept. Not really intercept, but appear to be the good dog owner who is surprised at her dogs' failure to obey. "They're friendly. They won't hurt you," I yell to the man.

He bends over and pets the dogs and they immediately stop barking and start licking. Some guard dogs. "Hi, I'm Jack. The Smiths told you I'd be house-sitting for a couple weeks?" The Smiths' home is a blue hexagon on stilts (very cool) on the other side of the annoying rental property.

"They did. Nice to meet you." We look out for each other here in the country. As I'm introducing the dogs, Kody starts growling, looking toward the rental house. I grab his collar just in time, though my shoulder regrets it. Over his barking, I say, "Sorry, I need to take him inside. Let me know if I can help you with anything." As long as it's not peace and quiet.

Dogs safely behind a closed door, I'm retrieving my laptop from the porch when they start growling and barking again. Sheesh they're persistent. Dog-hater from next door is walking toward his dock, talking on his phone, or pretending to so he doesn't have to acknowledge me. Wow, when did I become so judgy? I push the dogs back and squeeze inside, yelling at them to hush, which is funny when you think about it.

They calm, until Dog-hater comes back from the dock, then they go crazy again. Maybe Kody's not so smart after all. I write and re-write the article the rest of the afternoon, while throwing balls off the dock for Pep to retrieve. Kody's not a swimmer, so I occasionally toss one for him to catch. Dog-hater doesn't reappear. Perhaps Kody scared him off. Which should make me feel bad, since he paid for this vacation, but doesn't, because I paid for this house and if there weren't new people every week, there'd be much less dog-drama.

When my husband arrives with the pizza, we eat on the dock. "Did you finish your article?"

"Almost." It's not a complete lie, but I will need to work more. Pep-the-tireless brings another ball, but not one I've seen before. This has a large blue dot on it and feels different. Neil handles it. "Must be some kind of practice ball." He bounces it once on the dock. "A little bigger and less bounce." He throws it into the water,

Pep retrieves it and swims to the ladder, where Kody awaits her safe return. Soon she's back, waiting until she's within range to shake. Lucky us.

Neil throws the ball several more times, but inevitably it disappears in the weeds when Pep hesitates too long. The number of tennis balls we have donated to the Earleton environment would support Wimbledon for decades.

As the sky shifts from blue to pink to red, we talk about work, and our kids in college, and our upcoming vacation, until the mosquitoes send us inside. Pep has another ball in her mouth. Again with the blue dot. It must have floated back.

The full moon is a bright streak in the water as I stare out from our second floor bedroom. The exhausted dogs are sleeping soundly, at last. But someone isn't. A boat motor purrs in the distance, but I see no running lights. Lake Santa Fe is popular with fishermen, but not this late at night.

An hour later I hit send on my article. That took way more time than it should have. As I close my laptop, I notice people on the Smiths' dock. It's far away, and fairly dark, but I would swear they had SCUBA tanks.

***

Despite my late night, I'm up to photograph the sunrise. It's gorgeous—orange and blue, with bright wedges cutting through from the horizon. Pep can be only so patient with my hobby and soon drops one of the new tennis balls at my feet. This one has a green dot. "Where are you getting these, Pep?" She has a history of stealing toys from neighbor dogs. I'm not proud of it.

I'm startled when Kody tears off down the dock, unrecognizable in his anger. Here we go again.

I chase after both dogs. Dog-hater grabs Pep's collar. Maybe he's coming around. He tries to pull the ball from her mouth. She doesn't give up a tennis ball easily and turns her head from side to side. I laugh. So many try to be nice and throw the ball for her, somehow she doesn't realize she has to release it first.

But this man isn't smiling.

I grab Kody's collar, order him to be quiet, then tell Pep to sit, and she actually obeys. "Drop it," I say, and she obeys again. The wonders never cease. The man picks up the slimy ball with a disgusted expression, then turns back to the house. Not a word. He doesn't throw the ball, just takes it. I suppose it could be his, but what's one lousy tennis ball? Or two maybe. Whatever.

I release the dogs and return to retrieve my camera. I glance back to see Pep run around the corner of the neighbor's shed. She must have seen a squirrel. Jack is on the Smiths' dock. I wave, but decide not to ask about his nighttime visitors. Either I was dreaming, and therefore will sound crazy, or I wasn't, and therefore will sound nosy.

By the time I reach the back door, Pep's there...with a ball. It's like she's burping them up. I take it from her, again with the tell-tale dot. "You little thief. You're going to get me in trouble."

The man had been so unfriendly, I decide to let Pep play with it for a while. I'll return it to his porch later, when he's not home.

An hour later, I realize I never fed the dogs. Kody comes running at the tell-tale clang of kibble, but no Pep. I find her under the kitchen table, tennis ball at her side, sound asleep. Nothing, I mean nothing, keeps Pep from her food. I try to wake her. No response.

My heart pounds, my face heats, tears prick my eyes. "Neil?" I pull Pep from under the table. She's breathing, but won't wake up. I pull up her eyelids, her pupils are pinpoint.

"What's wrong?" Neil squats beside me as I wipe a white powder from her face. He picks up the ball. "It came from this."

I call Art, our neighborhood vet. "I think Pep ingested something, maybe heroin." Neil's eyes widen.

"I'm on my way." Country folk are awesome.

"No wonder he wanted his stupid ball back." I sit with Pep, watching each slow breath.

At last, Art arrives in his golf cart, syringe at the ready. He examines Pep's eyes, her pulse, her breathing. "It does look like heroin." He pulls the cap from the needle and injects Narcan into Pep's thigh.

Moments later, my beautiful dog's eyes open. Glassy, but open. "She'll be okay?"

"Could the heroin have been contaminated with anything else?"

My pulse pounds behind my eyes.

I storm from the house, Neil on my heels. I follow Pep's path around the neighbor's shed and find a hole dug under the wall. In the hole are several spotted tennis balls.

"Can I help you?" It's a male voice, and he doesn't sound much like he wants to help. Or maybe it's the gun Dog-hater's pointing at us from ten feet away. He holds out his other hand. "I'll take that ball."

I toss it to him. Not my best toss, considering. As he reaches forward to catch it, a large black fur ball beats him to it, slamming into his arm and knocking the gun from his hand. With the ball triumphantly in his mouth, Kody stands over drug-running Dog-hater, growling and drooling on the man's red face.

He shoves Kody back and reaches for his gun.

"I wouldn't do that if I were you." Jack holds a gun leveled at the man. "DEA. Keep your hands where I can see them."

Well that explains a lot.

"Is it pure heroin?" I demand.

Jack raises an eyebrow. "Yes. How did you—"

I run back to the house and tell Art.

"That's good. Well, not good it was heroin, but..."

"Yeah."

Neil arrives with Kody, who sniffs and nudges his sister. I sit with both dogs' heads in my lap, and let a few tears fall at the close call.

Art leaves me with extra Narcan. Country folk take care of each other, even the four-legged ones.

Jack appears. "I'm sorry about all that. I wish I could have warned you. We had no idea how he was smuggling the heroin."

"The SCUBA divers last night?" I ask.

"You saw us? He always rents houses on water." He shrugs. "We didn't find anything."

"Pep did," I say.

She whines and tries to get up, pulling toward the rental house. Other DEA agents have opened the shed and tennis balls rain down. It's doggie heaven for Pep. I hold on tight. No doggie heaven quite yet.

Sometimes what appears to be heaven-sent, isn't. And sometimes people aren't who they appear to be. If in doubt, ask a dog, especially a rescue.

Tammy Euliano's writing is inspired by her day job as a physician, researcher and educator at University of Florida. She's received numerous teaching awards, ~100,000 views of her YouTube teaching videos, and she was featured in a calendar of women inventors (available wherever you buy your out-of-date planners). Her short fiction has been recognized by Glimmer Train, Bards & Sages, Flame Tree Press, Flash Fiction Magazine, and others. Her debut novel, a medical thriller entitled "Fatal Intent," was published by Oceanview in March, 2021, and the sequel, "Misfire" is coming January, 2023.

The Marks of Zorro

Michael Allan Mallory

N o, not him. Nor her. Or them. That guy? Nope.

Officer Suki Ogawa sighed. None of these people looked like a pickpocket. Though, to be honest, she had no idea what the suspect actually looked liked. Gingerbread brown eyes scanned the hundred plus craft fair attendees in her line of sight in search of a phantom. A phantom who could be anyone in the slow moving tide of sunhats, T-shirts, shorts, and sundresses. It was like playing a real life version of Where's Waldo without knowing how Waldo was dressed. Spotting a skinny dude in a candy cane striped shirt and knit wool cap in this bunch would've been easy, if their thief was outfitted in Waldo's traditional togs.

"Anything?"

Suki turned toward the mellow masculine voice next to her. "Nothing so far," she said without enthusiasm.

"It's a long shot," Sergeant Joe Romero's warm voice reassured. He was short and chunky, solidly built and somewhat moon-faced. Deep laugh lines stretched around his mouth as he half-joked, "If we're lucky, our guy may not even be here today."

Fine with her. This was Suki's first year working the Pine Haven Beach Craft Fair and she'd be happy with a quiet, uneventful shift. No drama. Definitely no drama. But she knew the venue was popular and drew in lots of visitors ripe for the picking from a skilled pickpocket. She could only hope for a relaxing few days walking among the booths by the ocean under the summer sun.

Yeah, like that was going to happen.

She looked to Romero who seemed to be drinking in every sight around him, not so much searching for their thief but, it seemed, appreciating the experience for itself. "You work the craft fair every year, don't you?" she said.

"Every year since it started. Going on ten."

"You must like it."

"Five days outside by the water. Great people watching. Food vendors. Usually nothing happens. What's not to like?"

"You gonna miss it?"

Silly question. Of course he'd miss it. Retirement didn't mean one's life stopped. She'd asked the question more as a chance to get the usually closed-mouth sergeant to open up about his after life from the job.

Romero sighed blissfully. "I will miss these."

They had paused in front of a mini donut cart where she was met with the enticing aroma of fresh deep fried pastry dusted with cinnamon. She basked in the smell.

"Sergeant Romero, my best customer," greeted the curly-haired man behind the cart as he topped off the batter loader. "The usual?"

"One small bag," the other said. "And no jokes about cops and donuts, Ogawa. These suckers are a once a year indulgence." A minute later as the officers continued on their rounds, the sergeant held out the little bag to Suki. "Have one?"

She politely declined. Reluctantly. She was on track to lose ten pounds and was determined to make her goal weight. Some of her colleagues trained for marathons or iron man endurance events to stay in peak physical condition. Not her. Just the thought of those grueling workouts freaked out her inner couch potato. She was upping her exercise regimen, just not to the point of insanity. Sure, she was a whisker on the plump side, but she had less exhausting methods to improve her fitness. Like giving up the deep fried goodness of a high-calorie donut.

The pair continued to patrol the craft fair. Four acres of white tents and tables made up a temporary village at one end of a large parking lot near the shoreline. The officers strolled along the wide avenue between booths at a lazy pace so that their uniforms might act as a deterrent to would-be troublemakers.

Romero stopped when they reached a particular booth. Three long folding tables were arranged in a U shape. A long nylon banner was draped from the edge of the front table bearing the words: Pine Haven Animal Humane Society. Atop this table sat a display rack of brochures, a donation box, and a plastic bin with small trinkets for sale. The table to the right held a wire cage with a floppy-eared bunny. Romero hovered by the table opposite, the one making up the left arm of the U. He smiled like a kid at the occupant of the wire cage, a sable-colored ferret who sat up, bright-eyed, studying the human in front of him with keen interest.

"Hey, Joe," came a pleasant voice from across the table, a woman clad in a green polo shirt and tan shorts. Her gray-streaked hair hung in a long French braid.

"Hi, Mindy."

"I hear this is your last year working the craft fair." She observed his interaction with the ferret.

"Yeah. Hanging up my shield in two weeks."

"We'll miss you." Mindy turned to Suki with a playful wink. "We're Joe's favorite booth—or so he tells us. He spends a lot of time here. Every year."

Suki looked skeptical. "I thought the mini donut stand was his fave."

"A close second," he corrected, adjusting his duty belt to squat down to eye level with the animated tube of fur.

Mindy returned a motherly smile, even though she was, by Suki's reckoning, at least a decade younger than him. But some women—no matter their age, be it sixteen or sixty—project a maternal tenderness toward everyone. "What'll you do with all your free time, Joe?"

He gave a dismissive grunt. "Staying clear of idiots and troublemakers"

"That's ambitious," she quipped.

"I deal with those jokers every week. The numbers wear you down. Looking forward to some serious quiet time."

"We can always use volunteers at the shelter."

"Well, that's an option."

Mindy smiled at that. Then tilted her head toward the ferret. "You seem taken by our little friend here. Interested in a companion animal like Zorro?"

"Zorro, huh? I get it, the mask."

"Not just for the mask. He's a rascal. Smart, curious, a bundle of energy, affectionate. A real sweetie."

"That he is." The sergeant leaned in closer. "Hey, little guy."

"Got him three weeks ago. His previous owner had to move overseas for work and couldn't take Zorro with him."

"That sucks."

The ferret sat up taller, fuzzy triangular ears angling toward Romero. The sweet masked face was pegging the cuteness scale. Smiling too. At least that was Suki's impression. Or maybe the little guy had gotten a whiff of cinnamon donut and wanted a handout. Whatever the reason, the sergeant looked smitten.

As was she. Zorro was irresistible. That adorable face! She extended her index finger toward the cage.

"Don't!" Romero and Mindy cried out in unison.

Too late.

Zorro's paw had already swiped out.

Suki jerked back her hand with a gasp.

"You OK?" Mindy said, concerned.

"I'm fine." Suki inspected the four shallow parallel scratches on her finger.

Mindy breathed easy when she saw them. "Barely broke the skin. No blood. Good. Just so you know," she added for reassurance, "Zorro has had his shots."

"Smooth move there, Ogawa," Romero mocked. "Next time read the sign." He indicated the small placard fixed to the base of the cage: KEEP FINGERS AWAY FROM CAGE.

"Lesson learned." Suki averted her eyes, embarrassed this had happened in front of her mentor. In these last weeks before his retirement, she had wanted to leave a strong positive impression for him to report back to their captain. Scratch that. She sighed.

Mindy hastened to add, "Zorro is friendly. He's usually very mellow. But he's in a strange environment with a lot of noise and strangers. Animals don't like sudden movement. The sign is there to protect him and us from the public."

"We get that," Romero agreed. "We deal with knuckleheads all the time. I bet those teeth of yours could handle 'em, little buddy."

Zorro's pink nose twitched back.

The interplay between them delighted Suki. "Mindy's right, Sarge. You should adopt Zorro. You live alone."

Broad, rounded shoulders gave a noncommittal shrug but he did not say no, a point not lost on Suki. That told her he was open to the idea.

As if he'd read her mind, Romero suddenly stood up and started walking. "Time we moved on," he said with a last glance toward Zorro and Mindy.

They didn't get far. At a pottery booth a minute later a distressed middle-aged woman in a floppy yellow hat shuffled over toward them. "Excuse me, officers," she said in a thin, hesitant voice. "I think I was robbed. My wallet's gone from my bag." She displayed the inside of a wide-mouth canvas tote bag. "It was there earlier." Her eyes darted anxiously between them.

Sergeant Romero's usually jovial face grew stern. "When did this happen?"

The woman's heavily penciled eyebrows knit together. "Um, I'm not sure. I noticed it five minutes ago when I was at that wood carver's booth over there."

"Is that where you think it happened?"

"I guess. Someone bumped into me."

"Man or woman?"

"A man."

"Young or old?"

"Young, I think."

"Can you describe him?"

She shrugged sheepishly. "Not really. I was looking at a horse figurine."

"How was he dressed?"

"The horse?"

"The man."

"Oh. All I remember was a white baseball cap and a cloth bag slung over his shoulder."

"Color of the bag?" Romero prompted with long-practiced patience. Suki admired how good he was at herding witnesses, keeping them from straying too far from the point.

The woman in the floppy hat pressed her lips together. "Um...army green. I think."

"OK, thanks. We'll keep our eyes open as we make our rounds. Give Officer Ogawa your contact information. We'll be in touch."

"Looks like our pickpocket is working today," Suki said later, after the woman was out of earshot.

"It does, doesn't it? Though if he were smart, he would've been long gone by now. A smart thief knows when to quit while he's ahead. Some are too greedy. Like our guy, if he's still working the crowd."

Her gaze swept across the shoppers milling about at the crawl of molten lava, many shoulder to shoulder. Perfect targets for a pickpocket. "How d'you want to do this? Split up and cover more ground? Sarge?"

Romero didn't answer, distracted by something in the distance. "Hold on," he said a moment later, squinting to confirm what he was seeing. "This way," he motioned.

Maneuvering between a cluster of teenaged girls in tank tops and short shorts, too wrapped up in themselves to notice the traffic around them, Suki followed as the sergeant made a beeline to a nearby booth filled with acrylic paintings of sunflowers and mountain landscapes.

"Meatball Lewis," Romero chortled, hands on hips. "It is you. What the hell are you doing here?"

The man behind the table looked uneasy. "It's Dan, Sergeant Romero. I haven't gone by Meatball in five years." Forty something, hair pulled back in a ponytail, and sporting a loud Hawaiian shirt, Lewis exuded a smarmy, high-energy TV pitchman charm.

Romero eyed him skeptically. "Into art now, are you?"

"Up to my neck. I painted all of these."

"You did these?" Romero seemed taken aback.

"Every last one. I'm an honest citizen now, Joe."

"For real?"

"Yes, for real."

Clearly these two had a history. A second later Romero enlightened her. "Meatball—sorry, Dan is no stranger to the station lockup. In his day, he was a lucrative shoplifter. I arrested him a few times."

"That you did," the other acknowledged without rancor. "After the last time, I took a hard look at my life. Made changes. It took a while but I'm doing pretty good now." He swung out a slender arm toward his artwork display.

"I must say I'm impressed." Romero looked at him with pride.

The man previously known as Meatball stood straighter. "You didn't know I was an art school grad. Top of my class." He cleared his throat meaningfully. "That was before I started supplementing my income with my other sideline."

"These are nice. I'll have to get one for my den."

The corner of Suki's mouth pulled back. It was educational watching how easily the sergeant connected with people. Not something that came naturally to her, but a skill she needed to acquire if she wanted to succeed at this job. Like now, how he seamlessly transitioned from art admirer back to investigator. Romero lowered his voice as if confiding to a friend. "Just so we're clear," he said, "you've been at your tent all day. Right? There's been a report of a pickpocket."

Lewis looked injured. "You don't think I—? Seriously? I told you I gave up that life."

"If you say so."

"I do. And besides, I was a shoplifter not a pickpocket. Those guys rob people. I lifted merchandise from businesses," Lewis replied with a glimmer of professional pride.

"True. It is a different skill set."

"Thank you."

"Let me ask you this. Have you noticed any suspicious looking people hanging about?"

What the art vendor saw they never found out, for Romero didn't wait for the answer. Suddenly his head snapped round at the sound of a familiar voice in distress.

"Hey come back! Stop him! Help! Someone stop him!"

It was Mindy.

Romero and Suki dashed off at full sprint toward the Animal Humane Society booth where they found Mindy jumping up and down in distress. "Joe! Help!" Her fingers tore through her hair. "This guy distracted me and stole Zorro. He ran that way!"

They tore off at a dead run in the direction she pointed.

Mindy shouted after them, "He's got a white cap and a bag!"

Same guy, Suki thought as her legs cranked hard against the asphalt. The officers charged through the crowd in hot pursuit without a clear bead on their suspect until—

"There!" Romero called out. "That's him."

Suki struggled to see around the shoppers. So many of them. And she wasn't that tall. But she caught a flash of movement. A runner! The only runner in an ocean of meanderers. He also had a white cap and what looked like a green bag. He glanced over his shoulder.

He'd seen them and amped up his pace, pulling ahead farther.

Suki's heart sank. The guy already had eighty yards on them. Plus he was young and ran like a frightened deer. If he made for the parking lot, they'd lose him in all the vehicles. How much longer she could keep up this pace, she wasn't sure; her heart was already beating like a kettle drum. And Romero was wheezing. If they didn't catch this guy soon she was worried that Romero would either drop out or drop dead.

But luck was with them. Seconds later, to avoid crashing into a large family with baby strollers, their suspect veered away from the parking lot toward a line of food trucks at the periphery of the fair. Suki locked eyes on him as he ducked between a taco truck and a Philly cheesesteak truck, scrambling into the vendor prep area. A forlorn groan escaped her when she saw the lanky runner clamber up and over a tall wooden fence. Seconds later, as she closed in on the fence, her concern ballooned into dismay.

The damn fence was eight feet tall!

You're not built for this! She sucked in her resolve and attacked the fence in one fierce jump. Her duty boots scrambled for purchase on the planks. The climbing grooves in the soles found a grip and, with a mammoth effort, she hoisted herself up and over. Suki dropped to the sandy ground like a bag of cement, exhausted, panting hard, amazed she'd actually taken the fence. A heartbeat later she was amazed further when Joe Romero's chunky frame collapsed next to her with a heavy thud.

On hands and knees, he complained, "I'm too old for this shit."

Normally she would've made a joke. Instead, she pointed to the ground near his feet where a white ball cap and olive green book bag had been discarded. "Look," she said, breathless.

Romero snatched up the items then struggled to his feet.

In front of them stood the backside of a long outbuilding. Beyond the far edge, Suki could see a beach. The sound of surf and voices rang in her ears. Many voices. Another crowd for the pickpocket to lose himself in. Both she and the sergeant were exhausted. And the situation just got more difficult. The cap and book bag had been their only way of identifying the suspect.

"Do you remember what else he was wearing?"

"Negative," Romero wheezed.

That didn't bode well. Trotting along the side of the outbuilding, she lamented, "How're we gonna find this guy in this crowd?"

As they rounded the building and faced the open beach, Romero laughed. "Oh, I don't think it'll be that hard."

Suki broke into a wide smile when she saw what he saw.

Before them stretched a wide beach populated by dozens of people. Young. Old. Men. Women. Some sat in lounge chairs. Some built sand castles. Others swam in the warm water. A few walked along the sand. All of them—each and every one—had one thing in common: they were buck naked. All of them save one young man trying to hide behind a plastic trash container, the only person on the beach wearing clothes.

"It's a nude beach!" Suki said.

Romero nodded. "It is. I should have remembered."

They closed in on their suspect, stick thin with rough features, dressed in a short-sleeved linen beach shirt and khaki cargo shorts.

"Get up," Romero ordered. "Hands where we can see them."

The young man—he couldn't be older than twenty, Suki realized—slowly got to his feet. Savage deep set eyes glared back above a petulant nose. "What you bothering me for? I ain't done nothin'."

Romero was panting like a dog, barely able to talk. He waved for Suki to take over.

She stared down their suspect. "If you didn't do anything why were you hiding?"

"I wasn't hiding. I was resting."

"Don't give me that. You were running from us. You're out of breath."

The brooding youth defiantly folded his bare arms across his chest. "You got the wrong guy."

And then Suki noticed something. "Sarge, open the bag."

The book bag was draped across Romero's shoulder. He shifted it to the front and pulled open the flap. Out popped a masked furry face with a what's-going-on-out-here expression.

Suki's voice hardened. "You stole this ferret. And I bet there's a few stolen wallets in your bag as well."

"I've never seen that thing before and that ain't my bag."

"If that's true," she came back, "how do you explain how you got those?"

She pointed to his crossed forearms and four deep fresh claw marks.

A tense silence followed.

Suki grunted derisively. "What? Nothing to say? Dude, you got caught. You've been marked by Zorro. You're coming with us."

Stroking the ferret's head, Joe Romero gave an approving nod. "Good one, Ogawa. Nice job."

Michael Allan Mallory is the co-author of two novels featuring mystery's first zoologist sleuth. Lavender "Snake" Jones first appeared in Death Roll and returned in Killer Instinct, which Mysterical-E called "a tale that will enchant you and even keep you guessing." Michael's short fiction has appeared in numerous publications. His story "The Man Who Wasn't There" appeared in the Bouchercon 2019 anthology, Denim, Diamonds and Death. He is a member of Mystery Writers of America, Twin Cities Sisters in Crime, and the Mystery Short Fiction Society. He can be found lurking at www.snakejones.com.

Wag More, Bark Less

Jayne Ormerod

T he fence gate emitted an ear-piercing squeak as Chandy Oliver pushed it open, granting her access to the beautiful English garden inside. She raced along the winding oyster-shell path in an attempt to reach the front door before Scrapper picked up her scent. Scrapper was one-hundred and sixty pounds of overly affectionate Great Dane who loved to put his massive paws on a person's shoulders as a friendly greeting. Chandy was not dressed to go eye-to-eye, literally, with Scrapper today.

"Aunt Mat?" Chandy called as she shut the door. "I got here as quickly as I could. What's the emergency?"

Matilda Fisher came through the back door, tugging mud-encrusted gardening gloves from her hands as she walked down the hall. "Thanks for coming. I've got a case for the best PI in Heron's Ridge."

"I'm the only PI in Heron's Ridge. What's up?"

"Sit, sit." Matilda motioned toward the dining table, which was covered with boxes of promotional material and envelopes waiting to be stuffed. Yet another solicitation on behalf of the local SPCA, of which Matilda was president. "On second thought, let's go into the kitchen."

Matilda's kitchen was the quintessential definition of cozy, wrapping Chandy in memories of many happy family meals. She closed her eyes and took a deep breath. Yes, the aroma of Aunt Mat's healing chicken soup seeped from the painted wood cabinets and faded chintz curtains. This is what a home should smell like, Chandy thought. Hers did not. Yet. That may be because she hadn't cooked a full meal there. Yet. But it had only been two years. These things took time.

Matilda bustled about the kitchen, getting glasses and filling them with ice and tea. A plate of homemade peanut butter blossoms appeared from the bread drawer. Chandy was a sucker for PBBs, as she called them. But everyone knew Aunt Mat only made PBBs when she wanted something from someone. It made Chandy nervous to hear what case Aunt Mat was about to propose.

Once settled around the Formica kitchen table, Matilda explained the reason for summoning Chandy to her house. "At nine-forty-five this morning, I set fifteen flower arrangements on the long table on my front porch before rushing off to volunteer at the animal shelter. Great exercise for both me and the pups, you know."

Yes, Chandy knew. Aunt Mat had been trying to get Chandy to sign up to walk shelter dogs, but there weren't enough hours in her day. When she wasn't working full time at Ye Olde Ice Cream Shoppe, she spent every waking moment trying to get her PI business off the ground. Let's face it, there wasn't much call for a private investigator in this small riverside town, so she'd developed an active (albeit time consuming) social medial campaign to convince people they needed her services. Anything from tracking down lost loves to locating missing pets. No clients yet, but people were starting to recognize her. She needed to prove she could do the work. This case could be her big break!

Matilda rose to fetch the ice tea pitcher. "And who knows, you may find your fur-ever friend by volunteering to exercise with the mutts."

"As much as I love Scrapper, and the fact you rescued him, he's a cautionary tale of big dogs from cute, squiggly puppies grow."

"I wouldn't trade him for the world." Aunt Mat returned to the table. "Rescues make the best pets. But I know you've heard my spiel before." She tapped the table with her gnarled finger. "So, back to my case. Helen Jenkins was supposed to pick the arrangements up at ten and carry them to the clubhouse for tonight's Wag More, Bark Less black-tie event. But when she arrived, the vases were all gone! Not a dropped daisy petal to be found. So, you need to find out who stole all the flower arrangements and get them back. And you need to do it fast. The event is in…" Matilda glanced at the kitchen clock, "…three hours."

That was a tall order for a freshman PI, but Chandy felt up to the task. She pulled her cellphone from her cargo pants pocket and prepared to take notes. "Can you describe the arrangements?"

Matilda nodded. "I repurposed old metal sprinkler cans to use as vases, chalk-painted a light purple. Most of the flowers were from my own garden. Sprigs of lavender and stems of gladiolas, with few Shasta daisies to give them a pop of color. For greens, I used distinctive hydrangea and magnolia leaves. Helen brought me some purple asters she'd ordered from California. The arrangements were stunning, if I do say so myself."

"They sound stunning. But who would pilfer them right off your front porch?"

"I can tell you three people." Matilda used her fingers to count off her accusations. "Allie Bricker's daughter's wedding reception is at six at the church. I heard her florist up in Ashland cancelled on her and she was in dire straits."

Chandra had gone to school with the bride, Kelly Bricker. She only knew Mrs. Bricker by reputation...a woman who gets what she wants, no matter the cost.

"Then there's Miss Patty's eightieth birthday brunch over at the Elks Lodge," Matilda continued. "Steph Martin was in charge of decorations and you know how scatterbrained she is. Never did order the floral centerpieces."

Miss Patty loved a good party. Everyone knew that. And as past president of the garden society, there was no doubt in Chandra's mind that fresh flowers on the tables would be expected. Make that required. Miss Patty was known to walk out of a party if it didn't have fresh flowers on the table. It wouldn't be good for Steph's reputation around town if Miss Patty walked out of her own birthday party.

"Thirdly, there's the annual Mahjongg tournament down at the River House. Bitsy Newsome is running it this year. You know that woman squeezes a quarter so tight the eagle screams. Had this bright idea to use plastic flowers for luncheon tablescapes. She argued they could use them every year, thus saving money. But when Mahjongg Maven Jacelyn Winters found out, her head about exploded. 'Fake flowers? Not at my tournament,' she'd screeched loud enough to be heard three counties over. That was yesterday at five o'clock. I can't image Bitsy found a florist on short notice. On a Saturday in June, no less." Matilda pursed her lips and shook her head.

Chandy knew Bitsy Newsome by reputation only, as a social climber of the worst sort. She had been angling to get on that mahjongg tournament board for years. No way would she risk her status by not making the Mahjongg Maven happy.

"These are great leads, Aunt Mat. But a good PI always keeps an open mind to less obvious suspects. I'd better get going. Keep Scrapper out back while I escape out the front. I can't be interrogating witnesses with his paw prints on my shirt. It's not professional."

A tingle of excitement snaked up Chandy's spine as she climbed onto her motor scooter. Her first real case. She would not, could not, let Aunt Mat down.

Chandy zoomed down the narrow road toward Bradford Sound, the breeze blowing against her cheeks. She loved the freedom she felt when riding her pink PI scooter. And yes, she wore her matching pink helmet, even though it messed up her hair. It was a promise she'd made to Aunt Mat.

At the bottom of the hill, Chandy made a left at the one stoplight in town and headed toward her first stop, the Elks Lodge. Steph Martin seemed to have the most at stake for not providing flowers on the tables.

The brunch was over and the banquet room empty when Chandy arrived. Not to be discouraged, she headed for the member's only taproom. There were six aging Elks bellied up to the bar, drinking bottled beer, and swapping war stories. None were familiar to Chandy. She did spot an ally curled up in a sunspot by the front window. "Punchy," she called to the Siamese cat her aunt had fostered back to life. Aunt Mat had proclaimed Punchy the best mouser she'd ever seen, and with the rodent problem at The Elks Lodge, it had been a win-win-win situation.

The sleek cat, now pushing nine years old, rose, stretched, and sauntered down the bar where she arched her back against Chandy's extended fingers.

The man at the closest barstool leaned over and commented on the cat's piercing blue eyes. Soon, Chandy and he were chatting like old friends. It was the bar patron who brought up the topic of Miss Patty's eightieth birthday party. "You missed a good one," he said.

"I bet the decorations were wonderful," Chandy said.

"I guess. I don't so much as notice things like that. But she had an assortment of desserts that you wouldn't believe. I can personally vouch that every last one of 'em tasted delicious." The man patted his round belly while licking his lips.

All of the other patrons echoed the praises of the desserts, but not a single one confessed to noticing the centerpieces.

Chandy said her goodbyes, gave Punchy one last pat, and headed out the door feeling slightly discouraged that she wasn't any closer to finding the flower thief. She glanced at her watch. Time was running out.

Once in the parking lot, she slipped on her pink helmet and glanced around. Her lucky day! Steph Martin was just walking out the back door. Chandy trotted over to catch Steph before she got in her car and drove away.

Having no time for small talk, Chandy jumped right into the questioning. "Did you manage to get flowers for the centerpieces?"

A guilty look spread across Steph's face. "Uh, yeah. Mom cut every last hydrangea from her garden and arranged them in bowls. Guests took them home, but mom's yard looks so forlorn."

"Sorry to hear that. I hope they grow back." Chandy jumped on her scooter and headed for Mrs. Martin's house. Sure enough, not a hydrangea bloom to be found on the five mature bushes in front of the porch. Proof to Chandy that a mother's love knows no bounds.

Next, Chandy scootered over to the church. The basement was abuzz with wedding reception set-up. She counted tables. Fifteen round tables dressed in rose-colored linen set for ten persons each. No table centerpieces yet, though.

Allie Bricker stood on the small stage, barking instructions. "Archie, not there. The band should go in that corner."

Chandy approached Allie. "Things are looking festive, Ms. Bricker. I know this is an exciting day for you. And for Kelly. I hear her husband-to-be is a great guy."

"He is."

"I remember how Kelly had all the details of her wedding worked out by the time she was ten years old, to include grand floral centerpieces on each table. But I heard there was some trouble with the flowers."

Allie sighed, the big heavy sigh of a mother-of-the-bride when things don't go quite as planned. "We paid for imports. Flown in special. They should be here within the hour, the good lord willing."

Chandy asked Ms. Bricker to pass along her well wishes to Kelly and then left.

On the way out, she passed a white florist's van heading for the church. On a hunch, Chandy stood back and watched to see what kind of flowers would be unloaded.

She bit back a bit of disappointment when a young man began unloading lavish arrangements of pink and blue roses stuffed with baby's breath. A little heavy on the baby's breath, Chandra thought, but it wasn't her wedding.

Another dead end. She only had one stop left. At least as far as Aunt Mat's suspect's list went. But a good PI always kept an open mind.

A thought popped into Chandy's head. What if this was all a wild goose chase? And Aunt Mat hadn't really had her flowers stolen, but wanted Chandy to have a closed case to add to her resumé? If she returned to Aunt Mat's house, would she find the watering pots full of flowers, sitting in Aunt Mat's shed? And Chandy would get the credit for solving her first case? A definite possibility. Chandy rapped the heel of her hand against her head. Some PI she was, not pursuing the most logical explanation first, instead of wasting time on chasing wild geese.

But there was a niggle of doubt. She would follow up on the last lead before rushing back to Aunt Mat's house.

Chandy climbed on her scooter and headed back toward town. Final stop, the River House for the Mahjongg Tournament. Game play was in full swing, with tiles "chirping" and calls of "Pung", "Kong", and "Mahjongg" coming from the various tables. No flowers on the game tables as that would have interfered with play. No, the flowers would have been needed for the luncheon tables, which, it was obvious, was long over.

Chandy ran into party planner Bitsy Newsome walking through the empty dining room. The two had only ever spoken when Bitsy came into Ye Olde Ice Cream Shoppe. She was a woman of few words. Scoop of Heavenly Hash seemed to be the extent of her conversational skills.

But, like all good PIs, Chandy had a ruse to get the information she needed. "Hello, ma'am," Chandy greeted Bitsy. "I was hoping to get some photos of the luncheon for the Heron's Ridge Community Facebook page." Chandy held her cellphone, adding credence to her fib. "I've taken over social media responsibilities from Hilda. Looks like I missed the big event."

Bitsy nodded.

"I don't suppose you took any photos that you could send me?"

Bitsy shook her head. "Too busy."

Chandy knew Bitsy was reticent by nature, but something felt off about the way she spoke. "Oh, that's too bad. Jessica tweeted how lovely the centerpieces looked but didn't include a photo. If they're that great, I might want to engage your florist for my next event."

Bitsy chewed her lower lip.

"No trouble getting fresh flowers at the last minute?"

A shadow dropped over Bitsy's face. Her eyes narrowed. Her mouth puckered like she'd just eaten a lemon. "No trouble at all."

"Where are they now? I could still snap a picture and photoshop it onto a generic table." Chandy waved her cellphone again.

"All of the luncheon decorations have been loaded into the back of the van. I've arranged to have the flowers delivered to the senior center so that they may enjoy them. Now if you'll excuse me, there's a tournament I must oversee." Bitsy backed through the French doors that led to the tournament playing area.

That was a lot of words for a reticent woman. Almost forty, by Chandy's count. This situation required further investigation. She raced from the room and out to the parking lot. Her gaze swept the assembly of sedans, SUVs, and small trucks. Not a van to be found.

But there was a small U-Haul truck parked at an angle by the back door. Certainly big enough to hold decorations and floral arrangements. But with no windows, Chandy couldn't be sure. She approached it and found it locked up tight. Some television PIs might pull out a lock-picking set and get to work, but Chandy hadn't developed those skills. Yet.

Chandy kicked one of the truck's tires in frustration.

Her spidey sense was strong. Unignorably strong. The floral arrangements were in there. Chandy glanced at her phone. She had two hours to deliver them to the Wag More event. How could she get proof they were in the back of the van?

A nearby door slammed shut. Chandy flattened herself against the truck and peered around the back to see what was going on. But it was only Bitsy, carrying a garbage bag, heading for the dumpster.

And voilà, with one glance, Chandy had the proof she needed. She stepped out from behind the bush and called to Bitsy. "I know you pilfered the flower arrangements from my aunt's front porch."

Bitsy turned. Their eyes met across the grassy lawn that separated them. "They were set out farm-stand style, ready for purchase. I knocked on the door, but no one answered. I paid for them."

"No, you didn't." Chandy walked toward the woman and held out her hand. "If you give me the keys to the van, I will gladly run them over to where she needs them for her benefit for shelter animals. No questions asked, ok?"

Bitsy squared her shoulders. "I did pay for them. I left a check under the mat. A very generous one, as it saved me so much time driving from home to home asking to buy clumps of flowers from people's gardens."

Chandy shook her head. "There was no check."

Bitsy touched her fingers to her lips. "Maybe it blew away or something. Oh no, it must look like I stole them."

Chandy nodded.

"How did you know it was me, then?" Bitsy asked.

"I'm the best PI in Heron's Ridge. We have ways of figuring things out."

***

Aunt Mat met Chandy at the door to the hotel banquet room. Chandy had texted "Mission accomplished. On my way to deliver. Meet you there."

"Oh, honey. You did it! I knew you could! Tell me, how did you figure it out."

Chandy told her story while the two women unloaded sprinkling cans full of aromatic flowers and carried them to the banquet room. "I didn't have proof, at first, and Bitsy wasn't very forthcoming with information. But when she came out of the building and walked away from me, I noticed two very large muddy paw prints on the back of her yellow shirt."

"Scrapper prints?" Matilda asked.

"Exactly."

"He must have nabbed her on the way out. I hope she wasn't injured."

"She didn't seem to be. And when I confronted her with the evidence, she admitted she had been out driving around with the intent of gathering flowers from people's yards, with their permission of course."

"Heron's Ridge does have some lovely gardens, that's for sure."

"When Bitsy spotted the arrangements ready to go, she thought you had set up a roadside market. She knocked but no one was home. She assured me she left you a very nice check."

"Oh," Matilda said, then got that look on her face that meant she was puzzling things out. "That must have been the torn-up paper I found in my garden. Scrapper must have gotten ahold of it and chewed it to bits."

"He gave us the clue to solve the case, so I hope you forgive him."

"Of course I will. Now let's get this show on the road. There is money to be raised for our SPCA."

***

Chandy had just enough time to return the van to Bitsy and run home to change for the Wag More, Bark Less benefit. But she made a detour to swing by Aunt Mat's house and deliver a big indestructible rubber ball for Scrapper's enjoyment.

"Thanks, buddy," she said as she wiped pawprints from her shoulders. "I've always considered you my good friend but can now elevate you to paw-rtner in crime solving."

Jayne Ormerod grew up in a small Ohio town and attended a small-town Ohio college. Upon earning her accountancy degree, she became a CIA (that's not a sexy spy thing, but a Certified Internal Auditor). She married a naval officer, and off they sailed to see the world. After nineteen moves, they, along with their two rescue dogs Tiller and Scout, settled in a cottage by the Chesapeake Bay. Jayne writes cozy mysteries about small towns with beach settings. You can read more about Jayne and her many publications at www.JayneOrmerod.com.

An Educated Pig (as told from the pig's point-of-view)

Lesley A. Diehl

Anna Belle Lee, a young, female pot-bellied pig, considered her options. Most of her family had been racing pigs in carnivals and fairs during summers, winning blue ribbons and medals until the Crofton family living in Upstate New York rescued the pigs from the race circuit. The Crofton family was dedicated to giving this pot-bellied pig family a better life than the one they had being hauled around from one fairground to another and forced to perform for money. The family loved all the animals on their farm. Although they admired the pigs' prowess as racers and encouraged them to enter races if that's what the pigs wanted, they also knew pot-bellied pigs were intelligent and deserved a life that celebrated all their piggy talents. Two of their pigs had decided not to become racers but had entered the private detective business. Both gals, Desdemona and Willa Mae, were known for having long snouts (not common among pot-bellies) which they had used to sniff out bad guys, earning them the reputation of being stellar pig PIs and sought after by police departments and other law enforcement agencies. Now, that was the kind of occupation Anna Belle Lee wanted for herself, but unfortunately, she had one of the shortest snouts in the family. She couldn't smell rotting garbage if you sat it in front of her face.

"You're a swift pig, fast on your feet, and you know the ins and outs of the track. The Croftons won't force you to race, but you'd have a winning career, so what's the problem?" asked her mother.

Anna Belle Lee wrinkled up her stubby snout in disgust. "It's boring. You run around a track again and again, out distancing the other pots (pot-bellied pigs liked to call themselves "pots" or "bellies") and then you stop, pick up your blue ribbon, and enter another race." Anna Belle Lee rolled her eyes in disgust. "I want something more challenging, and don't tell me I'd make a good mother. I'm not ready for that yet, and besides, none of my male counterparts want to marry a pig who's so short in the snout. It makes me look fat."

Anna Belle Lee's mother was not an unsympathetic mommy pig. She knew her daughter was ambitious. It was just a matter of finding her daughter something to be ambitious at. "Well, racing season is over, and it's fall. Let's see what a few months bring," said Anna Belle Lee's mother.

The Crofton son, sensitive nine-year-old that he was, could sense the frustration in Anna Belle Lee.

"How would you like to come to school with me?" he asked. "I'll bet my teacher wouldn't mind if you sat next to me if you remain quiet and well-behaved. My classmates would love to have you there, too."

Mrs. Crofton called the school and talked to both Principal Javits and her son Billy's teacher, Mrs. Lamondo, and was granted permission for Anna Belle Lee to accompany Billy to school.

"You'll have to get permission from all the children's parents also," warned Principal Javits.

That was easy. All Billy's classmates were excited to have a pot-bellied pig as their classmate.

As for Anna Belle Lee, she sat quietly beside Billy's desk, paying close attention to all the lessons—reading, math and writing. Although she could not hold a pencil, she used her small, wet snout to trace damp letters onto paper, sad that the letters faded once they dried, but satisfied that she could at least copy the words. But her favorite subject was math. It all just made sense to Anna Belle Lee. It had order and could be manipulated in numerous ways—added, subtracted, divided, and multiplied. The only time Anna Belle Lee made noises in class was when she got the answer to a math problem sooner than the rest of the class. Then she snorted in glee. Nobody minded. They knew Anna Belle Lee was one smart pot-bellied pig, but they never could have predicted that she would use her learning to solve a crime.

April of the school year brought rain every day, keeping the children inside for recess, but the last Monday of the month, the sun finally came out, and Mrs. Lamondo gladly shooed the class outside for their playtime. Next to the school stood the town's local bank. As the children ran around the playground, engaging in races, kicking balls, and riding the merry-go-round and teetertotters, they heard a car come to a screeching halt in front of the bank. Two men jumped out of the car and ran inside. A few minutes later, a loud bang came from within the bank, and the men rushed out, masks over their faces and carrying a bank bag. Anna Belle Lee and her classmates watched the car drive off. The door of the bank banged open and one of the tellers ran outside, watching the car speed away.

"The bank was robbed, and the bank manager shot," the teller cried. "Did anyone get the license number of that car?"

The children and the teacher shook their heads. Everything happened so fast. No one, not even the teller, had memorized any of the numbers on the license, no one except for our smart little pig.

Anna Belle Lee nudged Billy's leg to get his attention. He patted her on the head and said, "I know you're scared, sweetie, but not now. Something bad has happened. Here come the police."

The scene was chaotic, police ran in and out of the bank, an ambulance pulled up in front to take the bank manager to the hospital, and Mrs. Lamondo herded her class back inside to keep them safe.

Anna Belle Lee knew the license plate number. She had memorized it using her smart pot-bellied brain and her knowledge of math, but how could she tell anyone what she knew? She used her wet snout to imprint the numbers on the tablet that always laid on the floor beside Billy's desk, then nudged Billy again, but by the time she had his attention and he looked at the tablet, the numbers had dried up. But Anna Belle Lee was not to be deterred. She put one of her front feet on Bill's desk chair so she could reach his hand. She knocked his pencil out of his hand with her snout, grabbed it in her mouth and began to transfer the numbers of the license plate onto the tablet paper. It wasn't easy for her to move her head around and make the pencil trace the numbers, and before she was finished, Billy yelled, "Hey, Anna Belle Lee. Give me my pencil back." The pig jumped back, turned, and raced out of the room. Billy followed, face red with embarrassment at his pig's misbehavior. She ran all the way home and hid in the barn where Billy found her behind a hay bale.

"You've been a very disruptive pig, Anna Belle Lee. You know what the rules are. You were to sit quietly and not make trouble in class. Mrs. Lamondo now says you can't come to school with me anymore."

The shame of it. Anna Belle Lee had been expelled from school, and it wasn't even her fault. She had only been doing what any well-educated pig would do.

Sad as she was, she was not only a smart pig, she was a determined pig. She knew something that was important to finding the bank robbers and she wasn't about to give up. She ran about the village, grabbing pencils and pens out of people's hands. She wrote the license plate numbers on books and newspapers, pulled laundry off lines, and used the stolen pens to write the numbers on panties, shirts, bed sheets and towels. She grabbed handkerchiefs out of men's pockets and used her stolen pens to transfer the numbers onto them. Children who were trying to play hopscotch had their chalk pilfered by Anna Belle Lee, and numbers were written on all the sidewalks in town. No one, not even Billy understood why Anna Belle Lee was being so naughty. The numbers meant nothing to them, but when the robbers saw the numbers on laundry lines and especially on the town's sidewalks, they knew what the numbers were, and they worried someone would discern the connection between the numbers and the license plate of their car. The robbers scrubbed off the numbers on the sidewalks at night, but by the next day, Anna Belle Lee had replaced them. The robbers knew they had to find the pig and grab her.

The robbers hid behind a bush near the café in town and when Anna Belle Lee came the next morning to inscribe her numbers on the sidewalk, one of the men grabbed her and threw her in their car.

"Well, piggie," he said to her, "I don't know how you know our license plate number, but since you do, your fate is in a BLT."

The men drove to the outskirts of town to the butcher who lived there and told him they needed the little pig made into "chops, ribs, and bacon."

"Well," said the butcher who recognized Anna Belle Lee as the pig who had gone to school and then been expelled, "This is a pot-bellied pig, and they don't make particularly good bacon."

"We don't care. You butcher this pig, and we'll be back for it." The men left.

The butcher looked down at Anna Belle Lee who shook and trembled with fear.

"Don't you worry, little gal. I know who you are. What I can't figure is what kind of grudge they have against you."

Anna Belle looked around the butcher shop and spied a two-week-old newspaper the headline of which read, "Bank Manager Shot in Robbery." She reached up with her mouth and pulled it off the table onto the floor. She put her little hoof on it and looked up at the butcher. He read the headline and nodded.

"Okay. So?"

Anna Belle Lee read the article to herself and when she ran across the sentence that said, "No one at the scene got the license plate number of the getaway car," she pointed to it with her other hoof, then grabbed the butcher's pen with her mouth from his pocket and began to write the license plate number on the margin of the newspaper.

"Aha," said the butcher. "I get it." Well, he almost got it, but not all of it. He ran to the phone and called the police and told them about the pig who read the headlines and had been kidnapped for bacon by the robbers. The police decided to stake out the butcher shop and wait for the robbers to come back for their pig, but after five days they didn't reappear. The butcher could only provide the police with a vague description of the thieves because he was so shaken with their request and worried they would do something to him also. And Anna Belle Lee was no help at all describing them.

"Now what do we do?" asked the Police Chief Brody. "We don't know who they are, and they may never come back."

Anna Belle Lee, now decidedly impatient with humans who supposedly were always smarter than pigs, stomped her little hoof on the floor and grabbed the marker the butcher used to label the packets of meat. Deftly wielding the marker in her mouth, she wrote on a piece of wrapping paper, "License number of robbers is" and completed the number.

"I can't believe it," said Chief Brody. Anna Belle Lee was about to nip his foot with her tiny piggy teeth when he continued, "But what do we have to lose?"

He picked up Anna Belle Lee and whisked her off in the police car to the station where he called in for the owner of a car with the license plate number she had written for him.

"Got it," he said. "Since you solved this case, Anna Belle Lee, do you want to come along?"

She squealed in delight. Wow! She would be in on the capture.

If the police had any doubt about the guilt of the men at whose house they found the car with the license number Anna Bell Lee had given them, they were convinced when the men yelled, "Get that pig out of here!"

The robbers tried to run for the back door, but Anna Belle Lee pursued them along with the cops. Because she had racing pig genes in her, she ran faster than everyone and placed herself in front of the door so that it couldn't be opened. When one of the men tried to kick her, he missed and slammed his foot against the door frame, breaking his toe. The other one ran into his partner, fell backwards into the kitchen, and hit his head against the stove.

"Nice work, Anna Belle Lee," said Chief Brody. "We could use you on the force."

Anna Belle Lee grinned up at him. At least it might have been a grin. It's hard to tell on a pig's snout.

Everyone in the village celebrated the capture of the robbers and the part Anna Belle Lee played in apprehending them. Never again would anyone doubt the detecting ability of this little pot-belly.

As for joining the police force, Anna Belle Lee, now reinstated in Billy's classroom, decided to engage in police work part-time until after she had obtained her degree. She liked the atmosphere of the classroom and valued book learning; school was important for honing her already keen intelligence. But she also discovered that her foray into detecting work taught her lessons she couldn't have learned in the classroom, lessons she valued and could use in her future detecting vocation. First, people didn't always value the intelligence of a pot-bellied pig. Sometimes they didn't even believe a pot-belly could be smarter than a human. And most surprising, being a swift-footed pot-belly could come in handy in situations other than racing at county fairs. It meant a little pig was faster than a robber any day.

Cows, Lesley A. Diehl learned growing up on a farm, have a twisted sense of humor. They chased her when she went to the field to herd them in for milking, and one ate the lovely red mitten her grandmother knitted for her. Determining that agriculture wasn't a good career choice, instead she uses her country roots and her training as a psychologist to concoct stories designed to make people laugh in the face of murder. "A good chuckle," says Lesley, "keeps us emotionally well-oiled long into our old age." She is the author of several cozy mystery series and numerous short stories. Find out more: www.lesleyadiehl.com

The Show Must Go On

D.L. Rosa

Foxy was led to the end of the stage, and the audience cheered. With her tawny tail wagging, she looked up to her handler. Mary was wearing an elegant dress of the early 1900s with chewy treats hidden in the palm of her hand. Mary curtsied and gave Foxy's lead a light tug.

Mary whispered, "Good girl. Come on. Good girl."

Once they stepped back and joined the cast assembly line, Foxy twirled and danced. Mary reached down to slip Foxy a small reward for a job well done.

A few more actors came from the wings. The cast formed a long line of waving hands and smiling faces but as soon as the curtain closed, bodies moved quickly around each other in every direction. Mary swooped down to pick up Foxy from the floor. It was just in time, as a tech hand stumbled right into the space Foxy had stood. He was juggling an arm full of microphone packs and neglected to see the Pomeranian under foot. The tech stopped after regaining his balance and looked at Foxy. He frowned with his eyebrows pulled together in deep concentration. He started to open his mouth to say something when a battery pack slipped from his grip. He caught the pack by the cord and returned to his original task without a word.

"That was close." Mary said and pulled Foxy under her chin for a cuddle.

Lights turned on, exposing the working parts of the theatre. Chairs, tables, and artificial plants were grouped for scene changes. Nearby, the wine glasses on the prop table shook as Ms. Vicky pushed her hand against the table to peek underneath. She rose and looked around the floor. Her eyes darted back and forth. Finally, she saw Foxy with Mary and smiled.

"Foxy!" Ms. Vicky yelled and approached with arms open wide.

"There's your momma!" Mary positioned herself to show Foxy the woman approaching. "Oh, Ms. Vicky, she did such a great job. I know you were unsure if the audience was going to throw her off but, Foxy didn't miss a single command."

Ms. Vicky wrapped her arms around Mary and Foxy. Her wool sweater was scratchy on Mary's skin and smelled of dog shampoo. "It was so lovely to watch.

This little old lady is having the best time of her life. I'm sure of it. Who knew she would be in a play! A little doggy thespian."

Ms. Vicky released her grip and took a step back. She started to take Foxy from Mary's arms but stopped. Her eyes focused on something in the distance. Mary tried to turn around to see what had stolen Ms. Vicky's attention when Ms. Vicky pushed Foxy back into her arms with a thrust.

"You can take her to meet the audience if you want. If you'd also promote the adoption of Poms that would be great." Ms. Vicky spoke fast. Foxy barked while Mary fumbled to hold on to the almost weightless bundle of fur.

Ms. Vicky brushed past Mary. Her long black and gray braid swung behind her. She hurried her short legs to the opposite side of the stage and disappeared behind the set wall.

"Okay, then. Um, do you have to go potty?" Mary asked Foxy.

Foxy's large dark eyes stared upward. Her small pink tongue slipped out of her mouth and licked her nose.

"I'll take that as a no. Do you want to meet people and play?"

Foxy turned her ears forward and she placed her front paws onto Mary's chest.

"You want to meet people and play? Do ya? Do you want to play?"

The small dog kicked her paws and her tail wagged at such a speed it turned into a blur. Mary set Foxy down. Once on the floor, Foxy danced in circles and let out a few excited barks. With the lead in her hand, Mary walked Foxy to the meet and greet.

People packed the lounge area. Family and friends hugged those who were part of the production, cast and crew alike. Mary felt a wave of hunger as the smell of popcorn floated in the air. A hard tug came from Foxy's lead and broke Mary from her food trance.

"This little rat chewed off my button." Carl had done his own stage makeup and it was applied in thick patches around his face. The combination of heat from the stage lights and his proclivity for sweating profusely gave him the look of an angry melted candle.

"What?" Mary asked.

Carl was holding Foxy under his arm like a football. He pointed with his free hand to his large belly. The buttons on his suit were strained and the fabric stretched. One gap in the middle exposed a white shirt underneath. Without a doubt, one button had lost the fight and relented to the physical forces it couldn't overcome.

Mary suppressed a smile. "Foxy doesn't chew buttons. Who knows how many different times this costume has been worn before you? I'm sure the thread is old and it's just time the buttons be re-sewn or replaced. Look at mine." Mary lifted the bottom of her dress and pointed out the lace accents were different patterns, and one strip was a brighter white than the others.

Foxy had given in to the football hold and let her legs hang free while she panted. Her tongue hung out the side of her mouth and her ears faced forward but every few seconds one would move to the side as they scanned the room for curious sounds. Carl had a less amused expression and sweat continued to drip down the side of his cheeks.

"I know something was in my dressing room."

"It's the men's dressing room. Not just yours."

"Don't argue details with me. Something was in there. After the dinner scene I went for my costume change, but my button was missing. So was a sock."

"Why are you only blaming her for the button and not the sock?" Mary reached for Foxy. Carl twisted his body so the small fur bundle was out of her grasp. Foxy wagged her tail, the fluff disappeared then reappeared in rapid repetition from behind Carl's arm.

"It was the ghost." Ann approached with a headset still perched on her head. She looked at Carl and nodded. Her curly hair bounced with every movement. "The ghost likes to take small things. I'm told he's been very active today. You're not the first to be missing things. I lost a pencil earlier. A few techs said they saw the curtains moving, too."

Carl stared with his mouth open. Mary stepped between the two and slipped Foxy from Carl's arm into her own. She hugged Foxy and in return, Foxy gave Mary a lick on the chin.

"Ann, there is no ghost." Carl pointed to the missing button. "That thing chewed my button. I don't think it could eat a sock. My socks are bigger than the dog is. The sock is somewhere but the button, I know it ate it."

"Last spring, during the musical, the piano would play a few notes by itself. Then the lead said she saw herself on the opposite side of the stage. A full copy of herself just standing there until it walked away on its own! This place absolutely has a ghost." Ann stood firm and crossed her arms. "Ask anyone about it. It's happened before! Today is no different!"

Mary felt a small hand pat her arm. Happy to leave the conversation of missing buttons and ghosts, Mary turned to see a girl standing next to her. Behind her stood more children around the same age. All of them were there to meet Foxy. Mary took the children to a place against the wall where they could sit in a circle and let Foxy run between them. They took turns petting Foxy and playing a gentle game of tug-o-war using her lead. The crowd grew bigger as adults joined in to ask questions about Foxy. Mary took the opportunity to talk about adoption as Ms. Vicky had requested. By the time the crowd started to disperse, Foxy was bright eyed and full of energy from all the attention.

"That was fun, wasn't it? You deserved it." Mary reached into her dress pocket and pulled out a treat. Foxy sat down and concentrated on Mary's hand. She placed the treat on the ground and gave Foxy a little scratch behind the ears. "This one's for you. But this one's for me!" Mary pulled out a bag of popcorn a volunteer had slipped to her as they were giving away the last bags for the night.

"Oh, there you are!" Ms. Vicky came through one of the theatre doors. "Time to go!"

Ms. Vicky walked quickly toward Mary though she seemed already out of breath by her loud breathing. A strand of hair fell loose from her braid and her cheeks were flushed. There was a dirt smudge on her chin.

"Are you okay?" Mary asked.

Ms. Vicky gave only a simple answer. "Yup."

"Okay, well, anyway I have a question for you. Has Foxy ever chewed buttons before? Or stolen socks? Carl thinks Foxy has been in the men's dressing room."

"Foxy? Not Foxy, no. Is call at the same time tomorrow?" Ms. Vicky walked forward and picked up Foxy. She didn't wait for an answer before she turned toward the exit door.

"Yes, but I'll be here earlier to help with wigs if you want to bring Foxy sooner!" Mary yelled. Ms. Vicky waved and signaled she heard Mary's answer with a thumbs up.

Mary returned backstage and went into the green room. The walls were lined with makeup mirrors and the center of the room had tables and chairs. Normally, the tables were covered with bags and coats. By now it was getting late and many of the cast members had already changed. The tables started to clear as they gathered their things. Only a few remaining actors were seated at their mirrors where they cleaned off makeup with wipes and cold cream. Mary waved and set her popcorn down on a table. She offered to share her food with everyone before she made her way into the woman's dressing room. There, she found herself alone.

Mary slipped off her dress and hung it on a hanger labeled with her name. After putting on her street clothes, she looked down to pick up her shoes when she noticed something white under the costume rack. Mary lowered herself onto her hands and knees. Under the long dresses was a large men's sock. She reached in to pick up the sock, but it appeared to be stuck. She pulled a little harder. The sock gave some, but a tension pulled it back. Mary tried one more time with a firm tug. The sock pulled back and a low growl came from under the dresses. Mary let go and pushed herself away. She hit her head on the bench behind her and released a yell in a shock of surprise more than pain.

"There are no ghosts. There are no ghosts. There are no ghosts." Mary repeated to herself. She leaned forward and pressed the dresses to the side to find a Pomeranian with a sock in its mouth. "Foxy?"

The pup looked up at Mary and released the sock from its mouth. Mary reached in when the pup growled again. She didn't pull away but held her hand steady. The pup sniffed at her hand and smelled the popcorn she had been holding before she came into the dressing room. It started to lick her fingers, getting braver and braver with each taste.

"Are you Foxy? Come here." Now, the pup allowed her to wrap her hand under its belly and pick it up. "You don't feel like Foxy. You're a bit of a chunky monkey. Who are you?"

Mary put the pup in her lap. This Pom was a boy and while smaller in size than Foxy, he was heavier with a big round solid belly. His fur was the same color but where Foxy had white around her eyes and snout, he had dark markings. Foxy had also been groomed for the play. Her hair was purposefully trimmed into a Pomeranian show cut. Her tail air blown to be high on her back and her scruff long and voluminous, similar to a lion's mane. This little guy's fur was trimmed to be short and even all over his frame resembling more of a teddy bear than a lion. He wore a collar, but no tags were attached. Mary tried to give him a hug but he wasn't interested and kicked at Mary. She then flipped him over and started to tickle his belly. He continued to kick and growl while gnawing on any one of Mary's fingers he could get a hold of.

"You, sir, have a spark in you. Question is, where did you come from?"

Mary took the pup to the green room where she found Ann and a few other people chatting.

"Ann, I think Ms. Vicky left something behind." Mary held up the pup still gnawing her fingers. "Also, I found Carl's sock."

"Wait, what? The dog is named Carl's Sock? Carl was looking for a dog? Who names a dog Sock?" Ann asked.

A crew member next to Ann tapped on the headset still on Ann's head. She rolled her eyes and slipped it down around her neck.

"I found Carl's sock and I found this guy. Both were in the women's dressing room hiding under the costume rack." Mary clarified.

"Could this be an omen? How strange." Ann whispered. "Can I hold him?"

"It's not an omen. It's a puppy, I think, and yes." Mary handed the pup over.

Ann squealed as the pup kicked and barked at her while she playfully moved her hand side to side in front of his face.

"I have to call Ms. Vicky real quick. Keep an eye on him. He has a ton of personality and lots of wiggles. Hold on to him tight but watch your fingers." Mary warned.

"This dog is the cutest little thing I have ever seen. My goodness and solid, too.."

Mary started to make her way to the phone in the director's office when Ann called out to her.

"Wait! I'll find Ms. Vicky. You're still covered in hairspray and makeup. Go home, take a shower."

"Are you sure?" Ann was right. Mary had started to feel like Carl looked with the makeup weighing heavy on her face. She could also feel her hair as it sagged slightly to the left side of her head. The pins used to keep it up had started to pinch. Even though she was now in her personal clothes, the storage dust smell of her costume still lingered on her skin. "A shower really does sound great right now. But, you won't find her. Ms. Vicky left already. She took Foxy and I watched her walk out the front door. You'll have to call her."

"No, I'm pretty sure she walked down the hall just a second ago. She had something in her hands. Really, it's fine. Go. I'll see you tomorrow night."

As Mary picked up her things, she noticed Ann had set the puppy on the floor and was using the lanyard from her keys to trick him into chasing it. She fought the urge to search for Ms. Vicky herself. As the pup wagged his tail and gave playful barks toward Ann, Mary couldn't bring herself to send the mystery dog home just yet.

The next day, Mary arrived back at the theatre looking for either Ms. Vicky or Ann to find out what happened to the puppy and why it was at the theatre. Neither had yet arrived. Mary busied herself and helped re-pin a few wigs before she had to sit to have her own hair and makeup done. She studied her lines and peeked over her script from time to time to see if Ms. Vicky, Ann, or Foxy would appear while her hair was being tugged, back combed, and sprayed to create the big hair she wore for her character. Even with all the distractions around her as more and more people came in to prepare for the show, her mind was on Foxy. As soon as her hair was finished Mary rushed into her costume and then out to the stage.

Several techs walked by and Mary asked if they had seen Foxy or Ms. Vicky. One of the techs poked around a curtain and lifted it up to look underneath it every few feet. Another rushed by her with a broom and dustpan full of what looked to be pillow stuffing. Both only took a quick moment to answer. Neither had seen Foxy or Ms. Vicky. Mary found Ann digging through a box full of prop throw pillows while holding one in her hand.

"Ann! Have you seen Ms. Vicky and Foxy? They're usually here by now." Mary's voice shook a little.

"Foxy's missing, too? I don't understand what is happening. Look at this." Ann showed Mary the pillow she was holding. The corner of it had been torn off or, no, Mary thought, chewed off.

"That's strange. Anyway, did you talk with Ms. Vicky last night? Did she tell you she would be late today?" Mary asked.

"No. She scooped the puppy up when she found him in the green room and took off. No idea what that was about, but I did find out his name was Mosey." Ann grabbed Mary's arm. "Are you wearing your mic? Go to the sound booth and finish getting ready. I'll take care of finding Foxy."

"What if she doesn't show up in time?"

"It'll be fine, we'll adjust. Go on." Ann led Mary to the side of the stage and gave her a little shove down the stairs. She pointed to the sound booth in the back before she jogged back in the direction of the green room.

Neither Ms. Vicky nor Foxy showed up before the house opened. The audience filed into their seats and the white noise of conversation filled the air. The tech crew and cast were pulled in the green room for their before show warm up and pep talk. Mary felt as if her stomach was tied in knots. The director made no mention of Foxy missing before he left to sit in the audience. The only note he had for the night was to keep in the green room when not in the scene, some backstage movement last night was distracting.

Ann looked to Mary and whispered, "Ghosts."

Mary shook her head.

Unable to sit and wait, Mary paced backstage. She ran lines in her head and thought on how to alter them as needed while she watched the back entrance. She hoped Ms. Vicky would come around from the shadows with Foxy at any moment. The time came when she couldn't wait any longer. She stepped on stage with her cue to deliver her lines without Foxy in her arms.

The scene consisted of Carl giving a long monologue about family squabbles. Mary was to sit and pet Foxy while she shared looks of annoyance with another member of the cast. She found herself at a loss of what to do with her arms and crossed them. She looked to her castmate with a smirk and a raised brow when she noticed something tawny backstage.

"Foxy!" She yelled.

The audience gave a small laugh.

"Excuse me, dear, but no, that is not the word I would use to describe Mother." Carl ad-libbed and glared at Mary.

A small dog ran out on stage. The audience released a mix of giggles and awes. Mary ran over and grabbed the dog.

"There you are my love." She waved a hand at Carl. "Not you. Please, continue with your whining."

"Very rude, Ma'am." Carl scoffed.

Mary pulled Foxy up for a snuggle but instead was met by a paw to the nose. Mary looked down to see it wasn't Foxy in her hands. Rather, it was the pup. Mosey was his name according to Ann. *You again?* She thought.

The lights dimmed as the scene ended, and the audience clapped. Mary ran backstage while techs rushed in to move set pieces. She hurried to Ann's station to show her she had Mosey when she saw Ann had not one, but two Pomeranians on her lap. One of them was Foxy who attempted to jump out of Ann's arms when she recognized Mary.

"Who's that?" Mary whispered looking at the third dog while she and Ann swapped Mosey and Foxy. This dog looked similar to Mosey but had deep black markings around her eyes and dark sections throughout her coat.

"No idea. They found Foxy in the green room, probably looking for you. Mosey just trotted out here, no idea from where. This one almost got stepped on, it was just napping backstage behind set pieces. The sound booth techs told me over the headset they saw the director stop in, scan the audience, and leave. They weren't able to get his attention and don't know where he went."

"That was very unprofessional. You should have waited for the dog until after my speech." Carl approached with a finger pointed at Mary."

Mosey barked at him.

"Where did you come from?" Carl asked.

"We need to get back. By the way, the one who doesn't like your tone? That's the little guy who stole your sock." Mary rushed on stage just as the lights came back up.

"Wait! What? Oh no!" Carl chased after her but slowed to a walk right before stepping into the lights.

"I don't think your approach is going to win any favors." Mary delivered her line and pet Foxy before she settled into a chair. She gave Foxy a kiss and was thankful for not getting another paw to the face.

"My approach is exactly the approach which needs to be taken with Mother. She has raised me in the image of Grandfather and any shortcomings would clearly be on her shoulders and not mine. I do believe..." There was a crash and the sound of glass breaking offstage. Carl stopped in the middle of his line and looked off stage.

Mary tried not to break character and continued to pet Foxy until a white sheet came into her view in the wings. It was being pulled along the ground. A tech ran and stomped on the end of the sheet to prevent it from being pulled any further. The opposite end was still being tugged, but Mary could not see what was doing the tugging.

Carl continued. "I do believe she is past her time and her capacities are less than mine."

A black Pomeranian darted across the stage.

Mary froze. The dog was completely dark head to tail. She wasn't sure if her eyes were playing tricks and she really saw a dog or a shadow in the lights. A long silence followed before Mary realized it was her line.

"How does one measure capacities?"

"Excellent question." The dog returned and this time Carl saw it. He reached down, grabbed it, and stuck it under his arm. The audience laughed and he continued his line with a dog, its pink tongue hanging out and tail wagging, stuffed in his armpit. "I have capacities and Mother has none. It's very simple."

Mary stood from her chair and walked to a bookshelf. She removed a book and moved across stage to hand it to Carl. "You're being quite childish. Perhaps you need to read more. This one might be of your level."

Carl looked at the cover of the book. "*The Wonderful Wizard of Oz*-? Honestly."

The audience laughed.

Mary smiled and turned to sit in her chair only to find another Pomeranian had taken the seat for its own. This one looked the most like Foxy with identical colors and markings but was by far larger. Mary moved Foxy to her hip to free a hand and picked up the other dog. Taking a lead from Carl, she shifted both dogs for one to be under each arm. Behind her, she heard shuffling of feet and the audience laughed much louder than before. She looked to Carl. They stared at each other. Each holding two dogs, one under each arm. Carl's newest companion was a second black pup.

"You're not the Queen of England, you know. One dog is plenty." Carl ad-libbed.

"Wrong decade." Mary whispered.

Carl shrugged.

Mary turned toward backstage for help. Ann was kneeling on the floor with Mosey and the other unknown dog. She smiled, released the dogs, and shooed them on stage. Mary looked over to the other side of the stage and saw a tech in the wings with treats in his hand to bait them over. The puppies ran across the stage. The laughs and claps from the audience were deafening. Mary put down her extra companion. He happily trotted over for a treat inspection. A dog emerged from under the chair Mary had been sitting in to follow the rest. This one seemed older and had a bit of a limp. Carl leaned down and let go of the two dogs from his arms but only one left his side. The smaller of the two sat in the middle of the stage and looked around.

The show continued on with dogs popping up from time to time. Mary scanned the audience and backstage when she could. She never saw Ms. Vicky or the director. She also didn't see any crates or people trying to capture the loose dogs. Mary couldn't help but hold Foxy tight against her. She was afraid there were so many dogs and confusion, she might lose Foxy in the shuffle.

Intermission finally came. As rehearsed, Mary would go to the green room where Ms. Vicky would be waiting. She would hold Foxy and Mary would change her costume except this time, Ms. Vicky wasn't there. Mary yelled out to several people in the green room, asking if they had seen her. But again, no one knew where she was.

"Oh, I wish you could tell me what is going on!" Mary said to Foxy.

Foxy just looked back at Mary with big brown eyes and panted happily.

Mary walked to the director's office. It seemed a long shot but maybe calling Ms. Vicky would be the thing to do. When Mary walked into the office, she found something else entirely. She flipped on the light and saw the room was full of small empty travel crates.

"Hey, give me Foxy so you can, wait, where did those come from?" Ann spoke from behind Mary.

"This must be where the dogs came from, but how did they get here? Why so many?" Mary started to count the crates when Ann interrupted her by removing Foxy from her arms.

"I'll see what I can find out. You need to get changed. I'll be backstage waiting for you. The only notes for the cast are to improvise. Act natural and go with it."

Mary nodded and rushed toward the dressing room.

The second half of the show went on the same as the first. Mary asked Ann for updates any moment she had between scenes but Ann didn't have much to share or was busy and couldn't answer. By curtain call, each actor had a dog in their arms as they took their bow. One by one, they held their dog out in front of them like a doggy curtain call. Only this time, after the cast bowed together the curtain didn't close. From the audience came the director and Ms. Vicky. Meeting them at the center of the stage was Ann holding Mosey and a microphone. Mary handed the microphone to the director.

"Thank you for coming in for our special performance this evening. I would also like to thank our special performers today. Here to introduce them is their rescue mom, Ms. Vicky."

Ms. Vicky took the microphone and looked at the director. Mary noticed her hand was shaking. The director nodded and pointed to the audience

"The performers tonight were Foxy, Mosey, Lacy, Teddy, Chloe, Gidget, and Raisin. They are Pomeranians and all are up for adoption, looking for loving homes. If you're interested in learning more about adoption from my rescue, or the other shelters and rescues in the area we're partnered with, please see me out front after the show." Ms. Vicky turned to Ann. Ann took the microphone and handed Mosey over to Ms. Vicky.

"Special recognition for performance tonight goes to Mosey!" As Ann spoke, the audience started to clap and whistle. Mosey barked. "Mosey, was brought as a last minute understudy last night for our little girl Foxy over there. Ends up, Mosey is very good at opening his crate. In preparation for our after show Ms. Vicky brought in some more little friends. Guess who is also really good at opening his friends' crates too?"

Ann gave Mosey a little poke on the side and he barked again. The audience laughed and Ann handed the microphone to the director.

"On behalf of myself and our dear theatre friend Ms. Vicky, we apologize to you, our cast, and our crew, for the mishap both in informing our cast and crew about the extent of our after show event and, well, to keep an eye out for one very mischievous puppy. Though, I hope all of you found our friends entertaining. Ms. Vicky set up an information table out front during the show. Come join us! And thank you again, you've been a great audience."

The audience clapped as they rose from their seats and began to move toward the aisles. Mary pushed her way through the cast and crew to reach Ms. Vicky.

"Is Foxy up for adoption?" Mary yelled over the commotion.

"And Mosey?" Ann asked. She reached over and pet Mosey still in Ms. Vicky's arms.

"I also have questions." Carl spoke loudly behind Mary. She turned to see him holding a tiny black dog Mary guessed was Raisin.

Ms. Vicky looked at Mary and smiled. "I was hoping you'd consider adopting Foxy, she's already chosen you."

D.L. Rosa is a graduate of Ferris State University and a member of The Grand Rapids Region Writers Group, a group focusing on writing education and goal achievement. She's recently joined the Grand River Writing Tribe to review and critique individual projects with other local writers. Currently, she resides in the Grand Rapids area with her family and two adopted pets: a cat named Potter and Hooper, a corgi mix.

He Was Framed, I Tell You!

Sandra Murphy

I pulled into The Haven's crowded parking lot and snagged a spot under the tree. It was at the far end, a fact Avery, my Cairn/Yorkie diva, didn't appreciate. "Count yourself lucky," I said. "We are walking farther but you won't burn your paws and behind on a hot car seat when we're ready to go home." I got a dirty look before she refused to move. Carrying a twenty-five-pound dog, who should weigh twenty pounds at the most, when the temperature is over 90 degrees, isn't a job I'd wish on anyone.

Saturdays, there are tour groups and volunteers on hand. This branch of The Haven is miles away from the city shelter where the small animals are housed. Here, horses have plenty of space. Donating their time, veterinarians are kept busy bringing the dozen or so malnourished and abused horses back to the life they were meant to live.

Personally, I'm a dog lover. Don't be confused by the fact there are five cats in the house too. It's not my fault. Avery came from the shelter. Apparently while there, or maybe before, she developed an affinity for cats. Her first, and really her only cat, was Reilly, one of a litter from our irresponsible neighbors. Every day Reilly met us as I took Avery outside and then he followed us to the door. One day, he just came in with us.

After that, any time Avery saw a cat in the yard, on the sidewalk, or trying to cross a busy street, she'd bark until I caved and brought the kitty into the house. The new cats were then my responsibility. Reilly was hers.

So, you see, I'm a dog person. My dog is the cat person in the family. You'll notice I didn't mention anything about a horse. Here's why. I was invited to attend the annual Catholic school picnic with my cousins. Every year a man would bring a Shetland pony to the picnic grounds and with a ticket or two, kids could ride the poor pony around in circles.

I tried but when the man said get on and I swung a leg over the pony's back, my legs were longer than the pony's. It didn't matter how young I was, I was banned from riding. That was my entire experience with horses of any size.

I volunteer at The Haven's city location but was asked to help at the horse barn where a litter of kittens needed their medicine. Someone had dropped off a semi-feral cat to live in the barn without mentioning she was pregnant. I buckled Avery's seat belt and off we went. Little did I know where that would lead.

Kittens are pretty elusive and fast. Avery to the rescue, literally, as she pointed me in the right direction to find the sneaky youngsters. Of course, I wasn't quick enough to catch them but she's empathetic enough that they came right to her. Showoff.

We managed to get all but the little orange boy who I swear had tunneled an escape route through the hay bales. I promised to come out the next day, Sunday, to try again. Before we left, I did pet Eddie, a sweet reddish-brown massive horse. At least he seemed big to me. I wondered if it would be tacky to take his photo to my hairdresser. I'd love to have the same color hair or at least highlights.

On Sunday, Avery and I went back to the barn. It took all afternoon, but the little orange boy finally tired himself out and I was able to scoop him into a crate without even waking him. Of course, by this time, Avery decided she liked horses and trips to the barn. There's no arguing with her.

It was pretty funny to see a curious horse lean down to sniff at Avery. She loves attention, no matter the source, so she was happy. Somehow, I'd been put in charge of making sure all the barn cats were spayed or neutered. We spent the majority of our weekends out there and got to know people and horses.

Fred was Avery's favorite person, mine too. An older man, he was gentle with the horses, willing to help anywhere in the stables, and never seemed to mind mucking out stalls. Avery adored him.

Volunteers were in and out all the time, to ride, train, feed, water, walk the horses, or just spend time with the skittish ones who had suffered neglect or bad treatment. Church groups, 4H, and Scout troops all came to visit, some to volunteer, by the day or week. Through it all, Avery ate up the attention from everyone except Pete, the stableman. She wasn't obvious about it, but I could tell she didn't like him.

Pete was popular with kids, especially the teens who thought they were extra special. I'd have put them on pooper scooper duty, which is probably why my job is working with cats.

I could tell the kids were up to something. When I asked, they said they wanted to organize a hayride for a Saturday night, and maybe a late-night picnic after, in a couple of weeks. I volunteered to chaperone, but they just laughed and walked away.

Meanwhile, I spent a good part of my time with Fred, who taught me to brush Eddie and get him to come to me, which was better than chasing him. Eddie's fast and stubborn. When he doesn't want to do something, it's hard to change his mind, at least unless you have a piece of fruit for him. I'm better at bribes than running.

"Horses are naturally curious. They also spook. In the wild, there are predators. That's why their fight or flight response is flight, to get some distance, and then assess the situation. They'll fight but only when it's necessary." Fred used his pocketknife to cut up an apple for Eddie. "This guy has a fine sense of humor. We had to change his stall to one away from the door. He watched us turn out the lights in the evening and decided he could do the opposite. Ran up the electric bill something awful until we figured out who was leaving the barn lights on at night."

I laughed. "He must have gotten a kick out of that! Did you send him to bed without his supper or take away his television time? That was always my punishment."

"Nah, Eddie's a good boy, just bored. He knows other tricks too." Fred ran a hand down Eddie's neck. "Don't you, big fella? I taught him to play games, like soccer. Wanna go a few rounds with him? I'll warn you he stepped on a ball once with his front feet and popped it. Now he headbutts it or kicks with his rear feet, never the front, just so you know."

"I'll take it easy on him. Come on, Eddie, let's play! Avery, you keep score and stay out of the way." People don't believe dogs can do the eye roll, but she's got it down pat.

Eddie had a large Pilates kind of ball and a net at one end of the corral. I thought it would be easy to block his goal. I was wrong.

Eddie never touched me but he'd headbutt the ball right into the goal and then would take a victory lap around the corral. Showoff. I didn't score any points or block any of his. "Come on, Eddie, this one is mine," I called. "It's not going to be a shutout." Famous last words.

From my position flat on my back in the dirt, Eddie looked down at me and hopped from one front foot to the other. "Sure, go ahead and happy dance, you got lucky." How embarrassing to lose to a horse. Not that I was ever any good at sports, even in high school.

Back at Eddie's stall, I brushed him down to remove all the dust, wishing someone would dust me off too. I overheard voices just outside, but I couldn't see who was talking.

"So, we'll have barbequed steakburgers, chunky fries, corn on the cob, watermelon for after. My dad knows a guy, he's trucking them up from Arkansas, homegrown."

"The Haven is vegan, man. No burgers."

"Yeah, who's gonna know? Besides, the best part will be the watermelon. I've got a secret ingredient. They'll be here Friday night and they'll have time to mellow by Saturday evening." The voices moved away, and I couldn't hear any more.

"What kind of secret ingredient can you put on watermelon?" I asked Eddie but he didn't know either. I did mention to the coordinator that burgers were on the menu. The steakburgers quickly turned into veggie burgers despite protests from the guys who claimed they needed extra protein.

Since we weren't invited, Avery and I spent Friday night doing a load or two of laundry, eating popcorn, and watching television. Well, mostly she ate popcorn. I think her excuse is, being a Cairn/Yorkie, she's not tall enough to reach the washer or dryer. I tried showing her videos of a Jack Russell terrier who pulls clean clothes from the dryer and puts them in a basket but she looked the other way.

Saturday morning, we went to the barn early, just in time to see an ambulance roar out of the drive, siren wailing. Avery barked and strained against her seatbelt. "We'll go up to the barn and find out what happened. Probably one of the riders took a fall or got stepped on." I parked in the grassy area next to the buildings.

"What happened?" I called to Pete. He ignored me and walked on. Inside, I could hear a horse screaming and pounding hooves against a stall. "Stay here, Avery." Of course, she didn't listen but raced ahead, me right behind her.

"It's Eddie," I yelled. Avery already knew and was flying as fast as her short little legs would go. "Stay back, he's hurt or scared." She ran to the stall, where trainers were trying to get a halter on Eddie, who was having none of it.

Avery skidded to a halt, looked up, and barked twice. Eddie looked around, wild-eyed. She barked again, forcing him to focus on her. At least he stopped screaming and rearing. That's when I realized half the people standing around were police officers.

"Somebody tell me what happened!" I turned to the nearest official-looking guy, Joe Samson, according to his name tag.

"Horse went nuts, tried to stomp an old man, did a pretty good job of it. EMTs didn't look like they had much hope when they tore out of here," he said. "They're talking about shooting the horse with a tranquilizer gun."

"The hell!" I dodged around him to where Avery sat. Eddie was calmer but still wild-eyed. "Eddie, want to play soccer? There's a good boy. Come with me."

"You can't take him anywhere. He's got evidence on his feet. We need a blood sample too," Detective Samson said.

"Then I'll go in with the vet, keep him calm, we'll get your samples." I saw Luke, one of the gentlest vets, standing by. "He needs to get out of that stall."

I paused between every step I took, reassuring Eddie that I was coming for him. "We'll just clean you up first. Then we'll play, I promise. Come on, good boy.

Avery, by me. Watch his feet." She probably knew what to do better than I did but when I told the story later, I said she obeyed.

The smell of blood was strong plus there was another sharper odor. Avery wrinkled her nose. Her sense of smell was thousands of times better than mine, so I knew I wasn't imagining things. Luke was right beside us.

Eddie nosed my pocket where he knew I kept peppermints for him. "That's a good boy. Luke, okay for him to have a peppermint?"

Samson had to chime in. "Don't give him anything. We need to test him."

"Yeah, yeah, one piece won't distort your test and it'll calm him down." I slipped the candy from my pocket and leaned in to hand it to Eddie. He snuffled and slobbered on my shirt, smelling like my Uncle Hubert on Thanksgiving, right before he started an argument with my dad. I was beginning to understand what happened or at least I had the beginnings of an idea.

Luke got the blood sample while Eddie checked my pockets for more candy. We cleaned his feet while Samson bossed us around from outside the stall. There was a lot of blood on the hay and Eddie's front feet. None on the back. Odd. He'd kicked his stall walls but apparently, not Fred.

Luke and I walked Eddie to the corral. I told him what to look for in the blood sample. "Avery, you stay with Eddie. Don't let anybody near him." Luke waited with them while I went exploring. Sure enough, behind the barn, I found what I was looking for. One sniff and I knew what had happened.

"Detective Samson, would you come back here, please?" He was more used to telling people what to do than being asked, but he followed me.

"What the hell?"

"Pick up a handful and take a whiff. Tell me what you smell."

"Whoa, that's gotta be 80 proof. You think the horse got into this?" Samson shook his head. "The horse was drunk? Where'd this come from anyway?"

I explained about the watermelons and what I'd overheard. "I think Eddie was framed. I'd bet Pete, the stableman, supplied vodka for the kids. They cut out pieces of the watermelon, poured in the liquor, plugged the piece back in. By tonight it would be saturated."

"I wouldn't think a horse would like the smell."

"Knowing some of the kids aren't sticklers for rules, Fred must have stayed late. If he caught them doctoring the watermelons, he'd have threatened to call their parents, the police, anybody he could think of." I paused, examining one of the more intact melons. "One of the kids or Pete must have clobbered Fred, then mashed up the melons to look like Eddie did it and put Fred in Eddie's stall. A head wound would have bled a lot and would have really upset Eddie. If they crowded him, he'd have stepped in the blood, trying to get away from them. His breath smelled like vodka which also probably freaked him out. It would take an awful lot to get a horse drunk, if you could make him drink. Pete must have poured it on him."

"Maybe I should talk to this Pete. Where is he?" Samson made notes.

"He was just here." I looked around. "There. Headed for the blue pickup truck."

Samson whistled, caught the attention of a uniformed officer, and signaled him to stop Pete. There was a bit of a tussle, but Pete was outmatched.

With the threat of a murder charge if Fred died, Pete confessed. As I thought, Fred had caught Pete and a few of the boys in the act of dousing the watermelons. One of Eddie's other tricks was to open his stall door and wander around. He smelled the watermelon, wanted a bite, and interrupted the argument between Pete and Fred. Pete suggested they walk Eddie back to his stall but when they got there, Pete hit Fred over the head and threw him in with Eddie.

The odor of blood had set Eddie off. When Pete came back with bottle of vodka, he poured it on Eddie's face and in the stall which made Eddie smell like Uncle Hubert. The kids weren't part of beating Fred, but they'd paid Pete to get the vodka and hadn't called an ambulance when they had the chance. They were in a lot of trouble and their parents were screaming about their innocence.

Avery and I spent part of our weekends and evenings at the hospital, convincing Fred to get well. I sat in an uncomfortable chair while Avery climbed in with Fred, nice and comfy. Fred pulled through and was able to go home after a month.

Pete went to jail, the kids were banned from the barn and, better still, had community service hours to complete. They also couldn't be around animals of any kind without supervision.

There was a ceremony to welcome Fred back to work. He thanked the police officers, the volunteers, and Luke for all they did. And me for driving Avery to the hospital to visit. At least I got an honorable mention. Avery got a tiara and a necklace with a little medal on it. She was going to be impossible now.

As we walked to the car, Fred called for me to wait up.

"Don't get a big head or your tiara won't fit," I told Avery. Her eyes lit up as she looked behind me.

"I wanted to show my appreciation," Fred called. He was leading the smallest horse I'd ever seen, about the size of a Great Dane. "This is Marco. His people couldn't keep him, so he ended up here. He's housebroken, a certified therapy animal, and Avery will love having a horse of her own." Fred grinned. "Eddie's going to stay here as a Haven ambassador. It all worked out."

Before I could react, the back of my little SUV was filled with food for Marco, a bridle, and all the equipment. "Lucky you've got such a big yard and no near neighbors, huh?" Fred grinned and opened the rear passenger door. Marco hopped in and sat on the seat as Fred buckled the seat belt. "He loves car rides. I know he's in good hands with you. Avery deserved a reward and this is the best I could think of for her."

I am a dog person despite the fact there are five cats, one orange kitten, and a miniature horse living with me. Marco comes in to watch television and eat popcorn with us but thankfully sleeps in his own bed. On the enclosed porch.

At least he's not on my bed. With five cats, an orange kitten, and a diva dog, I'm already hanging onto the edge of the mattress.

I was sleep-deprived, but I couldn't have been happier.

Sandra Murphy lives in St Louis, Missouri, where dogs and cats of all ages, sizes, and colors have found their way to her door. She shares living space with Ozzie the Westie-ish boy, Fetcher of Toys and Louie the Tuxedo Cat, Clock Monitor for mealtimes. Sandra's the editor of Peace, Love, and Crime: Crime Stories Inspired by the Songs of the '60s and A Murder of Crows where crimes occur but animals are never harmed.

Firebug

cj petterson

"**M**uffin, how in the world did you get up there?"

Standing on the top rung of the stepladder, Libby Sams gripped the edge of the roof with one hand, held her breath, and stretched as far as she could but still couldn't reach the kitten.

None of her pleas, threats, or kitty treats enticed the tiny cat close enough to grab. Libby couldn't decide what frustrated her more, letting the calico kitten escape through the door or having to call the fire department for a rescue.

"Oh, no," Libby groaned as she heard the fire truck's siren wind down in front of her home. She threw her hands up in frustration when she bumped into her ex-fiancé, Tyler James, as she rounded the corner of the house.

"Did you have to use the siren? I didn't say there was a fire," she said and pointed a finger at the bulky, turnout gear the firefighter was wearing. "I said my kitten is on the roof, and I can't reach her."

The twinkle in his eyes betrayed his amusement, but he answered her complaint with a sober tone. "We have to use the siren on official runs, Libby, and even something as non-emergent as a pet rescue is an official run. Where's your crisis?"

"Around back," Libby said, as Tyler and another firefighter followed her around to the patio. "Her name is Muffin."

"Guess I won't need this gear," Tyler said and dropped his heavy coat over one of the patio chairs.

"Another foster kitten?" he said and stepped onto the bottom rung of the ladder that the other firefighter steadied.

Can't keep anything secret in a small town, she thought, and Glen Eden, Alabama, is definitely a small town. She hugged her sweater tighter against a gust of cool October wind. "I keep saying I'm not going to foster anymore, then the shelter calls, and I can't say no."

Tyler was up the ladder and back down with his fingers wrapped gently around the mewing kitten before she finished her sentence.

"Thank you," she said and motioned to the garden storage shed when the other firefighter asked where to store the ladder on his way back to the fire truck. "I have no idea how she got up there."

Tyler pointed to the bush with branches overhanging the eave. "Probably climbed that camellia on the corner. If you don't cut it back, you'll have more than cats up there."

"Between working and fostering two cats and a special-needs puppy, I'm always out of time. I hired a neighbor boy to rake the leaves in the front yard. Since we have a burn ban until after November 1, he bags them for trash pick-up. Maybe he can trim back that bush, too."

"What's a special-needs puppy?"

"Harley was hit by a car and had to have a hind leg amputated." She immediately regretted her matter-of-fact tone when Tyler winced. She knew she'd reminded him of comrades who'd lost limbs while serving in Afghanistan.

"I've had her only a few weeks, but she's doing great. I'm helping the Pet Rescue Center get her a prosthetic leg. Or rather, they're helping me."

"Awesome."

She cuddled the kitten close to her chest. "Muffin thanks you for the rescue."

He stroked Muffin's cheek with gentle fingers. "Wish I were a cat," he teased.

"In your dreams, firefighter."

He chuckled at her response just as a call came across his radio about someone setting fire to a pile of leaves, and the homeowner being worried that it was close to her house. He spun on his heel and headed through the gate at a dead run, grabbing his turnout coat on the way past.

She kissed Muffin on the top of her head. "Okay, you little stinker. That's our big adventure for this month. I hope that fire isn't a big one. That makes the third or fourth one in the last week or so. Hope they catch the firebug before somebody's house goes up in flames."

***

"Don't start on me," Tyler warned when he heard a chorus of "wooo-eee" as he walked into the firehouse kitchen for a cup of coffee. He knew where the teasing was headed.

"What?" Sergeant Lyons said, with wide-eyed innocence. "Danny just told us the cat lady was your high-school flame."

"High school was a long time ago. Libby fosters cats, but she's also got a puppy that's had a hind leg amputated. It's going to get a prosthetic leg."

"That's wild," Lyons said around a mouthful of apple. "My wife is on Facebook, and she was telling me about how they can do that now."

Tyler poured a cup of black coffee, took a sip, and dumped the cup and the rest of the pot into the sink. "Whoever left this on the burner needs to make the next pot."

"That would be the chief," Lyons said. "High school may have been a long time ago, but I've yet to meet a woman who didn't hang on to a good man after being dumped."

Tyler counted scoops of coffee grounds into a paper filter. "That's not what happened. We kind of grew apart." There was no "we," he thought. It was all me. "No reason we can't be friendly."

"Friendly?" Danny said. "The look you gave her was a lot more than friendly. Doesn't hurt none that she's a squeezable, red-headed, five-foot-two cutie with green eyes."

"That's enough," Tyler said with an edge in his voice.

"You gonna try to get back together?" Danny shot back with a grin.

Tyler sent him a one-shoulder shrug. "She's a good woman, and to paraphrase Flannery O'Connor, 'A good woman is hard to find.'" He examined the tiny, red scratch Muffin put on his arm and mused aloud, "So are second chances."

***

As soon as Libby walked in the house, an ecstatic Harley yipped and bounced and almost knocked her down. She captured the wriggling puppy in her arms and held her close while avoiding a barrage of wet puppy kisses. When her cell rang, she groped around in the bottom of her purse to find it before it went to voice mail. Caller ID flashed a number she didn't recognize but thinking it might be a call about an adoption, she answered with a hopeful "Hello?"

"Afternoon, Libby. It's Tyler."

Haven't heard from him in a couple of years, and now twice in one day? "Hey, Tyler. What's going on?"

"Doing a little investigating. We've been getting a lot of calls in your neighborhood about someone setting fire to piles of leaves. Seems the homeowner rakes up their leaves, and then someone comes by and lights up the pile."

"Are they calling because they're worried about the no-burn policy?"

"Some of them mention that. They're also concerned the fire will get out of control in the dry grass and spread to their homes. I was wondering if you'd seen anyone or heard anything suspicious lately."

"Nothing other than noticing the smoke and smell of leaves burning. People are usually ready to blame some neighborhood teenager looking for excitement."

"Anybody come to mind?"

"The only teen in my neighborhood is Jason Olsinsky, the boy that comes to rake my leaves. But he's a shy, quiet kid. I like him. He stops by almost every day to see the fur babies and is especially taken with Harley. He even volunteers for her doo-doo duty. I don't know her other than to wave to, but his mother comes across as the total opposite. She was actually appalled by Harley having only three legs. She's also a strict disciplinarian from what I gather in my conversations with Jason. I doubt he's brave enough to risk getting caught and facing her wrath."

"Thanks. I'll have a talk with him anyway. Kids have a way of knowing who's doing what. Libby, I was thinking...wondering, if you're not seeing anyone special, would you like to join me for lunch tomorrow after church?"

Is it the invitation, she wondered, or the whisky-smooth sound of his voice? Whatever it was, it breathed life into a dark ember in the depths of her heart, and she tried, unsuccessfully, to stifle the heat it created.

"Sorry, I have to decline your invitation." Her automatic refusal sent her mind racing, and the truth followed by a lie tumbled over her lips. "There's no one special in my life right now, but one of the kittens is going to meet its forever family tomorrow."

"Next Sunday?"

Do I really want to risk getting hurt again?

When she didn't answer for several seconds, he said. "That silence sounds like a 'no'."

"It's just that my foster family doesn't leave me a lot of free time."

"Maybe next time," he said, disappointment in his voice. "See you at church."

When the call ended, she murmured, "Please forgive the lie about the forever home, Lord, but could you make it happen?"

The cellphone vibrated in her hand and another unknown number displayed. "This better not be a robo call," she muttered and answered.

Fifteen minutes later, she'd made a two p.m. appointment to meet a potential adopting family on Sunday afternoon. "Yesss." She pumped a fist. "Thank. You. Lord."

***

The doorbell rang promptly at two, and Libby opened the door for the kitten's audition.

When Libby was reassured there truly was a forever home waiting for her rescued fur baby, her throat began to ache and seemed to close as she planted a kiss between its ears.

"I'll miss you," she said in a croaky voice.

She handed the family a bag of kitty food and gave the kitten's silky coat one last loving stroke before he left. When she closed the door, she smiled in satisfaction, but the tears she'd been fighting back spilled over her lashes. She swiped at the wetness.

"Enough. He's going to a good home. One down, two to go, and then no more." Even when she said it, she knew it was a lie. There'd always be one more animal she couldn't refuse.

She logged on to her email account and opened the email with "Harley" on the subject line.

"The prosthetic is ready," Bobbie's note read. "Can you bring Harley in for a fitting tomorrow?"

"The adventure begins," Libby murmured with a smile.

"Tomorrow after work," she typed. As she hit send and signed out, the sound of a fire truck's siren coming closer caught her attention.

"Another one? What is going on?"

***

Libby watched anxiously as the technician fitted Harley's prosthetic leg, then removed, adjusted, and refitted it again and again until he said it was perfect. For her part, the puppy calmly accepted all of the handling without a whimper. Harley spent a brief time sniffing and examining the strange attachment before she tried a clumsy step. The prosthetic leg slid on the tile floor and Harley fell on her side and lay there a few moments before trying again.

"Oh, wow," Libby cried. "That looks so painful."

The technician assured Libby that Harley's first attempts at a stiff-legged walk were more painful for Libby to watch then it was for Harley.

"It'll take her a while to adapt. She'll do fine outside on the grass and on carpeting," he moved Harley to a line of carpet tiles where she took a few steadier steps. "You'll need to lay down throw rugs on your tile or wood floors." He handed Libby a list of do's, don'ts, and warnings and scheduled a follow-up appointment.

An obviously confused Harley made an awkward move toward the door. Libby immediately crouched to pick her up, but the tech shook his head.

"Let her walk. After the newness wears off, she'll be fine. You'll be fine, too," he said with a reassuring smile.

***

Two days after the fitting, Libby saw a glowing pillar of smoke in front of a neighbor's house, two doors down, and smelled the distinctive aroma of leaves burning. She also noticed Jason Olsinky gripping his mother's arm in the middle of the street, seemingly drawn like moths to the flames in front of them. Jason glanced in Libby's direction, ducked his head as if embarrassed to be caught rubbernecking, then said something to his mother before they retreated into the distance. Harley gave out a rare string of excited yips and yaps at the sound of the approaching fire truck siren. Libby figured Tyler was off-duty but on-call when he arrived in his pickup. It didn't take long for the firefighters to knock down the flames with a hose from the pumper truck, re-secure their equipment, and drive off. Now that the emergency was over, Tyler walked over to Libby's backyard where she and Harley had taken refuge.

"So this is Harley," Tyler said and chuckled while the wriggling puppy licked his hand.

"Yep, here she is," Libby said and unclipped the leash from Harley who immediately took off after a bird. "And there she goes."

"What kind of dog is she?" Tyler.

"Vet said she's probably a beago, and I can tell from the look on your face, you have no idea what that is. It's a mix of beagle and golden retriever. She's got big paws, so she won't be small. Probably more of a medium-sized dog."

Having missed her prey, Harley walked back and lay down next to Libby's feet, her tongue draped out of the side of her mouth, excited energy momentarily depleted.

"Harley, the Wonder Dog," Tyler murmured. "She looks like she's grinning."

"Wonder Dog is a perfect description. She's always grinning. Nothing seems to keep her down."

Tyler squatted to pet Harley then traced the outline of the prosthetic with his fingers. "This is amazing."

"They make them for all kinds of animals," Libby said. "I even saw a picture of an elephant fitted with a prosthetic leg. But the best one? The vet told me about a group of eighth graders who designed and 3D-printed a prosthetic foot for a disabled duck."

"You serious? Aren't eighth-graders about thirteen-years old? If those kids aren't walking on Mars in a few years, they'll be designing the equipment to get us there."

"If I know you, you'll be first in line for a seat on the rocket." The banter sounded like old times, and she laughed.

"I've got some buddies at the fire house who'd love to meet Harley," he ran his hand over the puppy's platinum-gold hair. "Could you bring her by tomorrow? Morning would be best, I think."

"Sure. The more people she meets, the better socialized she'll be. She's going up for adoption soon."

He continued to pet Harley as he looked up at Libby. "Please don't let that happen before you call me."

"I promise. By the way, I saw Jason and his mother in the street a few minutes ago, so I know he's home if you haven't had a chance to talk with him yet."

"I have not. But I'm not sure talking to him now would get me any info. He probably wouldn't open up in front of his mom. Call me the next time he's at your place, and I'll come by then."

***

The next morning, Libby and Harley arrived at the station in time to watch the on-duty crew conduct their morning equipment checks.

Libby wrapped her arm around Harley's neck and hugged her close.

"Harley girl, you're the best. It's downright peopley here, and despite all the commotion, you're as sweet as a mama could hope for. Look. There's Tyler." He walked toward her wearing a navy tee emblazoned with the fire department insignia on his chest.

I do love a man in uniform. When he took her hand, she jumped like he'd given her an electric shock.

"Come on. I want to introduce you and show Harley off."

Harley, who was panting nervously, lay down on the cold concrete next to Tyler's feet.

Tyler put his hand on the shoulder of the firefighter who crouched next to Harley. "This is Sergeant Joe Lyons."

"Nice to meet you, Miss Sams." Lyons returned his attention to Harley's prosthetic leg. "Technology is amazing, isn't it? She looks like a happy dog, despite the trauma."

"She's a very happy dog," Tyler said before Libby could answer. Libby listened as Tyler shared with the firefighters all the things he'd learned about animal prosthetics and about Harley in particular.

"Can I take a rain check?" Libby said when Tyler offered a tour of the firehouse. "I think Harley's had enough excitement for today."

***

When Libby and Harley stepped through her front door, Muffin scampered to greet them, weaving figure eights around her ankles, all the while complaining about being left alone. Libby removed the prosthetic so Harley could rest comfortably, while the kitten purred and groomed the dog's neck.

"That's sweet of you, Muffin. You missed your buddy, didn't you?"

The strong aroma of burning leaves caught her attention. "That's close," she said and ran out of the house to find fire in her front yard. The pile of leaves Jason had raked but hadn't yet put into bags was blazing, and he was dancing around the edge of the flames.

"Jason! What are you doing?" By the time she'd called 911 and dragged her garden hose around to the front yard, Jason had disappeared. The hose's half-inch nozzle did little more than propel burning leaves into the air and onto the dry grass like a thousand lit matches. She turned the hose on herself when one of the fiery missiles landed on her shoulder.

***

"Tyler, let's go," Lyons yelled as the alarm sounded. "Fire at Libby's house."

Tyler slid down the fire pole and made it to ground level before the overhead door finished its grind upward. Adrenaline sent his heart racing as he donned his turnout gear inside the cab while the driver headed toward the scene.

"This is one of the times I'm glad Glen Eden is such a small town," the driver said. "We'll be on-scene in just a couple of minutes."

Libby, soaked from head to toe, swung the water spray back and forth, attempting to stop the fire's hungry race toward her front porch. She dropped the hose only when Tyler pulled her away from the blackened trail of charred grass.

"We'll take it from here, Libby. Go tend to your rescues."

She watched the firefighters send gallons of water onto the flames and use rakes on the leaves to make sure there were no warm embers remaining.

"Did you see who did it?" Tyler said when the firefighters were cleaning up.

"It was Jason Olsinsky," she said. "I saw him dancing around the flames. Actually dancing."

"I didn't start the fire, Miss Sams, and I wasn't dancing." Jason's voice came from behind the camellia. "I was stomping on the edges, trying to keep it from spreading."

"If you didn't start it," Tyler said, "you must've been here quickly enough to see who did."

"I can't say," Jason said with a shake of his head. "I can't say."

"Then I will."

Libby recognized the man speaking as Eric Olsinsky, Jason's father.

"It was my wife, Olivia. I'm sorry everyone. Jason's mother is a firebug."

***

Two days later, Libby saw Tyler's number flash on her cellphone.

He responded to her hello with, "Have you had lunch yet?"

"I had a late breakfast."

"How about dinner? You still like Mario's spaghetti?"

"You're not going to give up are you?" she said, happy that he hadn't. She let out a melodramatic sigh, "Okay, yes. I still like Mario's spaghetti."

Mario's was as she remembered: tables with shiny polyethylene finishes, empty Chianti wine bottles stoppered with candles dripping wax down the sides, deliciously mingled aromas of garlic and basil, and a low hum of conversations that bounced and echoed between the hard floors and high ceilings. A feeling of familiar comfort washed over her.

She tore off a piece of warm, crusty bread and dipped it into a shallow bowl of herbed olive oil.

"Have you heard anything about Mrs. Olsinsky?" she said.

"I know she's out on bail, but what the future holds is up to the court. Hopefully she'll get the psychiatric help she needs."

She stabbed her fork into the spaghetti, twirled the limber strands into her spoon, and slipped the lump into her mouth. She murmured a contented "yum" when Tyler reached over and wiped a smear of tomato sauce off of her cheek. Yes, she thought as memories came flooding back. This is exactly the way I remember it.

"This used to be our go-to place," she said.

"This place and the frozen custard stand after football games. Those were the days."

"I think the operative word there is 'were.' You can't go back again," she said.

"But you can start anew. Life is not linear, except for the birth and death part. Things change. People change."

"A writer friend of mine says that when things don't go the way he planned or some disaster strikes, he yells, 'plot point' and changes direction . He says he never loses or fails, he simply sets a new goal and moves forward."

"How about you, Libby?"

"I'm good. I'm moving forward."

"You and I were special together. That once-in-a-lifetime kind of special that I didn't recognize until too late. I made the biggest mistake of my life when I broke up with you. Libby, do you think you could...maybe be willing to give me a second chance?"

She twirled her last few strands of spaghetti around her fork and stared at it for several seconds. The server took that moment to set their tiramisus and cappuccinos in front of them. "Perfect timing," she said, grateful she didn't have to answer that question yet.

Tyler decided to change the subject. "How long before you put Harley up for adoption?"

"Probably a week. As much as I'd love to keep her, I have to do what's best for—."

"I think I'd be best for her. I want to give Harley her forever home."

Libby felt her heart would burst. "You have no idea how much that means to me, Tyler. I've come to love that puppy dearly and hated the thought that I'd have to give her up to some stranger. Thank you. You've made me very happy."

"While we're on the happiness train, why don't you adopt Muffin? If you're her forever hu-mom, she'll still be able to spend time with her favorite dog, 'cause I'll be asking you to dog-sit when I'm on duty."

Libby laughed. "You must've read my mind, because I had already decided I was the best family for her. I told the Pet Rescue Center this morning I was going to adopt the little priss. Muffin and I'll be happy to have Harley with us while you're on your three-day shifts."

Tyler lifted his coffee cup. "A toast to second chances all around?"

"cj petterson" is the pen name of Marilyn A. Johnston. She was born in Texas, raised in Michigan, now lives in historic Mobile, Alabama. Marilyn writes contemporary romantic and paranormal suspense, a bit of mystery, and non-fiction and fiction short stories that have appeared in several anthologies. Marilyn began writing for pleasure after she retired from the auto industry. She is a member of the international Sisters in Crime writers' group and their online Guppy chapter, Alabama Writers Conclave, Alabama Writers Forum, and a charter member of the Mobile Writers Guild. Visit cj petterson's blog at www.lyricalpens.com

Notorious B.U.G.

Allison Deters

The black SUV was clearly an omen. I should have trusted that from the moment I laid eyes on it as I walked the fence line of my back yard, ruminating over all my current grievances. Perhaps I was too distracted by my grievances to fully take in the moment.

Most of the grievances were with the female human. First, she just "accidentally" sprayed me with the garden hose while she was washing patio furniture. My beautiful Yorkshire Terrier fur was now sure to curl unnecessarily in the humidity. This would probably make the female human jubilant, had she bothered to even notice my plight. Enter grievance number two; she made fun of the fact that my fur tended to grow straight up in uneven lengths, going so far as to tell me I looked like an overgrown rodent that had been electrocuted. Or a feathery bird, hence my name, Birdie. Finally, grievance three, my human father, my one true love, was out of town on business this week, and I was left in the incredibly mediocre care of his wife.

As I angry-pranced towards the fence line, I was forced to dodge Bug, the lump of a canine that the humans called my "sister." She was flopped on the concrete in a deep sleep, positioned in a way that made her look unmistakably like roadkill. Thankfully, Bug's flattened Pug-like face produced a permanently snorkly snore, so it was easy to tell she was still alive. Not that I actually cared that much. We were sisters in name, but not by blood --we hadn't even been rescued from the shelter at the same time. She had been the resident flat-faced, bug eyed canine and had been laying in the same lumpy formation ever since I came to live here. For over a year, we have maintained a general level of apathy towards one another, which suits us both just fine.

I marched the fence line, considering all of my woes, and that's when I noticed it. The black SUV. Normally, I wouldn't have given it a second glance; a rusted out peasant car like that parked outside my house wasn't something that would otherwise grasp my attention. But something was strange: the man in the front seat wore a hoodie, despite the warm summer weather and held binoculars to his eyes.

On instinct, I dashed behind a bush. Every E! True Hollywood Story I've ever watched told me that paparazzi encounters never lead to anything good for the subject. From my hiding spot, I peered back towards the road and realized it wasn't me the hooded man was examining, but my house.

"That's the second day he's been there." The voice behind me made me jump. I turned to find it was just Hamilton, walking atop the deck railing with his cat-like grace. Of course, his grace was cat-like because he was in fact, a cat. Hamilton was no house cat; he'd told me many times that no single residence could contain him and that the streets were his home. Granted, that was pretty tough talk for a feline who'd chosen a quiet street in a suburban neighborhood to roam. Plus, I knew for a fact that the female human routinely left food and water in the garage for him, so he wasn't exactly the lone ranger that he liked to project to the rest of the world.

Hamilton leapt down from the deck railing onto the grass with one eye on the female human. Like me, he wasn't her biggest fan, although his distain extended to all humans. "I think he's casing the joint," Hamilton said as he easily hopped on top of the fence to get a better look.

"What does that mean?" I asked, glancing back at the female human, who was still blissfully unaware of the SUV's presence, and Bug who was still fast asleep on the pavement like a gelatinous blob.

"Prepping for a B&E," Hamilton attempted to clarify, but his words were still lost on me. I could see the judgment in his eyes that I didn't follow his wise street-cat lingo. It wasn't my fault, though – sure, I'd done a couple of weeks hard time at the local animal shelter after my former owner passed away, but other than that, I'd lived a mostly pampered life.

"A break in, Birdie. He wants to break into your house and steal your belongings."

My life suddenly flashed before my eyes. Well, not so much my life, but all my favorite possessions. My glass food bowl. My collection of socks, stolen exclusively from the female human's laundry. My favorite pillow on the couch. I must have looked grief-stricken because Hamilton jumped off the fence, rubbing against me with a comforting purr.

"Calm down," he told me as he sauntered off. "It's the humans' stuff they want. Or the humans themselves. Good thing your favorite one is out of town." And with that, he jumped back over the fence and was gone.

My legs may have been tiny, but they could move quickly when I wanted them to, so I wasted no time. I sprinted over to the female human, making a split-second decision to alert her to the car's presence. It wasn't that I was worried about the female human, per say, but my growing collection of socks under the couch had me panicked.. What if the robber stole them? I'd have to start all over again. A year's worth of work, down the drain. Or worse, what if the robber stole the whole couch? Where would I hide them? Where would I nap in the mid-morning sun? These thoughts pulsed through me as I ran, yelling at the female human to look at the street. Maybe, just maybe, the female human would call the police, or maybe the robber would get spooked and choose another house.

"Birdie!" the female human scolded, reaching down and scooping me up as she cursed my name. As usual, I tried to wiggle free, but had no luck. The female human's grasp was too tight. "The whole neighborhood can hear you."

Well, that's the point, you dimwitted hussie, I thought to myself, but the point was lost on her as she continued to scold me. Even Bug lifted her flat face off-the pavement to see what was happening. Bug was partially deaf – or at least pretended to be, but a piercing yelp could usually get her attention. Bug let out an exasperated snort, clearly annoyed by the interruption and rolled over on the concrete, closing her giant eyes once more. She would be no help either.

I gave up with an exasperated sigh. The female human put me down and returned to her cleaning, and I walked back to the fence only to find the SUV was already gone. I craned my neck to get a better look up and down the street, but there was no trace of it. Maybe my barking had frightened him? Besides, Hamilton was probably wrong anyway. Maybe the guy was just bird watching or something. I tried to push my worries aside, but in the back of my mind I still plotted moving my sock collection to a more secure location. Better safe than sorry.

***

After dinner that night, I lounged on the couch feeling less than satisfied. My meal, the usual gruel that the female human haphazardly slung into my dish, hadn't been remotely appetizing, probably because my human father wasn't here to prepare it properly with a scoop of wet food or a morsel of chicken or cheese. But there was also this nagging feeling in the pit of my stomach that something just wasn't right.

"Hey Bug," I whispered. Bug was flopped against the female human in another roadkill imitation. Bug was rarely vertical, living her life nap by nap, only pausing for food and water. I often pondered how one could be so slothful and yet survive. But I knew better than to ask, Bug was incredibly sensitive about her weight.

"Bug," I tried again, not wanting to endure the female human's scorn if I interrupted her trashy reality television program. Would it kill her to read a book or watch a documentary occasionally?

Bug snorted, but I saw her eyes flicker open and dart across the sectional.

"I think someone is going to break into the house tonight," I confessed. Hearing the words out loud made my fur stand on end. Well, more than usual.

Bug gave another snort, full of the apathy that I expected from my fellow canine. As long as I'd known her, she'd been on an anxiety medication that sedated her into a general lack of concern for anything. The female human called it Bug's "sleepy cheese" as she hid the pill in a piece of sliced cheddar and Bug happily wolfed it down. It would be a cold day in hell before I'd ever let the human dose me like that. I even resisted my monthly heartworm pill, although it tasted like a treat.

"What if they hurt the female human?" I offered, attempting to tug at Bug's heart strings. As much contempt as I had for that woman, Bug loved her – well as much as a medicated baked potato with eyes was capable of loving anyone. Mostly, Bug loved the fact that the female human always snuck her snacks. Bug's love was easily bought, and I leveraged that now, watching her little pug ears perk up and her large eyes widen even further.

"We need to be prepared to defend this house," I said with more confidence than I actually had.

Bug lifted her head off the sofa in a halfhearted sign of agreement, her attention fully captured, so I gave her some marching orders. "Bug, whatever you do, do not eat your sleepy cheese tonight. I need you awake and alert." Bug snorted again in reply, which was her most common form of communication. I'd never actually heard her speak. She got by with an array of snorts and grunts in her very own Bug language, which I'd learned over the last year. This snort was clear: she was in. The team was assembled.

But Bug's commitment to the cause didn't help my churning stomach as I watched the clock behind the television tick forward. The female human wasn't much of a night owl, and I fully expected her to be in bed by 11 at the latest. I wasn't sure what I kind of hours night prowlers kept, but I imagined them lying in wait, patiently watching for the living room light and the television to flip off.

Sure enough, at quarter to 11, the female human began her nighttime routine, turning off the television and preparing Bug's nightly dose of sleepy cheese. I made eye contact with Bug, shaking my head to remind her of our pact. The female human picked her up from the couch and placed her in her crate, along with a big bite of cheese, her medication artfully hidden inside. Bug was crated nightly because she snored far too loudly to share the bed with the humans. It was the rare instance where I had a privilege that Bug did not share, and I reveled in it. However, now it presented a problem. I needed to break Bug out of her crate tonight. But I'd cross that bridge when I got there.

The female human turned off the lights and shuffled down the hallway to her bedroom to continue her nighttime routine, forgetting to shut the living room window. Barking, I ran after her, trying to remind her of her lapse in judgment.

An open window would be just what a burglar would be looking for, and the screen would be easy to pop out. But the female human just chastised me for barking again and went about the exhaustive process of taking her makeup off.

Defeated, I returned to the living room where I could hear a familiar sound. When Bug ate, it sounded like a pig slurping at a trough. It was unmistakable and made me gag. How was it possible that I was even the same species as that alien creature? But also, more importantly, what was Bug eating?

Panic soared through me as I realized it a moment too late – the sleepy cheese. Bug had not been able to resist the temptation. I ran up to her crate and peered through the bars. There was Bug, chewing the big orange slice like a cow with a cud.

"Please tell me you at least took the medication out first?" I pleaded, but I knew the answer as Bug chomped. Bug had no such restraint. She thought only of food. Why had I thought her capable of anything else? I slunk away from the crate feeling utter failure as Bug didn't even offer a snort of apology. Who was I to think I could protect this house? The female human dismissed me. Bug ignored me. I had no hope left.

"You look like you could use some help." The voice caught me off guard once again and I snapped my head around to see where it came from. Through the open window, I could see Hamilton in all his tom-cat glory, perched on the ledge, his orange fur glowing in the light of the streetlamp.

"You have no idea," I replied as I watched Hamilton pop the screen out of the window with a single swipe of his claws. It appeared he had done this before. "Bug ate the sleepy cheese and the female human went to bed with the window open and..."

"Child, calm yourself. I'm here to help now..." Hamilton purred as he propelled himself through the window, landing on the living room floor with the kind of grace I envied. He stalked over to Bug's crate and flipped the latch without effort. Bug stumbled out, looking confused, as if the cheese had already started to lull her to sleep.

"Well now, the gang's all here, what's the plan?" Hamilton asked. I had absolutely no answer. An embarrassing little whine escaped my mouth, the kind I usually saved for when the purity of the water in my fountain was subpar. I never imagined a day when things like that would mean so little. Now. I had real problems to deal with. And when faced with a challenge I was folding like a card table.

Hamilton ambled across the room, taking it all in. "Nice digs." He crossed into the kitchen, hopping up on the countertop. "I can see why you'd want to defend this place. It's cozy."

"But how do we defend it?" I asked, following him. Bug, whose legs had betrayed her, was now sitting by her kennel at an awkward angle, a line of drool trailing from the corner of her mouth. What a crack team I'd assembled.

"Have you ever seen the movie Home Alone?" Hamilton asked as he started systematically knocking things off the countertop. A stack of unpaid bills fluttered to the floor. A ceramic duck shattered as it hit the tile. A soup ladle danced towards the door. I would have been concerned with the noise, but the female human slept with a fan on, she likely heard no commotion. The mess however...

"No..." I answered meekly, staring at the kitchen floor and the utter mess Hamilton was creating as he scratched at the side of the refrigerator, pulling all the magnets down.

Hamilton cackled and shook his head. "How is that I, a feral alley cat have seen it, but you, a posh princess have not? That film is a masterpiece. But I digress. It's also central to our plan tonight. You see, in the movie, a young boy is forced to defend his home against burglars and sets a bunch of booby traps."

I blinked at Hamilton. I did not see his point. All I saw was Hamilton ransacking my kitchen as he opened the fridge and spilled a jar of pickles over everything. Panic started to swell up in me. I'd never be able to explain this mess to the female human.

"I don't get it," I said. Out of the corner of my eye, I could see Bug, who had nodded off in a seated position, startle at the sound of more shattered glass – this time a jar of jam. "I feel like you're just making a mess."

"Exactly," replied the cat, jumping back down to the floor. "In the movie, the boy uses household items to incapacitate the burglars. As you can see, I'm doing just that. Pickles and jam are quite slippery on the floor..."

Bug appeared, seemingly from nowhere, and began to lick the disgusting substance on the floor, but Hamilton jumped in front of her, hissing and batting at her with his front paws.

"Absolutely not," he insisted, his tail big and fluffy and his posture ridged. "We do NOT eat the props. For the love of God, Birdie, can you get this thing under control?" Bug backed away as Hamilton hissed at her again. She drew her paw back, stealing away a small clump of jam for her efforts.

I nodded, although I was unsure that any real effort of mine would stop Bug. But, I was starting to understand the genius of Hamilton's plan. Plus, I had this nagging desire for him to like me. He clearly thought of Bug as a useless lump of fur -- I didn't want him to regard me as the same.

"What about this?" I asked, walking back to the living room and dragging the base of the lamp under the window so the cord was lifted and taut. "If the burglar came through this window and took a couple of steps, he would trip, right?"

"Exactly!" Hamilton's face beamed with pride, and I could feel myself blush. It felt so good. I watched Hamilton, still in the kitchen, go for the carton of eggs. He rolled them across the kitchen island, like he was shooting pool balls into the side pockets. The eggs fell, creating a slippery circle of defense. I continued to work in the living room, although I didn't have the arsenal of fun props that Hamilton did. Nor the creativity.

Within fifteen minutes of chaos, the house was basically trashed – or as Hamilton called it, "ready for action." Bug's only contribution to the effort was peeing herself when Hamilton pushed a stack of plates out of a kitchen cupboard. I thought for sure the crash was loud enough to awake the female human, but she remained blissfully unaware of mess. And of the impending danger.

"Now... we wait," Hamilton whispered as he curled into a little orange ball in the center of the living room floor, with his head pointed towards the open window. It was eerily still and quiet in the house. The only noises to be heard were the sounds of crickets in the yard and the dull snore of Bug who had retreated to the protection of her crate. I paced the sectional with one eye on the window and the other on the door, ready to take action at the slightest movement.

I vaguely remember laying down on the couch just to rest for a moment, but the next thing I knew I was opening my eyes to the soft daylight of dawn as the sun peeked out of the horizon through the window. I reveled at it for a second; I was never up early enough to catch a magnificent sunrise. The moment was short lived however, as I gained my bearings and jumped to my feet, catching a glimpse of the clock. It was well past 6 a.m. and the female human would soon wake for work.

"Hamilton!" I called out, not seeing my partner in crime anywhere. My heart started thumping so hard I could hear it in my pointy little ears. Had I missed it? Had they taken Hamilton? Why, oh why, had I allowed myself to fall asleep?

I paced around the room, panicking at the site of it all. Torn and overturned furniture, spilled food, broken dishes... in the light of day, it really didn't look much like a boobytrap. It just looked like a giant mess. How would I ever explain this to the female human?

I could hear Bug still snoring in her crate. My one solace was that she was safe. That had to mean nothing bad had happened while we slept, right? I switched from pacing to scratching myself with my hind leg, which always brought me a certain amount of comfort. It was almost like getting ear scratches from my human father.

In a blur of orange fur, Hamilton leapt back through the window, landing on the living room floor in front of me, looking decidedly not kidnapped. Relief washed over me -- we were all safe.

"Hamilton, I'm so glad you're alright," I exhaled the breath that I didn't realize I had been holding. What a night!

"Of course, I'm alright," Hamilton's tone was confident. Something about his demeanor was off, but I just couldn't place it.

"What am I going to do about the house?" I asked, panicking about the next hurdle in front of me. The female human was not the forgiving type.

Hamilton shook his head. "Nothing. You can do nothing. You will do nothing." His voice came out in staccato as he drew out the last sentence as more of a command than the advice I was looking for.

"But the female human is going to lose her mind!" I cried. He clearly wasn't understanding the gravity of the situation. Maybe he'd hit his head last night. He didn't seem to be grasping the problem at hand.

"Exactly," Hamilton replied, sitting squarely in the middle of the floor, licking his paw for dramatic effect.

"What do you mean 'exactly?'" My heart started hammering again, because I was starting to realize the frightening truth. Hamilton, my handsome, street-smart, confident Hamilton, had played me.

"You know," Hamilton said with a snicker. He approached me with his trademark move, purring as he rubbed past me. But his aura was completely different now. Instead of friendship, I felt hostility.

"You set me up?" I said, instantly embarrassed by the emotion in my voice. But Hamilton was my only friend in the world right now. Bug was ambivalent towards me. The female human favored her and my human father was out of town. The deceit stung surprisingly hard.

"That I did," Hamilton purred, clearly pleased with himself as he sashayed around. "I knew I could convince you to trash this house. It just took the right situation to motivate you." I imagined he was about to cackle like a movie villain at some point.

"But why?" I asked, feeling my eyes moisten with hurt and rage.

"To get you kicked out of the house, of course," Hamilton replied, flicking his tail. "It was the perfect time to entrap you; the male human is gone and without him to defend you, the female human will put you out on the streets. You'll be lucky if she even bothers to drop you off back at the shelter. She'll probably just throw you out with the morning trash!" As he monologued, his voice got louder. It was clear this was an exciting moment for Hamilton, the culmination of weeks of work. But I still couldn't understand why. What did he have to gain from me being homeless? Or did he just enjoy creating chaos?

"And, of course, you fell for it," he continued, revealing more than he needed, like any true villain would. "You trusted handsome ole' Hamilton, the street-wise alley cat. Little did you know, he was an alley cat for hire."

I wasn't sure if he noticed his mistake; that he'd talked just a little too long, said a little too much. But I noticed.

"For hire?" I repeated his words, running them around in my brain, the same brain that the female human often claimed I never use. "Someone hired you to get rid of me?" My mind naturally went to the female human first, my obvious nemesis, but she wouldn't enlist someone to trash her own house. And my human father was blissfully out of state. That only left...

Bug chose this very moment to waddle upon our conversation, her enormous eyes were uncannily alert, without their usual fog of sleepiness. And then, it all came together.

Hamilton laughed again. "I'm proud of you for figuring it out – I'd always assumed you were a little dim, Birdie. Bravo."

"Why would you do that?" I asked Bug, my voice heavy with betrayal. Sure, we'd never truly been sisters, but she'd always seemed so apathetic towards me. It didn't make sense.

"She's hated you from day one," Hamilton continued, speaking for Bug as she stared at me with unblinking eyes. "This has been in the cards from the day you were adopted. We've just been biding our time, looking for the perfect opening to get rid of you. And when I saw that car yesterday, I knew the moment had come. From there it was easy to set the trap, with Bug playing along as your useless accomplice."

I looked at Bug, feeling my face crumple. "I was trying to protect you last night," I said. "You and your awful human." And, my sock collection, but I didn't feel it prudent to add that. "I can't believe you would do this to me..." And I really couldn't, mostly because I didn't think she was capable of such a feat. All I'd ever seen her do was sleep and eat. Egomaniacal house takeover was not on my Bug bingo card.

Bug blinked, and for a moment, I thought I saw a glimmer of remorse. But Hamilton ruined it by injecting himself back into the conversation.

"Bug and I have been friends for years," he continued. "Well, maybe not friends, but mutual beneficiaries. You wouldn't know it, but she's quite the mouse catcher. She pays me in carcasses from the basement and I bring her leftovers from the dumpster. I break in and let her out of her kennel most nights- how do you think I could unlatch it so fast?" The idea that my friendship with Hamilton was a ruse stung, but somehow his secret friendship with Bug stung even more.

"And now for the final act," he exclaimed. "Bug, my fat, fat, friend, get back in your crate so I can get out of here. We don't need you blamed for any of this. Birdie clearly acted alone."

Bug hesitated for just a moment, clearly upset that Hamilton had used the "f" word to describe her - even I knew better than to comment on a dog's weight. Her eyes locked on Hamilton, suddenly filled with scorn. In that hesitation, I saw a glimmer of hope... but Hamilton swatted Bug back with his sharp claws, making her scramble towards her crate.

I was done for.

"What in God's name..." the female human's voice startled us all from the hallway. Bug cowered in front of her crate while Hamilton leapt behind the dining room table. The female human couldn't see him.

My whole life flashed before my eyes. Everything was about to be lost. The female human would blame this all on me.

But then, Bug started to bark. In fact, she didn't just bark, she charged at Hamilton, flushing him from his hiding spot. He was front and center as the female human entered the room, startled and screaming as he zoomed past her. He made his break for it and flew through the window. But the gig was up. The female human had spotted Hamilton.

Bug and I locked eyes from across the room as the female human inspected the damage, wailing on the phone to my human father about a "wild animal" in the house.

"You didn't have to do that, you know," I said, feeling a strange wave of affection for Bug, despite the events of the past twenty-four hours. "You could have gone through with your plan and it probably would have worked. Why did you change your mind?"

Bug just gave me a quiet little snort, trying to look ambivalent as always, and shook her head before she returned to her crate. I think she meant girls gotta stick together.

Bug and I were never best friends after that night. We never snuggled together, or played with each other, or enjoyed each other's company. But somehow, after that night, we were finally sisters.

Allison Deters is the Director of Finance and Administration at Harbor Humane Society. She has always enjoyed writing as a hobby but this is her first published piece. She has a Master's Degree in Criminal Justice Administration, which she literally never uses. Allison resides in Holland, Michigan with her husband, step-son, and her four dogs: Hagrid, Minerva, Mando Boogs, and the infamous Birdie. She dedicates this work to her dearly departed pug mix, Bug, who crossed the rainbow bridge in October 2020.

Yo Ho Ho

Wendy Harrison

I t was the eyes that stopped her midstride. Jane Gray had jogged past the animal shelter a hundred times without a thought to the pet of the day showcased in the window. But this time, she turned her head to sneeze and hadn't gotten past the early part, the "Ah" that preceded the "choo," when she looked into the eyes of the parrot and forgot to finish the rest of the sneeze.

It wasn't the bright plumage, the yellow and turquoise and red, that left her standing mesmerized in front of the glass. It was the eyes. She knew those eyes. She didn't know how she knew them, but she knew they couldn't be denied. She meant to go on with her run. She had things to do, places to go, people to see. But she found herself reaching for the door and pulling it open. She walked up to the counter, and the woman working there looked up from her computer.

"Can I help you?" Her nametag said she was Alexandra and the manager of the shelter. Alexandra didn't show any surprise that there was a tall, slender woman with a lively dark ponytail, a dayglo pink jogging bra, and shiny black running shorts standing in front of her counter, dripping sweat on the tile floor. If she had thought about it at all, she would have thought sympathetically about how hard Southwest Florida was on athletic types. She much preferred her own version of exercise which consisted of squeezing squeaky toys for the myriad of dogs who passed through the doors.

Jane wanted to say no, of course you can't help me, I have no idea why I'm even here, but she heard herself say instead, "The bird? In the window?"

"You mean Napoli?"

"I guess so. Is there another bird in the window?"

Alexandra grinned. "Nope. Napoli has it all to himself."

"Napoli?"

Another smile. "He was brought in by the EMTs who found his elderly owner dead in her apartment. They told me Margaret, her name was Margaret Alessio, had no family they could find. They didn't know what else to do. When we asked the bird, 'Polly want a cracker?' he glared at us. 'No Polly.' He kept repeating it so we named him NaPoli after our vet's favorite city. Get it?"

Jane got it. She walked over to the cage. "Hi, Napoli."

He tilted his head. "Yo ho ho."

Jane laughed. "And a...." He joined her. "Bottle of rum."

This was no ordinary bird, Jane thought, but since this was her first encounter with a parrot, she thought she better not rush to any conclusions about him.

Alexandra and Jane discussed the care and feeding of parrots, their long lifespan, and that adopting one wasn't something to take lightly. Jane nodded as she asked herself what she thought she was doing. Each time she looked at the bird and met his intense stare, she continued the conversation and found herself agreeing to a trial run with Napoli.

After jogging home, Jane backed her car out of its allotted space at her condo, which was tucked inside a converted two-story warehouse. She drove back to the shelter to load up her new pet and a backseat full of supplies. After strapping Napoli's cage into the passenger seat beside her, she drove home, entertained by Napoli's occasional chatter but afraid to take her eyes off the road. That's all she needed, trying to explain to a traffic cop that her feathered passenger distracted her.

By then, it was dinnertime and her brother Dick would be breezing around the kitchen, tossing together a gourmet meal. The cooking gene had skipped Jane but she lucked out when her newly divorced older brother suggested they might share her large loft condo until he could put his personal life back together. That was two years ago, and the arrangement continued to suit both of them. Her busy schedule as a tv news producer meshed well with his more flexible work as a cartographer. But they never discussed adding another roommate. An avian one at that.

She took Napoli and his cage up to the second floor via the big industrial elevator, with no idea how she would explain to Dick why they would be sharing their home with a feathered intruder when she didn't understand it herself. As she stepped into the large living space, she called out, "Dick? Could you come here a minute?"

Tall ran in the family. Jane was 5'8" herself, and Dick towered over her at 6'4". He shared her dark hair and eyes and love for the outdoors. As he ambled in from the kitchen, he wiped his hands on a towel stuck into the front of his jeans to serve as an apron. He stopped short as he neared the front door. "Who's your friend?"

"His name is Napoli. I'll explain in a minute, but would you mind going down to the car and bringing up his supplies?"

She was fortunate Dick not only had the cooking gene but also inherited from their father a laid-back attitude toward life, also not a gene she shared. She put the cage on the large oak table Dick used as a desk for his mapping work. As she opened the cage door for the bird, Napoli stepped through the opening and climbed onto the top. Looking around the room, he seemed content to stay there. Jane was struck by how little she knew about parrots. Did he fly? Were his wings clipped? "Note to self," she mumbled. "Start a list of things I don't know." Napoli cackled. "Not funny, bird."

After dinner, and a long explanation of how Napoli had arrived that didn't answer the question of what had drawn Jane so inexplicably to the parrot, Jane cleaned up while Dick settled at the worktable, his maps spread out next to the cage. Napoli hopped onto his shoulder and stared down at the map of Useppa Island that Dick was working on. Napoli chattered to himself as he studied the map, but was interrupted when Dick said, "Polly want a cracker?"

Napoli glared at him and said, "No Polly!" before stepping back into his cage.

The next morning, after Jane left for work, Dick sat down again with his maps. The one he had been working on had a scratch in it, a tear in the shape of an X, near the middle of Useppa Island. "What the...?" Dick looked suspiciously at Napoli. "Did you do this?"

"Yo ho ho," was the answer. Dick felt a sudden chill. No. That would be crazy, he assured himself.

While Dick was searching his bookshelves for an old copy of "Treasure Island," Jane was taking a coffee break at the tv station and chatting with her co-workers. When she told them about Napoli, one of them suggested they do a human-interest story about the rescued bird. "Maybe it will bring more interest in adoptions at the shelter," Pamela said. An attractive blond with sparkling white teeth, she was the lead field reporter for the noon newscast. "You'll have fun."

"Me? I haven't been in front of a camera for years." Jane could hear the panic in her voice.

Roger, the lead anchor with equally dazzling teeth, joined in. "But maybe you'll even find out who his owner is."

"I'm his owner." Jane explained that Napoli's last owner died without any family around to take him in. She decided not to mention that the minute their eyes met, she knew Napoli belonged to her. That wasn't something she could share without having to endure months of teasing.

When she called the shelter, Alexandra answered the phone. "Alexandra? It's Jane."

"Oh no. Please don't tell me you want to bring Napoli back already?"

She was quick to reassure her. "Oh no. Not at all." When she explained the idea for a story about the shelter and the parrot, Alexandra happily agreed and they set a time for the next day.

As she prepared the stories for the next broadcast, Jane had time to regret agreeing to publicize Napoli. What if someone else showed up to claim him? But she realized it was too late to back out. When she returned home dinnertime, she went straight to Napoli who was perched on top of the cage. "Yo ho ho," she greeted him. His head bobbed up and down, and he jumped onto the table and the map of Useppa. "Oh no you don't," Jane said. "I don't think Dick would appreciate your walking all over his work."

"I'm not so sure about that." Dick walked toward her from the kitchen. He told her to sit down while he described his day. He had located the copy of "Treasure Island" and read with interest the story of Long John Silver, the pirate always depicted with a parrot on his shoulder and a peg leg. "That song, 'Yo ho ho?'" Jane nodded. "It was about fifteen men fighting over a dead man's treasure chest."

"Okay?" Jane didn't know where he was going with this.

"Treasure. Got it?" He pointed to the X marked on the map. "Napoli did this. I know it sounds crazy, but I think he may be trying to tell me something."

"You have to be joking."

Dick looked at Napoli who, with tilted head, squawked, "And a bottle of rum." He ruffled his feathers and began to preen, looking up at them each time his beak reached the end of a feather.

"Have you been drinking?" Jane stared back and forth between the two of them. "Dick, I mean you. Are you drunk?"

He sank into a chair. "I know how this sounds. But Jane. I know that area where Napoli made the X. It's deep in the woods, a perfect place to hide something. We don't know where he came from. I'm not saying he's the reincarnation of a pirate, but just maybe he learned a secret wherever he came from." He paused. "Or maybe I've just lost my mind." He leaped from the chair. "Okay, let's forget this ever happened. You know me. I'm into science and facts, not woo woo fantasies about treasure chests. No more. I promise."

The next morning, Dick helped Jane move Napoli in his cage down to her car, as he mumbled his objection. "No no no," he protested.

"Don't worry, Napoli, we're off to see Alexandra. It will be fun. Please, just be polite." She wasn't sure how extensive his vocabulary was, and they were planning a live shoot from the shelter. Was she tempting fate by putting an uncensored parrot on the air?

When they arrived at the shelter, they were met by a cameraman from the station. Jane reviewed her notes on what she was going to ask Alexandra and figured she'd be okay if Napoli cooperated.

Alexandra talked a little about the shelter and the need to find good homes for animals of all kinds. Jane took a chance and did her "Yo ho ho" act with Napoli who came through like a pro. The telephone number for the shelter was repeated several times, and they ended with a close-up of Napoli, who seemed delighted with the attention.

Just as she was leaving, a call came in. Alexandra answered and handed Jane the phone. "It's for you. About Napoli."

With a feeling of dread, Jane took the receiver. "This is Jane Gray."

A young male voice said, "My name is Jason, and I'm calling about the bird. He belonged to my grandmother. When she died, he disappeared. I'm sure that's her parrot." When she hesitated, he said, "I'm not going to be able to take him, but it would feel really good to be able to see him again. I didn't get a chance to say goodbye to grandma. This would be the next best thing."

"I have to get back to work now," Jane told him. "Call me at the station tomorrow, and we'll see what we can arrange." She hung up and turned to Alexandra. "Are you sure his owner had no family?"

"The EMTs said the police couldn't find any. They did their best. No one likes the idea of an elderly lady dying alone with no one to bury her."

Jane was still thinking about the so-called grandson the next morning after Dick left for work. He hadn't been happy about Jason's call when she related it to him, and he told her not to trust a stranger with Napoli. "You never should've exposed him this way."

"You're just worried about someone else finding the treasure," she teased, trying not to let him see how worried she was.

As she was getting ready to leave for the station, the intercom down at the entrance to the building rang. She clicked the switch and asked who it was. "It's Jason. I talked to you yesterday about the bird." At the sound of his voice, Napoli started pacing frantically in his cage. "Bad man. Bad man." Jane turned to him. He froze in place and looked at her. "No, Jane, no." It was the first time he had used her name. She looked through the Ring monitor and saw a tall man, in his 20s, attractive, with dark hair, almost to his shoulders.

"How did you find me?"

He looked straight at the camera and winked. "Google, of course."

"I'm not comfortable with this," she said. "Call me at the station the way I told you to."

She waited until she was sure he was gone. "C'mon, Napoli," she said. "I'm not leaving you here alone today."

She hated when Dick was right, but she was forced to admit that the tv appearance had been a bad idea. It was possible that Jason, if that really was his name, was just what he claimed to be, a grandson who missed his grandmother. Even as she thought it, she was shaking her head. She could feel something was wrong with the over-eager Jason.

Hoisting the cage, she walked into the elevator and headed down to her car, her head swiveling to be sure she was alone before she headed to her office.

After settling in at work, Jane turned toward the parrot who was crunching sunflower seeds with such enthusiasm that there were empty shells all over her desk. "If only you could talk." Wait. He could talk. But would he be able to answer questions? She looked around the newsroom to make sure no one was paying attention to her. "Napoli. Who is Jason?"

The bird looked at her over the large shell in his beak. "No Jane. No."

"I know you don't like him, Napoli, but why?" The parrot began to mutter and rock from one foot to the other. "Jason?" she persisted.

Napoli dropped the seed he had been eating and began to screech. She hadn't heard him make that noise before, and it drew the attention of everyone within hearing distance. She knew if it kept up, she'd be told to get Napoli out of there and not bring him back. She couldn't risk it. "It's okay." She lowered her voice. "Really, Napoli, everything is okay. Want another treat?" He stopped and eyed her, judging whether she meant it or not. When she offered him the largest of the remaining seeds, he took it gently from her hand.

"Good Jane," he told her and began crunching the shell to extract the seed.

Jane decided to try again, but at home where no one would be bothered if Napoli decided to tell her off again.

She arrived home before Dick this time. As she opened the front door, she stopped and stared at the destruction of the living room. "Uh oh," Napoli commented as she put his cage on a bookcase next to the door. Should she go in? Call Dick? Call the police?

"Hello?" She shouted so if anyone was there, they would hear her. "The police are on their way." Silence greeted her. Carefully, as if she were walking through broken glass, which she actually was, she methodically searched the apartment. When she returned to the living room, she let out the breath she was holding. The rest of the place had been untouched, but Dick's maps and books were scattered everywhere.

She heard a noise behind her and whirled to see Dick standing in the doorway. "What in the name of....?" He couldn't finish the sentence. "Are you okay?"

Jane nodded. "I am. I took Napoli to work with me, and we just got home. I checked. There's no one here."

"Did you check the Ring video?" She stared at him. How could she have forgotten about their modest security system. But she hadn't received any alerts all day.

Pulling her phone out of her pocket, she clicked on the Ring app and reviewed the video for the day. No one had come near the front door. "He must have come in another way."

Dick circled the room and stopped at the window that looked out on the small garden in back. The window slid easily when he opened it. "It wasn't locked." Jane decided not to remind him that in their division of labor for the apartment, that was on his list.

"But how did he get up to this floor?"

Dick shrugged. "Maybe a ladder. Maybe he has super Spiderman skills. Nothing would surprise me at this point."

"At least he didn't bother the rest of the place."

Dick shook his head. "That's bad news. It means he found what he was looking for." He walked to his worktable and searched the scattered papers. "Oh no." He looked over at Jane. "The map is gone. The one I was working on for Useppa."

"Jason." They said the name together. "Had to be," Jane told him. She described the visit from the stranger that morning. "He saw the Ring doorbell. He knew he couldn't get in past the door without being caught on it. He must've walked around to find another way in. Do you have a copy of the map?"

Dick nodded. "I have a picture of it, but it's not the same. I'm not sure it will show Napoli's addition to it." He grabbed his phone and pulled up his photos. When he found the one he wanted, he zoomed in with his fingers. "It's there. But it won't be hard for Jason to follow it."

"We should get there ahead of him," Jane said.

"He had all day," Dick reminded her.

"But he may not have been prepared to go exploring a place he's probably never been before and that you need a boat to get to. We should go now."

"It's getting dark out," he reminded her.

"But you know that place like it's a second home with all the mapping you've done there. And we have lanterns in our hurricane supplies."

Dick shrugged. "We should be calling the police, you know."

She was determined to get to Napoli's treasure. "We can do that later. C'mon."

***

The marina where they kept Dick's 17' custom workboat was quiet at night. They loaded up their supplies and Napoli and headed out to the Gulf. At the dock on Useppa Island, they tied up next to several other boats that looked as if they hadn't moved in a long time. There was no sign of any recent activity. Dick took the two shovels they had brought and the copy of the map he had printed from his phone. Jane took Napoli who bobbed up and down with excitement in his cage. They made their way into the woods with Dick in the lead, their footsteps crunching on the leaves lightly covering the path. After a half hour of walking, with the cage feeling heavier and heavier in Jane's hand, Dick stopped. "There should be a small clearing just ahead." They stood for a moment, listening, but the woods were silent.

The moonlight shone on a circular area bare of trees. "This must be it." He turned to Jane. "Stay here. If anything happens, make a run for it."

For the first time, Jane felt a wave of fear take her breath away. Were they completely crazy? If Jason was the one who had wrecked their apartment, what else might he be capable of doing? She put the cage on the ground and whispered to Napoli to be quiet, hoping he understood the command. She stepped forward to the edge of the trees and watched Dick study the map and then walk to the center of the clearing. He looked down, and back at the map before lifting one of the shovels and beginning to dig. Napoli began to bounce with excitement. "And a bottle of rum," he muttered.

"Hush." Jane didn't know how to quiet him. Maybe if she stroked him, he'd settle down. She bent over and opened the door to the cage to reach in. As she did, she heard a shout behind her. She whirled around, almost losing her balance. Dick was struggling with Jason who was trying to wrestle the shovel from his hands. "Run, Jane!" Dick shouted.

Instead of running away, Jane ran toward the two men. She wasn't about to abandon her brother. As she approached, she heard a screech behind her and a flash of bright colors flew past. "Napoli!" she screamed. "No!"

As she got closer to the struggle, she saw the bird fly at Jason. He held up his hands but it was too late. Napoli sank his claws into Jason's face as he screeched, "Yo ho ho!" Jason began to try to pull the parrot off him, but Dick picked up his shovel and pulled it back like a baseball bat before whacking the back of Jason's head. Napoli let go as Jason sank to the ground. Dick knelt beside the body and checked for a pulse.

"Is he breathing?" Jane wasn't sure what answer she wanted to hear. Napoli settled on her shoulder.

"Bad man," he told her.

"I know, Napoli, very bad man."

Before Dick could answer, Jason began to moan. As he struggled to sit up, Dick said, "Easy there," and pushed him down. He unhooked the strap on his binoculars and used it to tie Jason's hands behind him. "Now you can sit up, but take your time or I'll sic the bird on you again."

Jason struggled to a sitting position. "Keep him away from me." The blood around his eye began trickling down his face. Napoli chuckled. The rat-a-tat coming from his throat sounded eerily human .

"Let's start from the beginning," Jane said. "Who are you?"

"I told you. I'm Jason Alessio. The bird belonged to my grandmother."

"Let's try that again. Or the next person you'll be talking to will be a policeman."

"It's true," he insisted. Dick reached into Jason's pocket and pulled out a wallet. As he examined the driver's license, he nodded to Jane.

"Jason Alessio," he read. "Wasn't Napoli's owner Margaret Alessio?"

"See? But what I didn't tell you was that my father was the one who owned the bird. Me and Silver never got along, but dad sure loved him. He called him Silver after Long John Silver." When they both nodded, Jason's body relaxed. "Grandma kept Silver when dad went to prison for robbing a jewelry store. Before they caught up with him, he taught Silver to mark the place on a map where he buried the stuff. Then he burned the map." He paused. "Dad died in prison before he could get it back."

"How was he going to get Napoli...I mean Silver to help him find it again if he was in prison?"

"He didn't expect to die there. He told me the secret. If you say 'Bottle of rum' to Silver, he'll show you the right spot on the map. But you need to know which map to use and the words to say."

Jane and Dick looked at each other. What were the odds that they would have happened on the right combination? "We should be playing the lottery," Jane said.

"Why didn't you get him to do his trick after your father died?" Dick asked.

Jason looked down. "I would've but I was locked up myself. Following in the old man's footsteps, I guess. But mine was penny ante stuff. I was shoplifting, things like that. When they caught up with me, I pled out to a misdemeanor theft. Right before I got out, grandma died and Silver went missing."

"You'll do more time than that for attacking my brother," Jane told him.

"Yeah. I messed up. But before you call the cops, could we just look at what Dad buried?"

Jane and Dick hesitated, but their curiosity was as strong as Jason's. Each grabbed a shovel and began to dig, keeping an eye out for any movement from Jason. They both heard the thud as their shovels hit something hard. Dick lay on the ground next to the hole and reached in. He pulled on a strap wrapped around a metal box. As it slowly rose, Napoli became agitated. "Bottle of rum, bottle of rum," he squawked.

The box had a rusty padlock. A few strikes with the shovel and it broke apart. "Want to do the honors?" Dick asked Jane.

She reached down and pulled the clasp open. Lifting the lid, she gasped. Dick raised the lantern they had brought with them. As Napoli howled with glee, they could see the box was filled with birdseed and a folded piece of paper.

Jane opened it and read, "Sorry kid, but I hocked the jewelry to pay a lawyer. If you find this, give Silver a kiss for me."

"Yo ho ho," Napoli sang. "Silver want a kiss."

After a career as a trial attorney in Boston, Wendy Harrison moved to Southwest Florida and became an Assistant State Attorney, supervising the Juvenile Division and prosecuting juvenile sex and gun cases. Since her retirement, she has been writing short mystery stories which have been accepted by numerous anthologies, including *Peace, Love, and Crime*; *Autumn Noir*; *Crimeucopia*: *Tales from the Front Porch*; *Death of a Bad Neighbour*, and the upcoming *More Groovy Gumshoes*.

The Gentleman Thief

Mary Adler

Steam hissed, and glasses clinked, and text messages whooshed through the ether while I ordered the most complicated drink I could find. I was stalling. I hated confrontation, especially when I was angry, and nothing made me angrier than an innocent person being accused unfairly. I'd gathered members of my book club to keep me in check and provide moral support, but I wondered if they understood how much was at stake.

They looked so unconcerned. Rhonda gazed at her phone as if it revealed the secret to eternal slimness, while Lucy unrolled a giant cinnamon bun and ate it inch-by-inch. Meghan flipped her highlighted hair and smiled at an innocent tech type who closed his laptop on his thumb. He needn't have worried about her thinking he was nerdy. She'd already switched her attention to six feet of rugged-good looks with a bad boy vibe.

Only Serena, the object of my wrath, seemed to realize the probable consequences of her accusation. She drummed the table with her turquoise talons and stared at me. I stared back until she looked away, then I watched the barista add a single pump of mocha syrup to my coffee Frappuccino, then a half pump each of caramel syrup, vanilla syrup, toffee-nut syrup, and hazelnut syrup. My queasiness intensified with each pump and my stomach whirled in concert with the blender. Then she poured hot espresso over the frozen drink and topped it with whipped cream. What had I been thinking? I didn't even take sugar in my coffee.

When she called out *Anna*, I offered the sweet drink to anyone in earshot, and a bald man in unfortunate pink shorts threw his hand in the air. I bought a bottle of water and had barely taken a chair when Serena tapped a spoon on her glass. Customers looked over as if expecting a toast from the best man.

I glared at her. "Everyone in Starbucks doesn't need to hear you accuse Janice of being a thief. Especially since she'd never steal anything, least of all your ugly Gucci wallet."

"Please." Serena rolled her eyes. "You know as well as I do that she always needs money for those animals." *Animals* dripped with the disdain most people reserved for drug dealers.

She dismissed my reminder that she was in the book club only because of Janice's kindness, a virtue Serena lacked. If she were on trial, even the most compassionate jury would condemn her because of her past bad acts, starting with third grade, when she'd pushed Lucy's new bicycle into the Russian River.

"What about that new guy who helps her at the rescue? The one with the tattoos." Rhonda looked up from her phone. "He must have interrupted our discussion three or four times."

"Tattoo man *did* linger." Lucy leaped at the new suspect.

Meghan kicked me under the table, a warning not to mention that Tattoo and she had been doing some leaping of their own. She was only twelve years older than he was. I didn't see the problem.

"Did he come in while I was in the loo?" Serena looked around the table at our shrugs and don't know expressions. "You were probably talking about dogs and wouldn't have noticed Chris Hemsworth doing push-ups on the table."

"Who's Chris Hemsworth." Lucy licked icing from her fingers and gazed at the pastry case. "Is he the new obedience judge?"

Serena rolled her eyes. She is not, as she boasts, a dog person. Another reason she shouldn't be in our book club.

"Consider what you're asking us do to, Serena." I appealed to her better nature. Talk about a Hail Mary play.

"If I'm wrong, I'll resign from the book club," she said, her smile worthy of Cruella de Vil. "But if I'm right, we withdraw our support from Safe Haven Rescue."

"And what would you suggest we do with the money we'll raise at our book sale instead of giving it to the rescue?" I wanted to know what she valued more than animals in need.

"Mani-pedis, a spa day? Don't worry. We'll put the money to good use." She dabbed her lips with a napkin.

None of us, except Serena, would waste a spare sixty dollars on a manicure when we had so many doggie mouths to feed. Of course, the only mouth she had to feed was her own. "The money goes to the rescue, Serena."

She sat back in her chair and crossed her arms. "Then Janice resigns."

"If Janice resigns, I resign." Rhonda crossed her arms to a chorus of "Me too 's."

Serena lowered her voice. "Janice confesses, or I go to the police." She picked up the leather bag that matched her nails. "Tomorrow at noon at your precious rescue." The heels of her turquoise shoes clicked toward the door.

Why would anyone care if her fingernails matched her shoes? That matched her purse? Why did I care? Actually, I didn't, but I'd rather think about Serena's fashion choices than her threat to go to the police. Several dog rescues competed for a limited amount of local money. A hint of impropriety and Safe Haven would plummet to the bottom of the list. Unfortunately, an accusation of theft, even unfounded, amounted to more than a hint.

***

I called Janice and told her what had happened. Her long silence hurt my heart.

"I'm sorry I said *yes* when Serena asked if she could join the book club." Regret flattened her voice. "This is my punishment for not asking the rest of you first."

It was her punishment for being kind to the woman who had stolen her boyfriend when we were in high school. "She's sure her wallet disappeared at your house."

"The rest of you would have asked me privately if I'd seen it and believed me when I said no. And that would have been the end of it."

"Because we trust you. Serena doesn't trust anyone." Because she was untrustworthy herself? Be that as it may, it was no excuse for hurting someone as gentle as Janice. Again.

"The thing is" ––she hesitated–– "the thing is, Serena's wallet isn't the only thing to disappear recently."

"What else is missing?"

"My bank deposit and another wallet."

"How much? Never mind––it's none of my business."

"It was only eighty-eight dollars, thank goodness."

She operated on a shoestring. Independent bookstores had rosier financial futures than the rescue did. "Do you think it could be Tattoo?"

"Tattoo? Where are we? Fantasy Island?"

"The new worker with a mountain lion peeking out from his collar and a rabbit hopping down his arm. He's a walking promotion for *Wild Kingdom*."

"Do you mean Brent?" Her voice got dreamy.

Her, too? "Your illustrated man's tattoos look expensive. With his wages, he'd be hard pressed to pay for a tattoo of a mosquito."

"It's his Hogwarts Express wallet that was stolen. His niece gave it to him and he doesn't want to tell her he's lost it."

Maybe he said his wallet had been stolen to deflect suspicion. "When did things start to go missing?"

"About a month ago? Soon after our trip to the Porterville Shelter."

Porterville Shelter did its best, but it couldn't keep unclaimed dogs indefinitely, so Safe Haven and other rescues took the dogs whose time was almost up.

"I like one of the new dogs." She drew in a breath. "A lot."

"You don't need another dog." We always needed another dog. "Tell me about it?"

"Not it, him. You met him at our last book club meeting."

"Well, that narrows it down. We met six dogs that day."

"He looks like a border collie––long coat, floppy ears, but a bully head. He's pure joy. I don't think I can give him up. I named him Felix ."

"Felix suits a happy fella. He and the golden mix charmed us all." All but Serena.

"He's brought Buttercup, the golden, to life––at last. She might be in love." The gate bell chimed in the background and she said a quick good bye.

***

The next morning, I woke with a headache. A bad start to a day that promised to get worse. After coffee and two aspirin, I fed the dogs and we drove into town to pick up Janice's favorite apple tarts––something to sweeten the bitterness of Serena's accusation. It seemed churlish to expect Janice to cater her own trial.

Back at home, I worked in my herb garden, far from the siren song of cinnamon and pastry, while I waited for Lucy. Before she'd even turned into our drive, the dogs had run to the gate and sat perfectly, obedience-ring ready––except for the saliva pooling by Zoe's paws. Lucy never visited without something special for them.

"How's Janice supposed to prove she didn't take Serena's wallet?" Lucy passed out homemade salmon treats. "Trial by ordeal?"

"We'll convince Serena. Somehow. No one is going to the police."

When I opened the back door of Lucy's clunker to stow my tote, I disturbed a chicken who fluffed and mumbled as it nestled into a sweatshirt.

"Lucy?"

She looked across the car's peeling roof.

"You're taking free-range to a whole new level."

She frowned and hunched her shoulders with the little head shake that meant *What are you talking about?*

I pointed at the backseat.

"Rusty." Her voice caressed the hen she had nursed back to health after a bobcat attack. "Let's get you home, sweetie." She glanced at her watch. "Do you mind? We'll be a few minutes late."

"I'm happy to put off this meeting as long as we can."

***

Neither of us had much to say on the way to Janice's. We breathed in the pungent smell of eucalyptus that overpowered the faint odor Rusty had left behind. A few russet feathers swirled in the air while we drove through gentle green hills adorned with cows and sheep, the occasional discarded appliance, and ornate gates protecting multi-million-dollar estates.

Janice's rescue was on her grandparents' five-hundred-acre ranch, isolated enough that the noise from barking dogs wouldn't bother incomers from San Francisco and Silicon Valley who paid over-asking to live in the country, then complained when smells from a dairy farm lingered around their swimming pools or machinery clanked through the vineyards at two in the morning.

I told Lucy about Felix.

"No." Lucy groaned. "She's keeping him? How many does that make? Five?"

"Six." On the way to seven.

We were late, but still the first to arrive except for Serena, who was eager to rush to judgment. I set my tote on the floor and admired the six-burner range from the summer kitchen where Janice's grandmother had made jam and canned home-grown vegetables during the hottest days of the year. It reminded me of a slower time, when sheets smelled of sunshine and porch swings squeaked on violet-hued evenings. The ringing phone nudged me from my wistful thoughts. I answered the Safe Haven line before a potential donor or adopter skipped to the next rescue on their list.

"Safe Haven Rescue. Anna speaking."

My heart dropped and I asked the man to repeat himself. That's what I thought he said. He was Felix's owner. He thought he was just a few minutes away but had gotten turned around and needed directions. I stammered and asked him to hold while I called for Janice.

She'd been expecting him.

"After we talked yesterday, Brent scanned the recent batch of dogs." She smiled a rueful kind of smile. "The identification chips in two of the dogs had migrated. Felix was one of them. Brent got in touch with his owner, while I called Porterville and told them to re-scan their dogs. Immediately. They promised never to allow an inexperienced volunteer to scan dogs again."

I shuddered. Felix could have died despite his owner's best efforts to keep him safe.

Janice took the phone, and I followed the sound of angry voices to the patio. Rhonda and Meghan had arrived while I was in the kitchen. They stared open-mouthed at Serena and Lucy who looked as if they were about to come to blows.

"Be quiet and sit down. Both of you." I hadn't used that voice since I'd chaperoned a high school trip to Lake Tahoe. Apparently, it still worked. "Someone is coming for a dog. Not another word about why we're here until he's gone."

Lucy asked which dog and Serena rolled her eyes. When I said Felix, Lucy's eyes misted. I told them about Janice and Felix and the chip. We all knew how quickly a special dog could steal your heart and how hard it was to lose him.

"That has nothing to do with why we're here." Serena straightened in her chair.

"Stop!" Rhonda, who greeted the morning sun and gave gifts to the earth, shocked us with her tone. She waved a finger in Serena's face. "Don't say another word. We'll continue this charade tomorrow."

Serena's lip curled. "Today or tomorrow. She's still a thief."

I went for the coffee and found Janice sniffling over the sugar bowl. I took it from her and reached into my tote for a tissue. I wasn't one of those women who carried around everything from a Swiss army knife to false eyelashes, but I did have tissues. Tissues, but no wallet. Who'd been in here? The backdoor was open so anyone could have taken it. Tattoo? Despite what Janice thought?

I couldn't heap this on her now. I'd let her recover from losing Felix, or Raffles, as the man claiming to be his owner had called him. "Are you sure he's Felix's owner?"

"He knew he was missing a toenail." She wiped her eyes and now red nose. "He didn't know what had happened to it. They adopted him when he was about a year old."

The dogs barked. Our cue to put on brave faces and meet Randolph, Felix's owner. The Volvo station wagon had barely stopped when a man in jeans and a plaid shirt opened the door. Chris Hemsworth was probably safe, but Randolph would give Tattoo a run for his money. When Janice tried to smile at him, concern softened his expression.

"You've fallen for Raffles, haven't you?" He smiled, and Chris Hemsworth was no longer safe.

Before she could answer, a black-and-white projectile leaped into Randolph's arms and licked the tears that glistened on his cheeks, leaving us in no doubt who Raffle's heart belonged to. Even Serena wiped her eyes. Then she pulled down her upper lid to flush out a foreign body.

If any of God's creatures belonged together, it was Randolph and Raffles, so it surprised us when the dog jumped from his arms and took off. Randolph called for him, but he didn't come.

"Did you give him a toy?" His dark eyes looked like melted chocolate.

"Yes. A hedgehog."

"His favorite." He relaxed. "He probably went to fetch it."

"Come have some coffee or iced tea while we're waiting." Janice took his arm. "We aren't often lucky enough to hear the dogs' stories. Tell us about him."

We settled at the table. Even Serena sat and listened, although it was probably Randolph's dimples that had captured her, not the tale of his dog. No pun intended.

"My daughter and I found Raffles at the shelter. He looked like an alien. Like ET, all skin and wrinkles and enormous eyes. She fell in love with him, but I was hesitant to adopt a pit bull." His shrug was both sheepish and repentant. "We try not to let bad press influence us, but it does, subconsciously, and I'd never had a bully breed. Then Raffles threw his toy in the air and pounced on it, and we laughed out loud. We couldn't resist his joyfulness, so we trusted our instincts. And him."

"You adopted a bald dog?" Serena sounded appalled.

"Hard to believe now. His fur started to grow and didn't stop. We call him a pit-bull-in-disguise. Makes it easier that people don't fear him on sight."

"How'd you lose him?" When Janice asked, we all held our breaths. Except Serena. She didn't know how much we hoped this man had not neglected his dog or put him at risk.

"We came home one night––the dogs were in the house, of course––and the back door had been jimmied. Raffles was gone." Remembered grief shadowed his face. "We hoped he'd run and hid when the house was broken into, but he didn't come back. Then we found out a friend of his former owner, who was in jail, had stolen him."

"To reunite them?" I could almost forgive that. Almost.

"No. Because they wanted to use his special talents."

Meghan asked how he thought Raffles had ended up in Porterville and Rhonda wanted to know what special talents Raffles had.

Randolph nodded at Rhonda, a promise to answer her next. "We think the thief brought him south, and Raffles escaped. He can open doors and crates. Either that, or Raffles wouldn't work for him and he abandoned him."

"The vet said Raffles had a healed injury to his jaw that could have been made by being hit by a car." Or something else hung in the air, but we ignored it. Janice pursed her lips. "He wouldn't be the first dog who'd been abandoned when he needed vet care." Medical bills drained the rescue's funds, but she never turned away an injured animal.

Randolph looked around. "Where do you think he went?"

"He'll be back." Janice refilled his coffee. "The way he greeted you leaves me in no doubt."

He seemed pleased that she recognized how much his dog loved him.

Rhonda asked about Raffle's special talents again.

"We think the person who owned him originally, the one in jail, ran a street gang downtown."

"He was a drug mule. Dog." Crumbs flew from the tart Lucy waved around. "You know what I mean."

Randolph shook his head. "No, he was useful because––"

Barking interrupted our conversation. That happened a lot. Buttercup ran next to Raffles who carried a plastic bucket by the handle. He pranced toward us, his tail waving like a drum major's baton, then set the bucket at Randolph's feet.

"One of his talents." He removed Raffle's hedgehog and reached into the bucket. He held up my wallet and looked around the table. I reached for it.

"Your wallet, too?" Serena's eyes narrowed. She might have been contemplating a class action suit.

I nodded.

"When did that happen?" Janice held the back of her hand against her forehead.

"You look like the damsel-in-distress in the credits of *Mystery*. I mimicked the character's wan cries for help.

"Very funny." She rolled her hand in a *get-on-with-it* gesture. "Your wallet."

"It disappeared this afternoon. I didn't want to tell you with everything that was happening."

Raffles wagged his tail and looked proud of himself when Randolph produced a red Hogwarts Express wallet.

"That's Brent's." Meghan pointed, then stammered, "I think."

"Hmm." Rhonda raised an eyebrow.

Randolph interrupted Rhonda's inquisition of Meghan when he pulled out a bank deposit envelope and a wallet with interlocking G's.

"You stole it and the dog found it." Serena grabbed the wallet.

Randolph took Janice's hand. "I'm so sorry. Someone trained Raffles to take money from people's purses. He even lifted a wallet from a friend's back pocket without him noticing. We thought we had extinguished the behavior, but the people who took him must have used him to steal again."

"But why would he put them in a bucket?" Lucy furrowed her brow.

"He puts his toys in their basket at night. In his eyes, the hedgehog and the wallets were his." Randolph shrugged. "That's my best guess."

Serena counted the money in her wallet. She seemed disappointed so I assumed nothing was missing.

The silence stretched until I thought it would snap.

Randolph broke the tension. "I should be going." He pulled a leash from his pocket and dropped it on the ground. Raffles folded it and picked it up in his mouth. "Another of his talents."

We dog-people applauded.

Randolph handed an envelope to Janice. "There's nothing I can do to repay you, but I hope this helps you save other dogs who end up in... well, in the kind of place Raffles did. He would have died without your help. My card's in the envelope. If you ever need anything, call me. Anything. Any time."

Most of us teared up and hugged him and Raffles goodbye. He lifted the hatch of the station wagon and opened a variogate, a barrier crash-tested to keep dogs safe in a cargo area. Many people who traveled with dogs coveted them or variocages, but they were expensive.

Janice admired the gate and divider. "It's set up for two dogs."

"Our lab died a few weeks ago. She was fifteen." His eyes glistened. "You love them when they're young and think you couldn't love them more, and then the love deepens and deepens. There's something special about old dogs ."

Buttercup had backed away from the car and shrunk into herself. She seemed to be vanishing. Raffles looked at Randolph and woofed around the leash in his mouth.

"Raffles and Buttercup have bonded." Janice smiled, mischief in her eyes. "We can do the paperwork online."

Randolph knelt in front of Buttercup. "Want to go for a ride?"

She tilted her head. Raffles spun around and bumped her shoulder. She didn't move, and he bumped her until she wagged her tail. While Randolph helped her into the car, Raffles sat in front of Janice and raised a paw.

She hugged him and choked out a tearful, *you're welcome*, and Raffles hopped in next to Buttercup. I felt my heart lurch. Special wasn't the word for him. He was a once-in-a-lifetime-if-you're-lucky kind of dog.

We watched until the Volvo was out of sight.

"His name should have been a clue." My stomach growled, heeding the call of the apple tarts.

"Raffles. The gentleman thief." Trust Meghan to know about a gentleman thief.

"I thought Cary Grant was the gentleman thief," Lucy said.

"In a different era. Raffles was a contemporary of Sherlock Holmes." I took her arm and led her to the table.

"I see now why you do this." Serena's hand waved to include the rescue and the dogs. She gathered her belongings. "I should have trusted you, all of you. I'm sorry."

I looked at Meghan. She only had eyes for Brent, who had come for his wallet. I cleared my throat, and she gave me a *What?* look. I shifted my eyes toward Serena, and Meghan nodded. Lucy mouthed *okay* to Janice. Janice hesitated, then smiled. Rhonda picked up on the silent vote and shrugged *okay*.

I hesitated. Serena would have reported Janice to the police and put Safe Haven in jeopardy. Fortunately for Serena, we believed forgiveness is a gift you give yourself.

"You're welcome to stay, Serena. But it's your last chance."

I wished I hadn't seen the flash of victory in her eyes.

We poured more coffee and ate tarts, and Janice opened the envelope Randolph had given her. She seemed unable to speak. I leaned over and looked at the check. I didn't know what to say, either. Janice passed the check around.

Serena's eyes grew wide. "One hundred thousand dollars. That's a lot of mani-pedis ."

Mary Adler lives in northern California with her husband and their latest rescue dogs, Charley and Luc. She writes mysteries set in Northern California during World War II that feature homicide detective Oliver Wright and his German shepherd, Harley. The stories, set against the harsh reality of wartime, are tempered by the warmth of friends, of food shared, and, of course, wonderful dogs. Join her in starting each day with the question poet Mary Oliver poses:" Tell me, what is it you plan to do with your one wild and precious life?"

A Hare-Raising Haunting

C.K. Fyfe

T oot-toot!

Not again. Emma released an exaggerated sigh and dashed toward the front door. This time she would catch the pranksters in the act! Her bare feet slapped across the hardwood floor as she zigzagged through a trail of scattered moving boxes. Emma's chest practically bounced toward her chin, as her middle-aged knees crackled like a bowl of Rice Krispies and her thighs flapped akin to chicken wings. Determination trumping humiliation, she grabbed the copper train doorknob and yanked open the front door.

Nothing but nightfall and the rope pulley on the train-horn doorbell swinging in an autumn breeze. The crisp air nipped at her cheeks, and fiery orange and scarlet leaves rained down onto the ground. She listened for giggling resonating in the trees surrounding her property. Only an eerie silence prevailed.

Emma shut the door. Small-town living was supposed to be peaceful, unlike the noise of the city she'd left behind. So far that dream hadn't panned out. She'd moved into the train depot in Michigan's Upper Peninsula a week ago, and every night since, tricksters had been ringing the station's doorbell. Had the spirit of Halloween captured their attention early this year?

Returning to the living room, Emma paused to examine a wall mural near what used to be the train station ticket counter. Landmarks from the area, including Pictured Rocks National Lakeshore and Tahquamenon Falls, had been painted alongside a steam locomotive. Local legend claimed that when the locomotive's engineer died, his ghost remained trapped inside the building, haunting its halls long after the final passengers had departed, and the station closed forever.

Emma gulped. Was the engineer blasting the horn to frighten her, or for fun? The flames hissed in the stone fireplace, drawing Emma's attention back to the task at hand, namely unpacking the last load of boxes. A powerful sense of uneasiness engulfed her as she hustled into the bedroom .

Pepper, Emma's steel-gray Flemish Giant rabbit, lay at the foot of the bed chewing a plush raccoon. Pepper had come to her as a foster, but as the months passed, she had fallen in love with the rabbit's docile personality and quirky disposition. The arrangement had resulted in a total "Foster Fail" when Emma had decided to adopt her. Finally, Pepper stopped chewing her toy, but only to whimper.

The whimpering had become commonplace during the past week. Not to mention an episode or two of growling and thumping, which were unusual for her laid-back bunny. Emma worried that she'd made a mistake moving Pepper to a strange environment. Perhaps the change had been too much of a strain.

Emma petted Pepper's silky fur until the whimpering subsided. "Hey, sweet girl. I thought you were supposed to help me unpack?"

Pepper twitched her nose but didn't budge.

Somehow Emma doubted the rabbit felt guilty for slacking on the job. "All right. I'll finish emptying the boxes. Hope I won't be too tired to feed you a bedtime treat."

Pepper leapt to her feet at the magic word and jumped in short bursts, sending the myriad of stuffed animals off the bed.

Emma laughed and removed a knitting basket that had belonged to her grandmother from one of the large boxes. Balls of yarn had spilled all over the box. She tossed them on the bed and placed the basket on the floor. "Pepper, can you swat the yarn in for me?"

Pepper happily obliged and pushed a ball with her nose until it rolled off the bed and settled into the basket.

"Good girl." She smiled at Pepper. As she neared fifty, Emma's hair had begun to turn gray like Pepper's fur. Seeing how Emma didn't have a man to impress and her job as a programmer allowed her to work from home, there was no need spending money on hair coloring and touch-ups that were routine for daily life in a concrete jungle.

Toot-toot!

Here we go again. Emma sprinted through the obstacle course of boxes and belongings. She leapt over Pepper's playtime bunny tunnel; housewarming table linens with a turkey chorus line design too hideous to even use in Pepper's litter pan; and a stack of well-meaning books from her mom. The novels bore titles like *Reel him In, or Throw him Back?* and *Hunting for a Hero, not a Zero,* she hadn't yet organized on the shelves .

Emma hurdled another box and skidded on a braided rug in the foyer. Exhaling a ragged breath, she jerked open the door. "Leave me alone!"

Danielle lifted her head, peeking out from underneath a wide-brimmed hat. "Sorry. Thought you might like a little company, eh? I brought mini-apple pies from The Sweet Spot."

Relief washed over Emma. The visitor was her neighbor, who lived a mile down the railroad tracks. The two had met on the day Emma arrived in Conifer Falls in an embarrassing situation at a diner in town. Not being a Michigan native, Emma had ordered a traditional Upper Peninsula pasty, but she had mispronounced the name, enunciating it as "pay-stee" instead of "pass-tee." Danielle, her server, had been quick to correct Emma's faux pas as snickering from other customers wafted toward her table. The name had indeed puzzled Emma, considering there was a significant difference between a meat and veggie filled pastry and a woman's nipple cover.

"Please forgive me," Emma said. "Come in." She stepped aside and waved her arm for Danielle to enter.

"You sure?"

"Positive."

Danielle wiped her shoes on the rug and hung her hat on an antique coat stand. "What's going on? Why did you shout at me to go away?"

"I wasn't yelling at you. I was scolding the person, or ghost, playing a joke on me."

"Ghost?"

"Yeah. Follow me." Emma led Danielle down the hallway. Loose floorboards creaked underneath their feet and the spoke wheels on the kitchen's sliding barn door squeaked when Emma pushed it aside. She rummaged in the cupboards and drawers for plates and forks while her friend settled in at the dining table. In a flash, Emma set the items on the table and dropped onto a chair opposite Danielle. "I think the deceased train engineer is haunting me."

Danielle laughed and jabbed a fork into her pie. "You're not serious?"

"Oh, yes, I am. Someone keeps ringing the doorbell, but nobody's there."

"It's probably the wind. The U.P. is known for wild weather swings. That's the reason Michiganders always say if you don't like the weather, wait five minutes."

"No way. I don't buy that."

"Believe what you want."

Emma bit her lower lip and wrung her hands. "There's more. I've seen a man's profile hovering outside in the evenings. I know it's the same person because he has one leg that is shorter than the other. And according to my online research, the train engineer was a polio survivor who also had a short leg."

"Listen, I've lived in this town my entire life. I've never seen the train engineer, or any other specter." Danielle scooped the forkful into her mouth. "Mmm."

Emma's frustration mounted while Danielle devoured her dessert. Unassuaged by her friend's remark, she stood and turned to gaze outside the large kitchen window. She gasped and jumped back. A shadowy figure limped across the railroad tracks, veering toward the edge of the woods. Its silhouette loomed over a large hollow log blanketed with fallen leaves. Emma gaped open-mouthed, speechless, and gripped the edge of the farmhouse sink.

Danielle tsked. "City folk. Now what's wrong?"

"That's him! The man I told you about! He's here again." Emma pressed her nose against the window and squinted into the inky night. The man sidled into a sliver of moonlight too small for her to clearly see his face and stared at the depot. Emma's pulse pounded in her ears as the seconds slowly ticked by. Eventually, he pivoted on his heels and walked away. "I'm telling you. He's stalking me."

"Calm down." Danielle stood and peered out the window. "I don't see anyone."

Emma twisted her hair around her finger. It was a nervous habit she'd acquired in elementary school during those awful spelling bees. The pressure to spell words while hundreds of people gawked at her on stage was too much for her introverted personality. Now the same wave of fear from yesteryear resurfaced. "Maybe we should call the sheriff?"

"And tell him what? To come arrest a ghost?" Danielle steered Emma into the living room and over to the couch. "Sit. Relax. No one is stalking you. Dollars to doughnuts you saw one of the locals taking a stroll along the train tracks. It's not uncommon."

The pitter-patter of paws grew closer. Pepper entered the room, dragging her plush raccoon in her mouth. She laid the toy at Emma's feet and growled.

"What's wrong with your rabbit?" Danielle asked.

"I don't know."

Pepper stomped her back feet and lunged at the raccoon.

Emma patted the couch cushion. "Pepper. Come here. Use your ramp."

Pepper hopped up the ramp. After planting her paws on the sky-blue cushion, she looked fixedly at the ceiling.

"What a weird coincidence," Danielle said. "When I was younger, I had a cat who used to stare at the ceiling. Kind of freaked me out." She picked up the toy. "This raccoon is pretty realistic. Maybe that's why Pepper clobbered it."

"Or maybe she's trying to tell us something." Emma stood and studied the ceiling. Nothing there except the peeling paint she hadn't had time to fix and cobwebs the size of doilies tucked in the corners. She sighed and lowered her gaze. *What had frightened Pepper?*

Pepper flattened her ears and thumped her feet.

Eager to solve the mystery, Emma craned her neck once more. A dull, distant plodding sound reached her ears. The hair on her neck lifted, and her adrenaline spiked. "Wait! Did you hear that?"

"What?" Danielle rose and eased alongside her. "I only hear your heart beating out of your chest."

"Never mind my chest. Did you hear the footsteps? Someone's walking on the roof."

"Santa Claus? Boy, he's confused! The elves better make him a calendar for Christmas and tell him to lay off the eggnog."

"I'm glad you find the situation so amusing."

"Jeez-o-Pete! It's probably a squirrel, or the red fox I've spotted roaming the area."

"A fox? On the roof?"

"It happens."

"In that case, maybe you should sleep here tonight. It might not be safe walking out to your truck."

"Nah. I'll be all right. It won't attack me. Besides, my husband says I'm so doggone feisty that even wild animals wouldn't dare mess with me."

Emma chuckled. Her laughter floating between them appeared to calmed Pepper's anxiety, as the fluffball relaxed her rigid stance.

Danielle clamped a hand on Emma's shoulder. "Come on. Finish eating your pie."

Two hours later, when the pie, and Danielle, were gone, Emma lay awake in bed curled up with Pepper. Perhaps she'd taken the legend too literally and had imagined the shadowy figure.

A familiar creak resounded in the silence: the floorboards leading toward the kitchen. Someone was in the house! She snatched her cell phone off the nightstand. The battery icon blinked. *Don't die on me!* Her fingers fumbled over the numbers. She dialed 9-1... No! The screen faded to black along with her hope of summoning help.

She quietly slinked out of bed, not wanting to disturb Pepper. Standing in the middle of the room, Emma twisted her hair around her finger. What could she use as a weapon? Emma considered a handheld mirror laying on her dresser. Nah. The only horrifying thing about the mirror was her reflection in it.

Think! What else can I use? Emma crept around the room, passing on a pair of pink bunny slippers, a Tom Selleck coconut-scented candle, and a lace brassiere she assumed many men would call an over-the-shoulder boulder holder. If she had MacGyver's skills, she could convert the brassiere into a makeshift slingshot. Running out of ideas, Emma sneaked down the hallway to the bathroom and snatched a can of hairspray to spritz the intruder in the eyes. Knowing her luck, he'd be wearing glasses.

She stepped into the hallway and squinted toward the kitchen. Footsteps echoed behind her. Emma spun around to discover Pepper racing past her with a ball of loose yarn in her mouth. "Pepper, no," she whispered.

Emma followed the yarn trail in the dim glow of a nightlight. Pepper must have detected the intruder, too. However, Emma couldn't comprehend why Pepper would run into danger instead of hiding. She chalked it up to another behavior change caused by their move to the boonies.

"Pepper," Emma muttered, hoping to hear the familiar pitter-patter of paws in response. In the hushed silence, anxiety constricted her throat. *Terrific.* She'd lost track of Pepper.

Emma tiptoed along, panic bubbling up deep inside when she noticed the front door had been left ajar. She scrambled to the door and gently closed it. Her heart hammered against her ribs at the thought of Pepper having run outside.

Emma glanced around the room for her rabbit, but Pepper's gray fur proved difficult to discern in the dark. She continued tiptoeing down the hallway. The floorboards creaked up ahead. Emma's feet froze to the spot when the outline of a man's body appeared in the kitchen doorway. She gulped and raised her can of hairspray, wishing the intruder really was the train engineer's ghost. No such luck; the illusory figure that had haunted her from outside was unfortunately flesh and bones.

The man limped out of the kitchen and scraped his shoes across the floor, inching closer.

Emma trembled at the grating screech of each footstep heading toward her. To her dismay, the nightlight's soft glow veiled his visage in shadows, so she still had no clue who he might be.

"I've got you now," he said.

He took another step and fell to the floor with a thud.

Emma gasped and ran over to the kitchen door. She spotted Pepper hunched behind a box, with one end of the string of yarn in her mouth and the other tangled around the man's feet. Her stomach roiled as she firmly placed her finger on the spray nozzle and narrowed her eyes.

"Who are you? What do you want?" The words squeaked out while she looked down at him.

The front door crashed open behind her. Emma whirled around and spewed a shot of hairspray into the air. Even in the mist, she could see the wrong end of a shotgun. *Uh-oh.*

"Emma!"

"Danielle? Oh, thank goodness! What are you doing here?"

Danielle coughed and waved away the hairspray. "Decided to make a pitstop at your place on my way back from late-night bingo and saw your front door wide open. I must have forgotten to lock it when I left. Hurried home to get my gun. You all right?"

"I'm not sure. Turn on the lights."

The room brightened, and Emma stared at the man lying on her floor rubbing his neck. She'd never seen him before.

Danielle marched forward. "Colton? What in blazes are you doing on the floor, eh?"

"Wait. You know him?"

"Yes. He's the area wildlife rehabilitator."

Colton pointed at the gun facing his direction. "Mind putting that peashooter away first so I can stand up?"

Danielle nodded and lowered her shotgun. "Start explaining why you're prowling around the house and harassing my friend."

"I mean no harm to your friend. I was out searching for one of my critters who'd gotten loose when I saw the depot door open. Thought I better have a look and make sure nothing funny was going on. Anyway, I saw a furry critter run across the house, and I thought I finally caught the little rascal." Colton untied the yarn and turned his attention to Emma. "Sorry I startled you."

"Forget it. I appreciate you checking on me. It was sweet of you." Emma smiled when he blushed and slanted his gaze onto the floor. "Would you like Danielle and I to help you find, uh, what is it you're searching for?"

Toot-toot!

Emma seized Danielle's arm. "Come with me. Maybe you can scare the pranksters away." She bolted alongside her neighbor while Colton's footsteps thundered behind them. Crossing the threshold, Emma saw a masked bandit sitting on the porch bench tugging the train-horn pulley. She shook her head, and a loud laugh escaped her lips. "It's a raccoon!"

Colton pushed past Emma and tromped onto the porch. "Raidyn! Where have you been?" He plucked the raccoon off the bench and cradled it in his arms.

"Is this the animal you lost?" Emma asked.

"Yep. Emma, Danielle, meet Raidyn. The lil' stinker ran away instead of waiting until he was old enough, and big enough, to be released."

Danielle grinned. "Looks like Raidyn managed just fine. Would have been nice if he hadn't scared poor Emma by tooting the doorbell."

Colton stroked the raccoon's bushy tail. "Sorry about that. Raidyn loves ropes. He enjoys tugging and swinging on my barn rope."

"Forget it. I'm glad he's okay," Emma said.

"He was probably also drawn to the hollowed out log over yonder. The problem is that raccoons have multiple dens, which is why I had trouble locating him." Colton tightened his grip on Raidyn. "I better get him back to my place."

Danielle jiggled her keys. "And I need to get home, too."

Emma waved goodnight and strode into the depot. Pepper sat waiting on the rug beside the coat stand. "Good news. We can finally relax and catch some z's. How does that sound?"

Pepper hopped up, twisted in the air, and zoomed into the living room.

"Sounds terrific, huh?" Emma chuckled and followed Pepper. When she strolled by the mural, a shifting shadow on the train surprised her. She screwed up her eyes and winced. The ghostly engineer stood on the steam locomotive's steps and tipped his cap.

Emma swallowed hard. So much for their quiet night.

C.K. Fyfe has always enjoyed a good mystery. Fyfe's childhood love of Nancy Drew and The Hardy Boys led to a grown-up love of writing cozy mysteries with quirky, funny, and kindhearted characters. Fyfe lives in "The Wolverine State." Much like wolverines, Fyfe's villains have vicious dispositions, but the clever sleuths know how to tame their foes' tempers.

The Bust

Adam Sales

The mile markers flew by as I fumbled with the radio. "...another eleven overdose fatalities this week. We've got to attack this plague..." I tapped the off button, grabbed my coffee tanker for a swig, and returned it to the cup holder. It was my third of the day—one is usually sufficient. Sure, my left foot was dancing as my fingers drummed the wheel, but it was the only thing keeping me awake after being up half the night.

Steph had started awake for reasons unknown to me—those first minutes remain groggy. She kicked me out of bed to patrol the house. With fireplace poker in hand, I turned on the yard lights and reluctantly stepped outside. The black-and-whites showed up a minute later, but not at our residence, two doors down—Mark Adams, single, no kids. Shortly after that, the ambulance showed up, without flashing lights or sirens. He was wheeled out on a gurney covered with a sheet. His overdose wasn't a surprise; he'd been battling addiction ever since his knee surgery.

My phone buzzed again. It was in the console adjacent to my seat and the woman with the pleasant voice who lived behind the dashboard audio-visual screen asked if she could read the text.

"It's from Dad, yelling at me that I'm late again," I said to her.

She started, "From Dad, 'Where are you? I'm waiting.'"

"See, I told you it was from Dad." I took the downward ramp to arrivals and followed the traffic to passenger pick-up. I cut in to the curb with hazard lights flashing.

Dad remained in place until I parked. "I've been sending you texts. Have you been getting my texts? You're late."

I ignored his grumbles. "This is quite the piece of luggage for a weekend trip." I heaved the trunk into the back of the SUV.

"My toothbrush and a pair of underwear—that's it! Everything else is from your mother—every day is Christmas. And today at 9:00 in the morning, she was waiting at the pet store to get something for this orphaned dog of yours."

"He's not our dog and he's not orphaned. Mark didn't have a dog; he must have been pet sitting. We'll find the owners and get him back home," I said pulling away from the curb.

"Exactly, it's not even your dog, but your mother sends him presents anyway," he said.

"What did she send?"

"I don't know, but hopefully there's a watch in there for you so you can pay attention to the time once in a while. She also sent you a bong."

My jaw involuntarily dropped. "A what?"

"A bong," he repeated.

"Um...uh, do you know what that is Dad?"

"Yes, it's what your mother sent you!"

I hit the phone button on the steering wheel. "Call Mom."

"Calling Mom." I wondered if that magical voice started from a real person and if so, what she looks like?

"Hi sweetheart." Mom picked up. "Have you connected with your father? You know his flight landed early."

"Yes, I know, but I'm not sure he does," I said.

"He was late," Dad shouted from the passenger seat. "Tell him why you send so many presents that I can't even bring a pair of pants."

"Yes, I got him," I said. "Hey Mom? Dad said something about a bong?"

"That's because your Dad is hard of hearing," Mom said. "It's a Kong, and it's not for you, it's for that precious orphan you took in last night. Encourage your father to get hearing aids."

"The only reason I might need hearing aids is because you've been yelling at me for thirty-seven years," Dad said.

"Enjoy the gifts sweetheart and send pictures of Madelyn in her new outfits."

"Do I wear a brown uniform?" Dad was yelling at the dashboard again. "Do I drive a truck that says Amazon? This is work and there are people you pay to do it."

"Thanks for letting me know he got there safely, sweetheart."

***

Before the garage door was up, Steph stepped out of the house waving. "I was just telling Madelyn you would be home any minute."

I helped Dad move the trunk inside and turned the corner to the kitchen where Madelyn was perched in her high chair, with cottage cheese equally distributed across the tray and her face.

"We need to talk about him." Steph pointed to the back door where the canine we had agreed to care for at three-o-clock that morning was waiting patiently to come inside.

"You haven't found the owner yet?" I said.

"Yes, I did find the owner." She handed me a few papers. "The police left these for us."

I scanned them, stomach sinking. They were adoption papers from the local shelter. Mark wasn't pet sitting; this canine, Gus, had become part of his family yesterday.

"We can't keep him," I said.

"I'm not suggesting we keep him, but we do need to find him a good home. And for the record, there's no reason we couldn't keep him," she said.

"Why is he outside then?" Dad thundered. "Providing a good home means he's part of the family."

"Dad, please. You never let us have a dog when I was growing up."

"They chew, they scratch, they slobber. But if you have one, you take care of it. Let him in, I want a good look at the reason I don't have extra pants this weekend."

"Is it safe? What about Maddie?" I asked Stephanie.

"Yes, it's fine. They've already met and seem to be rather fond of each other." She opened the door, allowing Gus to lumber in.

"What the hell is that?" Dad said.

"Sam—Dad," Steph and I chorused.

"What? Just look at him."

"Language, Dad," I said glancing at Madelyn.

"Sorry," Dad shrugged his shoulders.

"The papers say it's a bulldog mix," Steph said.

"Mix—huh. I should say," Dad said.

Both Dad and I were equally taken aback with this genetic amalgam. His face was clearly bulldog, on a head the size of a bull mastiff. The top of his head was even with his shoulders and he had no discernable neck. Rather, the head simply transitioned into a thick tube of a body that was impossibly long. Undoubtedly, there was a dachshund somewhere in this hereditary mash-up. His six-inch legs barely kept his stomach from dragging along the kitchen tile. Most simply, Gus resembled a waddling tree trunk.

Gus immediately went to the high chair and sat down. "Gan-yeh, Gan-yeh." Madelyn smiled and threw cottage cheese to the floor where Gus quickly took care of it.

"Do you want to pet Gus?" Steph asked her. "Let's get you cleaned up." She carried Madelyn to the sink.

Minutes later, we were on the floor of the family room. Madelyn tackled Gus, and Steph was patiently teaching her to be gentle. Gus turned to face his newfound companion and licked the ever-present drool from her chin. He then curled up, around a still giggling Madelyn. Given his unconventional proportions he was able to make a full donut with a hole in center where Madelyn sat securely in an upright position.

"Gan-yeh, Gan-yeh." She smiled and hit him on the back.

"Gentle." Steph guided her hand as she stroked his fur. "Gus. This is Gus. Can you say Gus?"

"Gan-yeh, Gan-yeh." She flapped her arms, smiled, and slapped his back again.

***

After Madelyn was asleep, Dad retrieved his toothbrush and underwear from the trunk and left the rest for us. It was mostly for Madelyn—clothes, books, and toys—with a sprinkling of random gifts for the parents—a serrated knife, an alarm clock, bookends, and a hot glue gun. Of course, there was also the Kong. The package advertised "Genius Edition," and Dad's namesake for it was not entirely misguided. It was molded of thick rubber with a tube leading down into a bulb. There were holes and gaps so treats could easily go in, but only a canine of superior intellect would be able to extract them. We called it The Bong.

***

I balanced Maddie, my brief case, and lunch bag in one arm while fumbling for the house key with the other. The tumblers clicked in place and I gently twisted the knob and cracked the door. "Hey Gus. You need to back up. The door swings in, remember?"

His whine of anticipation came through the crack.

A couple of weeks had passed and we had not been successful in finding him a permanent home yet. He insisted on standing immediately behind the door—and he wouldn't move. I pushed the door gently, allowing it to contact his face, then more firmly, using the door to slide him out of the way. The bottom corner had become stained with his slobber. As soon as we crossed the threshold, his face came away from the door.

"Gan-yeh, Gan-yeh." Madelyn smiled and leaned down towards him. He sat as high as he could on those stubby posts. Given his dimensions, it looked like a mild cobra stretch where the back half of the cylinder was sliding back and forth across the wood floor trying to keep up with his tail.

I gave Gus a pat and placed Maddie down. Gus immediately enveloped her in the donut of his body and licked her face. I heard her laughter as I toured the house, diminishing my load with each stop. On days that I picked up Madelyn, Steph would stay at the office late. We played outside and read some stories before prepping dinner.

"Can you keep a secret?" I asked Maddie while I chopped cucumber. She was in her high chair snacking on Cheerios.

"Swin-got?" Her eyes were wide and she shrugged her shoulders.

"That's what I thought, but I feel like I need to talk this through and I'm not sure who else I can tell," I said. "Wait here." I retrieved my briefcase from the office, plopped it on the island in front of her, and popped the lid. "See that? Doesn't look like much, right? But it's made me the richest man in the world. Look around," I said, gesturing my hand casually around the house. "All of this is because of that," I pointed back to the briefcase.

"Bar-tan," she said, slapping the tray.

"Shh." I snapped the case closed and returned it to the office. "Remember, you can't tell anyone, it needs to be our secret," I said while washing mushrooms.

"Swin-got?" She shrugged her shoulders again.

"Especially Mommy. I'll tell her when the time is right."

"Swin-got?" She was dead pan.

"So why am I telling you? Good question," I said. "You ever have a secret and it's burning you up inside? You just have to let it out? I guess that's where I am. It's been a long time coming, but it's all gelling." I sprinkled the cut veggies over the greens.

"Swin-got, bar-tan." She stretched her arms overhead and looked at the ceiling.

"Yeah, maybe," I muttered. "Besides, I think you're trustworthy—for now at least. Thanks for listening, I'm glad we had this talk."

"Swin-got?" Another shoulder shrug.

"I love you too."

Steph arrived thirty minutes later, obviously down. "Hey hon," I said greeting her with a hug and a kiss. "What's wrong?"

"News," she said. "Sixteen more overdoses this week."

Ever since Mark's passing, these reports had become personal. "Come. Dinner is ready and Maddie is excited to see you."

After dinner, we had tummy time, play time, and stories before bath and bedtime. It was also the time I spent training Gus. He wasn't a bad dog, but he had some digging and chewing habits. Google said mental stimulation in the form of training might help. Steph's childhood dog Curly could fetch toys by name. I thought that sounded fun and decided to train Gus to do the same. We were only two days in.

"Gus, sit. Good boy." I gave him a treat, while the back half of his body slid back-and-forth across the floor. He loved training—lots of treats, minimal work. I extended the bong and gently tapped his nose. "Bong, good boy." Another treat. Another tap. "Bong, good boy." Another treat. Another tap. "Bong, good boy." Another treat. After a few minutes, I held the bong a foot away from him. "Gus, bong." He remained in place looking up at me, wagging his body. I pulled the toy away and tried again. "Gus, bong."

"Gan-ye. Swin-got." Madelyn sat across the room and added a firm head shake for emphasis.

Gus, waited patiently for another treat, but otherwise did not make any effort to reach for the bong. "I guess we're not there yet," I said, tapping him on the nose. "Bong, good boy." Another treat.

***

The next day I tapped Gus on the nose. "Bong, good boy." Treat. Repeat. From a foot away, "Gus, bong." He looked up, wagging his body.

"Gan-ye. Swin-got?" Madelyn bubbled her question through a mouth full of drool.

"I guess we're not there yet," I said, tapping him on the nose. "Bong, good boy." Treat.

***

The next week I tapped Gus on the nose. "Bong, good boy." Treat. Repeat. From a foot away. "Gus, bong." He looked up, wagging his body.

"Gan-ye. Swin-got?" Madelyn clapped her hands and wrung them around each other.

"I guess we're not there yet," I said, tapping him on the nose. "Bong, good boy." Treat.

***

Three months later, I tapped Gus on the nose. "Bong, good boy." Treat. Repeat. From a foot away, "Gus, bong." He looked up, wagging his body.

"Gan-ye. Bong." Madelyn pointed to the toy in my hand.

Steph and I locked eyes. Her jaw dropped; the corners of my mouth wavered before breaking. I couldn't stop laughing—Maddie's first discernable word.

A few weeks later, we had resigned ourselves to the embarrassment that was our daughter's first word and we worked tirelessly to teach her a second.

"Can you say Mommy? Please?" Steph caressed Madelyn's cheeks and leaned close to her face.

"Swin-got?" Madelyn smiled.

"I love you too baby girl," she said. "Keep working on it," she said giving me a one-armed hug and peck on the cheek. It was my turn to drop Madelyn off and Steph went in early.

As Steph pulled away, down the block, I ran back to the high-chair. "Do you remember what I showed you a few months ago?" Maddie returned a blank stare. "The shipment arrived yesterday. Wait here." I ran out to the garage, popped the hatchback, and brought the box inside, plopping it on the kitchen table. I lifted one of the packages out and put it on her tray. "This is the real deal—straight from California." Maddie giggled. "Yes, now you remember." She reached forward to grab it. "Gentle, gentle," I said. "Just like petting Gus."

"Gan-ye. Bong." She smiled and clapped, then grabbed the package again with both fists.

"That's right, gentle." I carefully pulled her hands away before returning the package to the box. "Remember, not a word of this to Mommy. She'll know soon enough, but for now, it's our secret. Promise?"

"Swin-got?" She was adamant.

"That's my girl." I gave her a kiss on the forehead. "Oh, I almost forgot—can you say Daddy?"

"Gan-ye! Boooong."

That night, we sat down for dinner. "I found Gus a home. A colleague of mine wants to meet him," Steph said as she dished out our portions. We said grace and took turns putting bite-sized nibbles on Madelyn's tray.

There was a thunderous knock on the door, followed by muffled shouting. We jumped up. Steph grabbed Madelyn. There was a second thunderous knock, a small explosion, and we turned the corner into the living room where the front door was collapsing inward.

"Police, freeze! Don't move, you are surrounded." They flooded into our home, complete with helmets, face shields, and rifles, scurrying from room to room, checking closets, bathrooms, and the attic. "All clear!"

"What the hell is going on here?" I said.

"Language," Steph muttered under her breath.

"It's an appropriately used curse word—Maddie will be fine," I said.

"Against the wall." The three of us were directed to the front corner of the living room. We were frisked sequentially so we could take turns holding Madelyn. "They're clean."

"What about the kid," a second one said.

"She's not packing heat in her diaper," I said.

"Check her," the second one said.

"Back off." I put Maddie on the carpet, opened the diaper, lifted her out enough for them to confirm.

"Diaper's clean," the first one yelled back.

"That's more than I can say for my shorts right now," I growled.

"One dog, friendly. He's secured in the laundry room." Another officer entered the room.

The presumed leader of the raid crossed our threshold—grey slacks with crisp pleats, a starched oxford with a narrow black tie. He inhaled deeply through his nose, lifting his head in the process. He exhaled while speaking, giving his voice a deep breathiness. "Vince McClure, narcotics taskforce." He held out his badge and identification for a moment before returning them to his pocket. "Igor, get in here," he shouted over his shoulder. A second man came running in, much younger—wrinkled khakis, a green Izod and maroon windbreaker. He presented a search warrant, the top leaves of the sheaf of paper on his clipboard. "My partner, Igor Stravinsky."

"Seriously?" I said.

"Hon—" Steph slapped my shoulder.

Again with the inhale. "Do you have a problem with my partner's name?"

"No, is that really— I mean, I wasn't sure—"

"Now this will go a lot easier for everyone if you tell us what we need to know," Vince said on the exhale.

"What is it you need to know?" I said, wondering if I should find a lawyer.

"Suppliers, routes, distributors, the usual."

I worked in supply chain management, but had enough savvy to recognize that wasn't what Vince was asking about.

"What in the world are you talking about," Steph piped up.

His head lifted for another lung full of air. "We've been tracking you for a while now. We know about the shipment from California—Mmm?" he nodded at us. "If you want to play dumb, go ahead. I was just trying to make it easier for all of us."

"I don't know what you're talking about." Steph said. "Do you know what he's talking about?" She slapped my shoulder again. I shrugged. She locked eyes with Vince, "We have no idea what you are talking about and we'd appreciate it if you'd take your friends and leave so we can return to our dinner now."

Dust motes were dancing in the waning sunlight that streaked through the vacant door frame—before being sucked into Vince's nostrils in preparation for his response. "No can do. If you won't cooperate, we'll do it the hard way. Tear the house apart boys," he called over his shoulder.

We sat on the couch while the they searched our home. They called Igor to check out "something strange," in the closet of the guest bedroom, and we gave them the password to the computer in hopes they would not confiscate it.

"Where's Howie and Snoodles?" McClure said, running his fingers through his graying hair. He had used enough product for it to resist being combed back, but he clearly used enough force that it was no longer laying to the side. Instead, his hair was sloping up in a quarter pipe curve to the right.

"They're coming," Igor said. Moments later another car pulled into our driveway.

Inhale. "Howie, I'm glad to see you," Vince said.

"Hi Snoodles," Igor said to the canine at Howie's side.

"Folks," Igor turned to us, "Snoodles is a fully deputized agent of the law, specially trained in narcotics. He will be assisting with this investigation."

"We need your help; we haven't found a thing." Vince said to Howie, exhaling the remaining breath.

"That's because there's nothing to find," I said from the sofa.

They both looked over and shot me daggers. Inhale. "Snoodles made the confirmation this morning, right?"

"Affirmative. He went crazy sniffing the girl's hands." Snoodles sat at attention waiting for a command.

"We need him to find the link here, otherwise, we have nothing. They have a dog in the laundry room; otherwise, the house is clear for inspection."

Howie nodded. "Hot spot Snoodles?" The dog immediately stood and simultaneously lowered his nose, over to the baseboard, around the perimeter, furniture, and passed in front of us before moving to the back of the house and then upstairs. The cacophony came from the guest bedroom. "Good boy, Snoodles. That's a good boy."

As if on cue, Gus let out a long slow howl reminding everyone that he needed affection too.

"We got us a box." Howie called from the top of the stairs.

"Yes!" Vince muttered and thumped a fist into his opposite palm.

"What in the world did they find?" Steph asked.

"I don't know," I lied.

The box was carried out of the house. "Go through it thoroughly," he told an agent. Vince wore a smug smile. "Now, it's just paperwork." Vince sat down with the clipboard from Igor. He was still on the first page when Igor returned.

"There's nothing there—it's exactly what's advertised." Igor handed Vince a label from the box.

"What's in there?" Steph said.

I shrugged and waved the question off with my hand.

Vince slapped the clipboard. "Yuppies, hiding in plain sight in the suburbs, pushing the biggest ring from here to San Antonio. We're missing something."

"He's missing something alright," I whispered to Steph.

Vince looked up, shook a finger at me and returned to the clipboard. "We're not beat yet—get Mutt," he said to Igor.

"But Snoodles—" Igor said.

"Mutt's better," Vince said.

While waiting for Mutt, we were permitted to finish dinner and bring some books and toys to the sofa to engage Madelyn.

Headlights arced across the driveway and a man with a pock-marked face and stringy black, shoulder-length hair wearing tattered jeans and a raggedy t-shirt walked in. Most notable was a nose that made Cyrano De Bergerac look well proportioned.

Inhale. "Mutt." Vince nodded his head in appreciation. "Thanks for coming. We need you—we're empty handed."

"No worries, I can use the pay," Mutt said.

"That's Mutt?" Steph barked. "Hon, go call us a lawyer—this is ridiculous." Vince locked eyes and willed her back to the sofa.

"Please, this will only take a minute." Igor stepped between them. "Mutt won't touch a thing." He tapped his nose. "He doesn't need to. He has the gift, thirty inches of olfaction—nearly twenty times human normal, even more than most dogs."

"It's his blessing," Vince said on the exhale.

"I prefer congenital anomaly," Mutt said. "Trust me, it's not all always a blessing." From the doorway he lifted his nose and sniffed the air. "Hmm," he nodded in approval. "Who's the chef?"

Steph raised her hand shoulder high. "I made dinner tonight."

"Sliced almonds on the green beans. Nice touch."

"Uh—thanks," she said.

"Bower's carries a garlic and tarragon infused avocado oil. Next time, try it with that. It's a bit pricey, but it's fantastic for green beans," he said. "Heart healthy too." He walked through the room, sniffing as he went. "I bet that threw Snoodles for a loop." He pointed to the box that had been brought inside.

Inhale, "Oh, he's good," Vince nodded to Igor.

"The dog—" he sniffed again, "in the laundry room. He had an accident." Mutt finally left the living room, moving deeper into the house, calling out tips as he moved from room to room. "Time for a bleach cycle on your washing machine."

A moment of silence. "Clear out the drain in the second sink of the master bathroom." True to his word he returned within minutes. "They're clean," he said to Vince. "You'll fix that, right?" He nodded to the door still propped against the wall.

"He's right," Igor said to Vince. "We don't have anything. We need to clear out."

Inhale. "But all the evidence—" Vince blew out his remaining air.

"What evidence?" I asked.

Vince shook his head, handed the clipboard to Igor, and walked out.

Igor glanced at the notes. "We received a tip from Blue Skies and Sunshine, where the caregivers noticed your daughter's zeal for her newfound vocabulary. Apparently, she speaks of nothing other than ganja and bongs all day long. That's clearly unexpected behavior for a toddler."

Much like that first occurrence, I got the giggles.

"That's what this is about?" Steph jumped up.

"I think we can clear this up," I said gaining composure.

Gus was allowed time for dinner and potty before we brought him into the living room where he circled into a donut and we plopped Madelyn into the middle.

"Gan-ye, Gan-ye," she smiled and gave him her version of gentle pets.

"It's not ganja, it's Gan-ye, with a Y." Steph was fiery. But listening closely, Maddie included a bit of sibilance and I understood how the name could be misunderstood.

Igor stepped to the threshold. "Vince, you'll want to see this."

Comfortably nestled within her companion, Madelyn was eager to perform, readily identifying both ganja and the bong where Gus wouldn't. She grabbed the toy, waved it around and let it fly "Bong," she giggled and then returned to patting Gus. I explained my tenacity and failure in training.

Inhale, "What about the shipment from California, and Snoodles?"

"That's the shipment from California," I said pointing to the box.

"What's in there?" Steph lifted a flap to peek inside. "Oh?" she smiled and lifted a hand to her mouth.

"Surprise," I said.

"Thank you." She gave a hug and kiss and we looked down on the remains of what had been four potted plants of golden poppies. They had been ripped from their pots, and the soil and roots torn apart in the search. The flowers and blooms were a bit disheveled from overnight shipping and their subsequent treatment, but still discernable.

The others looked at us expectantly. "Our fourth anniversary is this weekend. We met in California and our first conversation was on the legality of my picking the state flower, which I asked Steph to wear in her hair."

Vince had a hand on each side of his head, combing the hair straight up. "Your poppy supplier is also a suspected clearing house and money launderer."

"I was just looking for golden poppies," I said.

"But you showed them to the kid," Mutt said.

"Yes? This morning," I was cautious.

Mutt nodded. "That's why Snoodles went crazy."

"We had Snoodles at the daycare this morning and he confirmed the narcotics," Igor said.

"But he didn't," Mutt said. "He confirmed a poppy plant—which he's trained to do. But obviously he doesn't recognize the difference between the opium poppy versus golden poppies. At a fundamental level, all poppies smell the same."

Inhale. "So now what do we do." Vince paced the length of the room.

"We have the door fixed, and we go back to the drawing board," Igor said.

Vince exhaled through his words. "What about the report?"

"The truth," Igor said. "Ganja is the dog, the bong is his toy, and he's a slow learner."

Vince shook his head. "A word of advice. You might reconsider the names you've selected for your pet and his toys." He turned and left.

Igor and Mutt were both apologetic. Steph ensured the agents not only restored the door, but also cleaned up Gus' mess in the laundry room. She also got reimbursed for HVAC expenses since we had no door during the investigation. Vince and Igor stayed with it and finally got a real break in their case a few months later.

I can't help but wonder what would have happened if Gus had not been around to clear up that misunderstanding. Steph spoke with her colleague the next day to let her know we were no longer searching for a home for Gus—he already had one.

Adam Sales is a statistician by trade who works in pharmaceutical development. Although he is a closet writer of novels and short stories, he has earned awards for story-telling and speaking and served as an invited speaker. He is also a nineteen-year member of the Barbershop Harmony Society where he has served as an invited emcee for competitions and conventions.

Like a Good Neighbor

Joseph S. Walker

R uth Caldwell was just walking out her front door when her cousin Lemuel pulled into the driveway in his police cruiser. He got out of the car, hitched up his belt, and walked up to where she stood on the front porch, holding one end of Imogene's leash. The other end was attached to an elaborate harness snugly secured around the large black-and-white cat. Ruth had learned quickly that Imogene would slip from a simple collar with the nimble skill of a Houdini.

"Why are you the only woman in town who walks a cat?" Lemuel said by way of greeting.

"Imogene lived on the streets for her first several years," Ruth said. "She doesn't care to be kept indoors all day."

"So let her out the back door. That's what everyone else does."

Ruth sniffed. "I'll not have Imogene killing birds and being taken advantage of by feral toms, thank you very much. What brings you by, Lem?"

He glanced at the front door. "I thought we could sit and talk a few minutes.- You might have some fresh cookies."

"I do," she said. "But this is the time for Imogene's walk. You can come along or wait here." She stepped off the porch and set off, not waiting to see which he would choose. After a moment, there was the noise of his shoes on the sidewalk as he scrambled to catch up with her. They trudged silently half a block up a steep grade, stopping at the corner to check traffic before crossing Fairlane Road.

Fairlane was the central artery of Haverbrook, a small New England village clinging to a long hill overlooking the ocean. It was well named, because if you lived above Fairlane, you were rich. If you lived below Fairlane, you weren't.- Therefore, local wits had said for decades, if you were on Fairlane, you must be doing fair.

Ruth lived just half a block below Fairlane, putting her near the top of the jumble of single-floor homes and cramped apartments that filled the drop between the central road and the mostly abandoned warehouses at the shore.- Above Fairlane, the hill became gentler, the homes larger, and the lawns lusher as you climbed, up to the multimillion-dollar estates with their walls of glass facing specular views of the sea. Many of the people who owned homes above Fairlane actually lived in New York City or Boston, coming to Haverbrook for weekends, sometimes longer in the summer and fall. Whenever they arrived, the people who lived below Fairlane were waiting to cook their food, clean their pools, tend their lawns, and generally be of use. Ruth had run a maid service for the estates above Fairlane, until her retirement a few months ago.

Above Fairlane, the walking was easier. Imogene jumped into the grass, chasing a dead leaf skittering along in the wind. Ruth paused, letting the cat play rather than trying to drag her. She elbowed Lem. "What was on your mind, cousin?"

Lem started. "Right," he said. He'd allowed the cat's antics to distract him. "I guess you heard the Beckstrom place was robbed."

"I do read the paper," Ruth said. She gave a little tug on the leash, by way of warning, then started walking again. Imogene made a frantic effort to get back to the leaf, saw it was futile, and ran forward until the harness jerked her back into an easy amble at Ruth's plodding pace. "How's it bring you to my door?"

"Well." Lem stuck two fingers under his hat and scratched, thinking out how to say it. "The thing is, Bill and some of the boys thought I should come talk to you." Bill was one of Lem's deputies. "See if you could suggest anybody for us to look at."

"Me? You mean give you a suspect? How on Earth would I do that?"

"You gotta look at it from their point of view, Ruth." Lem started to tick points off on his fingers. "You're an eccentric little old lady who reads all the time and knits cardigans. You know everybody and you know everything that happens in this town."

"I am not eccentric," Ruth said.

"You're walking your cat, Ruth."

"You don't have to be a dog to enjoy a stroll."

"You're wearing flip-flops and a Snoopy sweatshirt."

"They match, don't they?"

"Look, this ain't me talking, Ruth. These are simple men. Everybody they've ever seen on TV who looks and acts like you also solves murders. So they said I should ask you for ideas."

"Oh, for—" Ruth stopped suddenly. "Lemuel, that is rank nonsense.- Stereotyping is what it is. Just because I'm a little old lady, I'm also a detective?- What sense does that make?"

"None," Lem confessed. "I'm sorry, Ruth," he said. "I probably wouldn't have bothered you except I wanted a cookie, like I said. Hey, how long is this walk of yours, anyway?"

"Two miles," she said.

"Lord, I don't have that kind of time. I'd better head back to my car."

He'd gotten a few steps away when she spoke. "Lemuel."

He turned, raising his eyebrows.

"You might talk to Herb Felson's kid," she said. "The boy who works at the Robinson auto yard. I hear he has a very fancy new car. Some kind of convertible, I believe. Not at all in step with his current salary." She shrugged. "It may mean nothing, of course."

Lem nodded slowly. "Well, all right, cousin. Maybe you're some kind of sleuth after all."

She clucked her tongue and turned back to her walk. "Nonsense."

***

Five days later, Lemuel pulled into Ruth's driveway again as she was leading Imogene out on her walk. She didn't bother to wait for him, but he hustled to her side, speaking before they'd even crested the climb to Fairlane. "The mayor's not happy, Ruth."

"I wouldn't be either, if my wife was carrying on like that."

"What?"

"The mayor's wife. I've heard shameful things."

Lem waved that away. "I'm not talking about rumors, Ruth. The mayor isn't happy because of the Felson boy."

Lem paused as they crossed Fairlane.

"We spent the better part of two days on surveillance," he continued. "He's got an expensive new car, he's spending money around town, taking his girl to places above Fairlane. A few girls, actually. So after a couple days we bring him in. Stick him in a room, get in his face, where'd the money come from? And he laughed in our face and told us."

Lem blew out air. "He hit big on a scratch-off ticket a couple months ago. Half a million. Oh, he'll blow through the whole pile in a couple years and end up back in a grease pit, but for now he's sitting pretty, drinking our coffee, and asking don't we read the paper. We looked like idiots, Ruth."

"I don't doubt it," Ruth said. "He should sue you all for false arrest."

Lem stopped dead and stared at her. "Sue us? You told us to look at him!"

Ruth wheeled to face him. "I didn't tell you to do a terrible job of it. Anyway, I never claimed to be a detective."

"Why didn't you know about the scratch-off?"

"Contrary to what your deputies think, I don't know everything that happens in town."

"I give up," Lem said. He threw up his hands and tried to stalk away, only to find himself falling, his arms pinwheeling helplessly, before landing hard onto the ground. Imogene had wound her leash around his ankles. A confused few moments ensued as Imogene and Ruth, frequently working at cross purposes, tried to untangle the leash, while Lem tried to untangle his feet and get vertical.- Eventually he was seated on the curb, catching his breath. Imogene found a patch of sunny grass, where she stretched out and was asleep in thirty seconds.

"You're not generally a clumsy man," Ruth said, watching her cousin mop his brow with a wrinkled handkerchief. "What ails you?"

"This case ails me," Lem snapped. "Fifteen homes hit in the last three months.- Security systems bypassed, safes opened. Every time just a few small things missing, but expensive. Jewelry, rare coins, things like that. All told we're edging up on five million in missing possessions."

He sighed and pushed himself to his feet. "It all seems pro, but pros move on. They don't hit the same town over and over again. Anyway, the homeowners are up in arms. Some of them want to sell, but they're afraid they'll take a bath because property values are sliding. And as go property values, so go taxes, which is why the mayor was screaming at me on the phone at six this morning. It'll be my job if I don't get this guy soon."

Ruth rolled her eyes. "And the best plan you can come up with is asking me for ideas? You'd be more likely to get results walking up to random people in the street and asking them to confess."

"I know," Lem sighed. "I guess I'm just desperate. We've got nothing. No fingerprints. Nobody on the cameras. This guy is like a ghost." He turned and started back in the direction of his car.

Once again, her voice stopped him. "Lemuel."

He turned.

"Ted Shaw," she said.

His brow wrinkled. "The pro golfer? His was one of the first places hit."

"Or so he'd have you think." She edged forward. "What better way to avoid suspicion than by being one of the victims?"

"But why? He's got plenty."

"Does he? Do you follow the sport? He hasn't won an event in five years. He hasn't placed in the top twenty in two. But he's got a lifestyle to maintain.- A private plane. Two ex-wives needing monthly payments." She raised her eyebrows. "Of course, that all may be nothing as well. Just an old lady thinking out loud."

"Right," Lem said absently. "Just an old lady." He stared into space, thinking, and abruptly turned and started back the way they'd come. Ruth grunted and sat on the curb where he'd been. No reason to wake Imogene. She had the right idea, enjoying the sun and the wide, quiet street.

***

It was more than a week later when Ruth opened her door and saw Lemuel pacing at the curb. She sighed to herself and led Imogene out. Lem fell into step beside her as they started up toward Fairlane.

"Another bust," he said. "We had to be careful. Media heard so much as a whisper that we were looking at Shaw, every golf reporter in the country would be here. We got the FBI to put a forensic accountant to work on him. You're right, he's in trouble. But then it all fell apart. Three of the robberies occurred when he is definitely and provably known to have been out of town."

"He flew back under another name for just a few hours."

"FBI says no. They keep pretty close tabs on flights these days."

Ruth spoke again after they crossed Fairlane. "An accomplice."

"None we can find. And he hasn't had any kind of influx of cash."

Ruth shrugged. "I guess I was wrong again."

Lem shook his head. "And while we were so busy looking at Shaw, another robbery happened. The Blake place. Guy took a diamond necklace out of a wall safe that Blake swears only he knew about. He says it's worth a quarter million all by itself."

"Yes, I saw. There seems to be quite an uproar."

Lem nodded grimly. "It's not just my job on the line. There's recall talk going around. The whole city government could get swept out over this thing, and I'm the one who looks like a stooge." He stopped dead, taking Ruth by the elbow. "I'm at the end of my rope, Ruth. I'm willing to chance it all for one more throw of the dice. Okay, your first two ideas didn't pan out. At least you had ideas. I've got nothing." He was almost crying. "Third time's the charm, right?"

"You're being ridiculous."

"Anything, Ruth. All right, you're not a detective. You're still the smartest person I know. Think of something."

"I wish I could. I'm sorry."

His shoulders slumped. He turned and began to slouch away, as Imogene stared up at him curiously. When he had gotten a few steps away, he turned and looked at her over his shoulder. Ruth sighed. "Lemuel," she said.

He turned, all eager attention.

"Sandra Kurtz," she said.

Lem was taken aback. "The deputy mayor?"

"Deputy Mayor now," Ruth said. "What if this purge you're talking about happens?"

"Why, she—" Lem broke off. Slowly he began to smile. "I'll be damned," he said. As he spun and went off toward his car, he was moving more quickly than Ruth had seen him move in decades.

She shook her head at his retreating back. "There goes the world's fool," she told the cat. Imogene looked up at her. "Come on," she said. "We have plans for this afternoon, don't we?"

Lem was already out of sight. Ruth backtracked half a block, turned the opposite direction from where she had just taken Lem and walked higher above Fairlane. Lem would have to be even more careful about Kurtz than he had been about Shaw. He'd be trying to investigate her quickly enough to have an answer before she could become mayor, but slowly enough that she wouldn't realize what he was doing. It should keep him busy for several days, at least. He wouldn't notice that Ruth had left town until it was far too late to do anything about it.

Three long blocks from where she'd last seen Lem, Ruth turned into a driveway leading up to a sprawling brick home. "Let's see if Mr. Lee ever developed an imagination," she told Imogene. She pulled on a pair of latex gloves.

At the garage door she opened the small panel concealing a keypad. Alan Lee was scrupulous about the passcode, changing it once a month. Since he needed to be able to remember it, though, he always arrived at the code the same way. Calculate the number of the month by the year. Subtract Alan Lee's age. Take the square root and round up to the nearest whole number. She'd run the numbers that morning and entered them confidently. The garage door rumbled up.

Alan Lee lived, for the most part, a rather Spartan life. He had only one real indulgence: he collected Superbowl and World Series rings. He'd been advised many times that they should be in a bank vault, but he needed to be able to go look at them anytime he wanted to. Ruth went to his office. She opened the second drawer of his file cabinet and lifted out several of the hanging files. The ring box was nestled in the space beneath them. Ruth lifted Imogene to the top of the cabinet. Lee had close to thirty rings, but Ruth focused on the six or so she knew to be most valuable. She wrapped each carefully in several layers of tissue and then tucked it into one of the little pockets concealed in Imogene's harness. This took longer than it should have because Imogene thought they were playing a game. She rolled onto her side and batted at Ruth's hands as they came and went.

Even with that delay, in five minutes Ruth was back out on the driveway. As she turned back toward home, she was running her own mental calculations. How much she thought she could get for the rings, added to the take from the previous jobs, divided by all the hours she'd worked for four decades keeping these big, ridiculous houses clean. Forty years of being ignored and condescended to, forty years of keeping her rates low so she wouldn't lose clients, forty years of no sir and yes ma'am. Forty years, during which she'd become so invisible that they would open their safes right in front of her, not even wondering how sharp her eyes might be.

When you spread it over four decades, it seemed very fair. Some of her pay had been deferred, and now she was collecting what she was due. Lee's rings made the tally complete. It was time to go. She supposed that her disappearance would be linked pretty quickly to the thefts, and that would probably make things look even worse for Lem. The police chief's own cousin, robbing the town blind.

"You know what, though?" she said out loud to the cat as soon as they had crossed Fairlane. "Lem was always a bully when we were kids, and he's not really smart enough to be the chief. He just looks like what people expect a police chief to look like. Maybe he deserves it a little, do you think?"

Imogene expressed no opinion. She leapt up onto a wall running along the sidewalk so she could walk in the sun. Ruth could hear her purring even out here in the street. She reached out and scratched Imogene's head, remembering the scrawny, sickly kitten she'd rescued. Such a big, healthy, happy girl now!

Ruth hoped the cat would be just as happy in Mexico.

Joseph Walker is an active member of the Mystery Writers of America, Sisters in Crime, and the Short Mystery Fiction Society. His stories have appeared in Alfred Hitchcock's Mystery Magazine, Ellery Queen's Mystery Magazine, Mystery Weekly, Tough, and a number of other magazines and anthologies. His story "Etta at the End of the World," from Alfred Hitchcock's Mystery Magazine, is currently nominated for an Edgar Award as best short story published in 2020.

Made in the USA
Middletown, DE
29 April 2022